HEALING KISS

AWARD WINNING AUTHOR
AMANDA UHL

Published in the United States by Amanda Uhl, LLC.
Healing Kiss. Copyright © 2023 by Amanda Uhl
www.amandauhl.com

Ebook: 978-1-952581-06-9
Paperback: 978-1-952581-07-6

Cover by Christian Betulan
www.coversbychristian.com

Interior formatting by 100 Covers.

*To those who heal or are in need of healing…
this one is for you.*

CHAPTER ONE

Lillian Milano clutched her younger sister's clammy hand between her palms. Hannah was only twenty-two. Too young to die. Lillian fought the panic pushing into her lungs, pressing on her chest like a weighted blanket. She dropped her head on the hospital bed rail.

Deep breaths. Keep calm.

Not the time to hyperventilate. Not the time to feel faint. Not the time for strong emotion. Strong emotion only weakened her healing ability. And without her life-saving gift, Hannah wouldn't survive the night.

"Did anyone see you?" Her dad sat on the opposite side of the bed, his glasses crooked and his hair going every which way, looking like he hadn't slept in days. God, how she'd missed him. The past two years had been the loneliest of her life.

"I don't know. I don't think so."

"You're taking a big risk coming to Cleveland. You should have stayed in Boston, where you'd be safe." His nostrils flared, but Lillian knew he wasn't angry. He held back tears. "I've already lost your mother. And now Hannah has this virus. I can't bear to lose either one of you girls."

"You're not going to. I promise."

"The healing has to work."

"It will. Hannah's gonna beat this." Lillian moved her chair until her knees touched the bed and squeezed Hannah's hand. "C'mon, Sis. Stay with me now. You don't have to do anything. Just rest."

Hannah didn't stir. The steady *drip-drip* of the IV, the *beep-beep-beep* of the heart monitor, and her sister's raspy breaths were the only sounds interrupting the tense silence. *She looks so weak. Too weak. Oh God, I hope I'm not too late.*

Lillian closed her eyes, focusing on Hannah. A dark shape formed behind her eyelids. Hannah's shape. Soft orange light wrapped around her sister's body like a warm shawl.

Deep breath in. The orange light pulsed and glowed.

Deep breath out, careful not to disturb the orange light.

Breathe in. Breathe out.

Breathe in. Breathe out.

Again. Again. Again.

Each of Lillian's breaths radiated healing light and power—energy she absorbed from others as easily as a tree absorbs sunlight. In the case of minor illness, the energy she released would have been enough to heal and comfort a patient. But this was no minor illness. And Hannah was no ordinary patient.

Orange light faded into the dark shape as Hannah's body absorbed the healing energy. Lillian opened her eyes to see Hannah's flutter, then open. Her gaze looked unfocused and feverish.

She squeezed Hannah's hand and released it. If she held it longer, the heat and light would transfer back to her, negating any positive effect on Hannah.

Breathe. Calm.

She stood and swiped a trembling hand across her damp forehead. Healing even a minor sickness sapped her strength. Tackling a severe illness like Hannah's could kill Lillian if she wasn't careful.

"Did that help her, Lou-Lou?"

She met her dad's gaze across the bed. The pet name almost had her falling apart. When had she last heard him say it? And in that scratchy timbre? She curled her toes to keep from crying.

"Yes," she said, projecting a confidence she didn't feel and pulling air into her starved lungs. "But it's not enough."

She turned toward Hannah. "It's going to be all right, Sis. I promise. I'll keep trying until you're better. You've got to hang in there."

Her sister nodded and coughed. Fear filled her coppery brown eyes. The hand Lillian had clasped never moved. *Not good.* Her sister's normally lustrous dark hair lay thin and limp, plastered against her sweat-slicked forehead.

Hantavirus Pulmonary Syndrome. The flu-like symptoms can be fatal.

Fatal.

The word rattled around in Lillian's head. As a nurse, she understood the seriousness of the virus Hannah had contracted. But as her older sister, the knowledge ripped through her mind with the stunning force of a tornado.

Breathe.

"Excuse me."

Lillian jerked her head toward the door at the masculine voice, bunching her muscles and straining toward the opening. She turned, fisting her hands at her sides. Her heartbeat drummed in her ears; fight or flight adrenaline took over.

"I didn't mean to startle you. I'm Dr. Beyton. Are you family?" He stood waiting in blue scrubs, a "this-woman-might-be-unstable" look on his face.

She expelled her breath in a rush, reaching a hand toward the bed to steady herself. Only a doctor. Hannah's doctor, not Kinetica, the dangerous underground organization who wanted Lillian as their lab rat.

"Not family, a friend." Over the past two years, she'd become accustomed to lying. And wearing a disguise.

She ran a hand over the straight, long blonde wig made from real human hair she'd paid a whopping sum for at a specialty shop. She scanned the doctor's body, connecting their energy fields, checking to see if she could use his energy to heal Hannah.

Insubstantial. She swallowed the bitter taste in her mouth. It wasn't the doctor's fault he had no more energy than anyone else she'd come in contact with today.

"How's our patient faring?" He flashed a brief smile and moved into the room without waiting for an answer.

He strode to Hannah, studying her charts and the machine monitoring her vitals.

"I have medical experience," Lillian said. "I've seen worse than Hannah. She's going to beat this," she added for Hannah's benefit.

"Well, we're certainly doing everything we can for her. Can I speak to you for a moment?" He gestured to her father. "Let's step out in the hall."

"I'd like…Zoey to come with me." Her dad used her alias.

"Okay," the doctor nodded.

Lillian and her dad followed Dr. Beyton into a small room with an examination table and a couple of chairs.

He closed the door and turned to her dad, his expression serious. "We're going to need to intubate your daughter to help her breathe. Her lungs are full of fluid, which makes it a struggle to take in oxygen. Her body can't focus on healing."

"Intubation?" her father questioned.

"He means they'll put her on a ventilator," Lillian said. "The ventilator will breathe for her." *About one in three patients never recover.*

"That's exactly right," the doctor spoke. "Your daughter needs time to fight the infection in her system."

"Is this like life support? Will she get better?" her father asked.

"That's our goal." The doctor sounded chipper.

Despite his optimism, Lillian knew there were no guarantees, especially for someone with extrasensory abilities. Hannah, a strong empath, held the grief, anxiety, and feelings of others in her heart and lungs. *She's dying.*

A wave of nausea flooded Lillian's system. She made a beeline for the nearest chair, which happened to be next to her dad, and sat.

"Can we stay with her?" her dad asked, leaning a hand against Lillian's chair.

"Not while we intubate. You can wait in the family room. We'll come get you in a few minutes."

Lillian nodded. They would put a tube down Hannah's throat. A harsh procedure for her dad to witness.

"Are you okay?" her dad asked after the doctor left the room. His curly dark hair carried a few more streaks of gray since she'd last seen him, and the lines around his mouth looked deeper. "You're not getting sick now, too, are you?"

Lillian took a slow breath. "No, I'll be fine. I'm tired, not sick." She shrugged, careful to keep her tone light. "She'll be okay. Let's head to the waiting room."

Not thirty minutes later, a nurse, who introduced herself as Dani, came to fetch them, and they returned to Hannah's bedside. A clear plastic accordion tube snaked into Hannah's mouth, feeding air and oxygen into her lungs. A large machine next to her bed beeped as it monitored her heart, respiratory rate, and blood pressure.

"She's a trooper," Dani said. "But the procedure's worn her out. She's been given a mild sedative to help her relax, and she's sleeping. Might be a good time for you to grab a bite and get some rest. I've got the evening shift. I'll be sure to keep an eye on her."

Lillian couldn't think of eating or sleeping, but a deep breath in revealed her father's vitality was low...too low. Neither one of them had eaten lunch. And he'd been at the hospital since yesterday. He needed a break from his worry and constant vigilance. "Let me take you home. You're exhausted and need to rest."

Her father took off his glasses and wiped them on his shirt. "You're right. I'm beat. Are you sure *you're* okay?"

"Yes." She attempted a smile but knew it was weak. She wasn't okay. She hadn't been okay for years now.

She drove her father's Cadillac, the glow of the headlights dim through the dank, gray fog. The damp weather seemed to infiltrate her body, blurring her thoughts until they all led to the same desperate conclusion. If she didn't heal Hannah tonight, her sister would die.

She parked the car in the driveway and turned to her father; his head lolled against the seat.

"Dad, wake up."

Her father startled and opened his eyes, his dazed look gradually clearing. "I'm sorry, I must have drifted off."

She peered around as far as she could see through the mist. Nothing seemed out of the ordinary, but she could never be too careful. Although it had been two years since she'd left, Kinetica could still be watching. "It's okay, Dad. Looks like the coast is clear. C'mon."

She shivered as she zipped her jacket and grabbed her purse. Her mother had warned that unless Kinetica believed Lillian was dead, they would never stop searching for her. If they were watching the house, they'd find Lillian and kill her dad if he got in the way.

She got out of the car and stayed alert to any sudden movement, but when nothing disturbed the silence, she let out the breath she held and followed her dad through the side door and into the kitchen. She sniffed the air, swallowing a pang. "Hmmm…it smells like coffee and waffles in here. Two of my favorite smells."

"It's good to have you home, Lillian, even if it has to be under such terrible circumstances. Are you hungry?"

"A little." The pang intensified into a physical ache when she spied the painted white cabinets and bright-yellow-flowered wallpaper she and Hannah had helped their mom pick out when they were little girls. She swiped at the sudden moisture in her eyes. Not much had changed over the years.

"You sit." She pointed to a chair at the small kitchen table. "I'll whip us up a late lunch."

Her father did as she asked. She'd never been much of a cook, but she made grilled cheese sandwiches and heated soup from a can she found in the cupboard, then cleaned up the dishes.

"Thanks, sweetheart. A little crispy, but it hit the spot."

Her father was being kind. She was so preoccupied worrying about Hannah and Kinetica, she burned the dang sandwiches.

He wiped his lips with a napkin, pushed his chair from the table, and stood with a small smile. "I see some things never change."

Pressure built behind her eyelids. How she'd missed her dad's familiar teasing.

"I'm going to bed for a little while." He wrapped her in a hug, the familiar smell of coffee and Old Spice aftershave enveloping her. "You should, too. You're safe here, and you need to rest."

"I can't stay, Dad. You know that. If Kinetica has any idea I'm still alive, this is the first place they'll look for me. It's not worth the risk. I'll stay at the hospital. Hannah needs me. I have to keep trying to heal her."

Her father touched her arm, fear and concern reflected in his dark-brown eyes. "I'm worried about you. But I'm not going to tell you what to do. Somehow, you've managed to stay safe these past couple of years without us. It's nearly killed me." His voice cracked. "Be careful, Lou-Lou. I couldn't bear it if something happened to you."

"Hey, I've survived this long, haven't I?" Lillian kept her voice light. "Don't worry, Dad. Nothing's going to happen, I promise." Lillian hugged her father and swallowed past the hard lump in her throat. She tightened her hand around the keys to his car. "Get some rest. I'll call you if anything changes."

Her dad nodded, then turned and shuffled to his bedroom, while she forced her shaky legs to move toward the kitchen table where she'd left her purse. She couldn't remain here and risk her dad's safety. That was true two years ago. It was still true today. And despite the ache in her heart for home and the people who loved her, it would still be true tomorrow.

She parted the curtains and peeked out the kitchen window. Thunder clouds lined the March sky, the fog blanketing her dad's car. She tugged on her lower lip. If Kinetica *were* watching the house, the fog provided cover. But would Kinetica still be searching for her after all this time? As far as she knew, they believed her dead. And they wouldn't come after Hannah since she hadn't inherited the healing gene, and Kinetica either didn't know or didn't care about her sister's other talent. If Lillian stayed hidden, she and her family would be safe.

She opened the garage door. Nothing moved, not even a tree branch. The silence seemed to lie in wait like a big cat ready to pounce. She hunched into her jacket and hurried to the car, careful to lock the doors as soon as she was safe inside. She grabbed the wheel with both hands to stop them from trembling.

What if I'm wrong? What if Kinetica knows I'm still alive and is waiting for me at the hospital?

The thought kept her heart racing during the thirty-minute drive. It didn't let up when she pulled into the visitor's parking lot and hurried toward the glass doors. They opened when she stepped in front of them at the same moment a tall man did.

"Oh." She gasped and stumbled out of the stranger's reach.

"After you." The stranger paused, gesturing for her to go in front of him, his deep voice causing her heartbeat to accelerate even more.

She hesitated, but he made no move to grab her, so she slipped by him. His height made it easy for her to bend her head and avoid meeting his gaze. Still, she caught a glimpse of a firm jawline, dark hair, and a black computer bag strung over one shoulder as she passed.

She continued moving toward the infectious disease wing where Hannah was staying, the beat of her heart matching the *tap-tap-tap* of her shoes against the floor. The man followed behind. No one else was nearby, so she could hear the soft tread of his shoes. She quickened her pace, her breath coming faster now. Her stomach did a flip, and her throat tightened, preparing her to flee or scream if the situation demanded it.

She reached Hannah's room. Bile rose in her throat when she realized the man's footsteps stopped when she stopped.

She grabbed the doorknob and glanced to the side. The man was no longer there. She let her breath out in a rush and leaned her forehead against the door to recover her equilibrium. *Get a hold of yourself, Lillian.* Not every strange guy was one of Kinetica's men, looking to grab her. She'd been so panicked, she hadn't even taken the time to check the man's vitality.

She pushed the door to Hannah's room open, closing it behind her. Her sister lay unmoving in the hospital bed, the ventilator huffing as it breathed for her. *Is she okay?* Fear squeezed Lillian's lungs, and she rushed forward, leaning over the bed, studying the still shape, drawing on her talent. Although she couldn't see anything with her eyes, in her mind, a thin, translucent wisp of white vapor escaped Hannah's lips.

Lillian's head swam, and she steadied herself against the bed to stay upright. Her sister was unconscious and weak but not dead. Not yet. And she wouldn't die. Not today. Not tomorrow. *Not if I can prevent it.*

She pulled the blanket back and grasped Hannah's limp hand in her own. She closed her eyes and centered her mind on the dark shape, which formed behind her eyelids. Hannah's body. A small amount of orange light pulsed and glowed around her.

Now to make it grow.

Grow until it covered Hannah's physical form. Until it overcame the virus in her system. Until her sister was no longer ill.

Lillian tightened her grasp on her sister's hands and opened her mind, letting healing energy flow through her fingertips and into Hannah. With every breath, the dark shape in her mind grew smaller, and the orange halo grew wider and longer. But not enough to smother the darkness.

She let go of Hannah's hands to swipe at the tears wetting her cheeks. No matter how many breaths she took, no matter how much she strained, no matter how long she tried, the orange light refused to spread to the size needed for true healing.

Tears came faster now, blinding her and soaking the blanket. A sob escaped her lips and she swallowed, releasing Hannah's hands. She grabbed a tissue from the cube on the hospital table and blew her nose. Despair slid a cold hand down her neck. She couldn't lie to herself anymore. Hannah was dying, and all Lillian could do was blubber like a baby.

She needed to do something, take some action, find someone with enough vitality to save Hannah's life. But people with that much vitality were as rare as a perfectly cut blue diamond. And she needed such a large, continuous quantity of energy to heal Hannah, it would be almost impossible to absorb what she needed from the hospital workers. Still, she had to try.

She tossed the tissue into the wastebasket and strode toward the door. She'd load up on caffeine, and then she'd walk every wing in the hospital, test everyone she came in contact with, absorb whatever energy she could. Short of harming another, she would do whatever she had to do to cure her sister.

The moment she stepped into the hallway, fear and pain slammed into her gut. She leaned against the wall, clutching her middle and struggling for breath. There was only one reason she would feel such intense agony. Someone suffered nearby. Someone who matched her body chemistry. Someone she could heal quickly, with so little effort it wouldn't impact her ability to heal Hannah.

She glanced at a room down the hall. The door was open, so she moved until she could see inside. A child lay in the bed, her thin arms on top of the blanket. Lillian figured she couldn't be more than four or five years old. An IV was taped to one of the small hands, wrapped in white gauze and an Ace bandage.

She should leave. If she lingered, someone might see and wonder what she was doing in the girl's room. Perhaps they'd call security, and she'd be questioned. But the girl gasped, and her suffering was a jolt to Lillian's overworked heart. How could she ignore the child's distress, knowing she could easily relieve her pain?

She moved toward the bed. "Sweetheart, it's okay. I'm here to help."

In answer, the child whimpered, her eyes unfocused. Lillian placed a hand on the girl's forehead and closed her eyes. Almost instantly, a dark shape formed in her mind's eye. She breathed, and orange light surrounded the shape, lengthening and widening. The orange pulsed and swelled until it covered the darkness.

"Are you an angel?" a tiny voice squeaked.

Lillian popped her eyes open to meet the child's puzzled gaze. Lillian smiled and withdrew her hand. "Just a friend. Do you feel better?"

The girl nodded and yawned. "Uh-huh."

"Good. Sleep now. You'll feel even better tomorrow. I promise."

"Okay." The child closed her eyes.

Lillian swiped a hand across the damp hair clinging to her forehead. A warm feeling moved through her body, soothing frazzled nerves, the after-effects of a successful healing. She'd like nothing more than to take a nap, too. But she couldn't. She had work to do.

She turned toward the door. The man she'd seen earlier—she recognized his computer bag and his towering frame—leaned against the doorway, his arms folded across his chest and one brow raised, like some sort of dark angel preparing to mete out punishment. She jumped back and let out a small shriek.

"What are you doing in here?"

Chapter Two

*O*h *my God.*

Now that Lillian got a good look at the man's face, she recognized him. He'd been on the local news for donating a large sum of money to the hospital. *Some kind of rich computer geek. Not one of Kinetica's men, thank God.* At least she didn't think so.

"I'm…I'm a nurse. The child was crying. I came to check on her." She flapped a hand toward the bed, grateful the darkness in the room covered the sweat probably gleaming from her forehead. "If you'll excuse me, I'll get out of your way."

This guy had a lot of clout. The last thing she needed was to have him asking about her at the nurse's station or for her to be seen chatting with a local celebrity. For all she knew, reporters could be following him right now.

She made to brush by him, but he simply moved a step to the right, his large frame blocking the doorway and the fluorescent light from the hallway. His eyes locked with hers, pinning her under his dark gaze.

"You're not dressed like a nurse. And you were hovering over the girl's bed like you were performing an exorcism."

With his wavy black hair, swarthy complexion, and broad shoulders, the man looked more like a spy ready for his next mission than a technology geek. He was even taller than she thought, and his eyes were black enough to blot her from existence.

Not a man to be ignored.

Lillian blinked and stepped backward, an annoying stab of fear in her stomach. If he was one of Kinetica's men, he wouldn't ask questions, she reminded herself. Kinetica struck first and asked questions later.

She kept as close to the truth as possible. "I'm not on duty. I was visiting with a…friend next door. I heard the little girl crying and went to investigate. That's all. I didn't mean to alarm you. She's sleeping peacefully. I think her fever broke."

She gestured behind her at the girl, and the man's gaze shifted, giving her poor heart a momentary reprieve. She used the second to take a breath, but that's all she managed before his hard gaze returned to hers.

"You work here?"

"No, not here."

"Where?"

"Denver," she fibbed, not daring to blink. She actually lived in Boston. But if there was one thing she'd become masterful at after two years of hiding, it was how to tell a believable lie. The secret was to veer from the truth only when necessary and never lose eye contact.

"What kind of nurse are you?"

"I'm an ER nurse." She hadn't worked in an ER since she'd left Cleveland, but he didn't need to know that.

"I see."

She flashed him the no-nonsense, attention-avoiding smile she'd perfected over the last two years. "If you'll excuse me, I really must be going."

This time when she moved forward, he paused for a moment before stepping aside. *Thank goodness.* But his footsteps sounded behind her. *Damn.* She didn't need to look to know he followed. *Damn, damn, damn.* All she needed was a nosy, rich computer guy asking questions. She moved toward the elevator.

"Do you always close your eyes when feeling a patient's forehead?" He had come up on the right side of her, his deep voice vibrating her insides.

Go away, Computer Guy. She stabbed at the down button outside the elevator. "Sometimes. When I don't have a thermometer handy."

The elevator opened, and he stepped inside, placing one hand on the door to keep it from closing. She had no choice but to follow him. Unless she wanted to create a scene, which she did not.

"Lobby?"

At her nod, he pressed the glowing L on the panel. "What's wrong with your friend?"

She watched the elevator doors close, nearly tearing her hair out at their agonizing slowness. "She's sick."

No need to panic. The elevator hummed as it moved toward their destination. The cafeteria and the exit were on the main floor. It made sense he'd head that direction, too.

"I kind of figured. Being that she's in a hospital and all."

The elevator stopped, and the doors opened. *Freedom.* But he followed close on her heels. "What's the matter with her?"

She kept walking. Her stomach tingled like he had the power to expose her secrets. The tingle widened, expanded, lengthened until she couldn't stop a shiver. She looked around at the cafeteria. The main section was closed, but a few people sat in the lounge where you could still get snacks and beverages. One of them looked up. *Ugh.* Already they were attracting attention.

She stopped walking, and he did, too.

She lowered her voice. "She has a virus."

Under the bright lights, his eyes were dark blue, not black. Although she wouldn't label him gorgeous, he was far from a geek. More like a confident tycoon—a suspicious one.

He lifted an eyebrow, as if to add an exclamation point to her thought.

"If you'll excuse me, I want to grab a coffee and get back to my friend's room." Lillian edged around the man and toward the coffee station. The high tinkle of a woman's laugh sounded behind her.

"Tristan King, I thought that was you. I didn't know you were coming back here this late in the day. Don't you have a party starting in a few hours?"

Tristan King; so that was his name.

Lillian glanced at the woman, who stopped in front of Tristan. She had high cheekbones and long red hair pulled into a sleek ponytail and wore a navy dress with an open neckline and cream-colored heels. Something about her polished, model look made Lillian suspect the woman was used to attracting attention.

The woman placed a slim hand with French-manicured nails on Tristan's chest and removed a piece of non-existent lint from his black shirt. Tristan's expression didn't change, but somehow Lillian sensed his laser focus. Whoever this lady was, she was important to him.

Now was the perfect time to make her escape. Lillian took a step, but a long arm snaked around hers, pulling her backward, so she nearly tumbled into him.

He caught her, his hands snagging in her hair. "Not so fast." Tristan smiled down at her, softening his harsh features. He winked, the movement so quick, she might have imagined it.

He turned to the lady. "Hello, Angelina." Tristan's sounded bored. "The fundraiser is still on. I only came to visit a friend. I'm heading out now."

Angelina ignored Lillian, leaning in close to whisper in Tristan's ear and giving him a good frontal view of her chest. Lillian could only imagine what she said. A promise of what might happen after the party?

Tristan wrapped his arm around Lillian's shoulder and tucked her into his side. He smelled of the sea and something else, something otherworldly, something magical, like tall evergreens under a full moon in a fierce winter snowstorm. He tilted his head and angled his face toward hers. His dark blue eyes were the night sky, swallowing her whole.

My God, what was happening?

And then she felt it. It began where his fingers grazed her arm, traveled along her spine, caressed sensitive nerve endings, and ignited a shivering, shaking, blazing trail through her entire body. White-hot scorching energy lit the space between them. His warm breath caressed her skin.

So energetic. So thrilling. So full of life.

Lillian stood transfixed under the enchanted spell he cast. Excitement curled and unfolded in her veins. She'd found a burner—the term her mother used to describe someone with immense vitality. Someone with so much natural power, he vibrated with it. Someone who could cure a room full of invalids if he'd let her.

Someone she could use to cure Hannah.

"Who's this?" Angelina asked, finally giving Lillian an ounce of her attention.

Lillian didn't answer. All she could manage was to lean against Tristan's side so she wouldn't collapse in a warm puddle at his feet.

"My date for tonight's party," Tristan said, his tone smooth, as if he hadn't just set her whole body on fire and left her a helpless lump of hot coal.

"Oh, I see. I didn't realize you had a date." Angelina shot her a dirty look. "If you'll excuse me, I need to take care of a few matters. I'll see you at the party."

"Of course," Tristan said, his gaze following Angelina's retreating form before returning to Lillian. He removed his arm from her shoulder. "I'm sorry I had to do that. Angelina won't take no for an answer. I needed to take drastic measures to get the message across. Thanks for playing along."

"You didn't give me much choice."

His grin changed his features from interrogator to co-conspirator. "There wasn't time—I had to improvise. But I'm grateful. May I get you a coffee?" He gestured toward a line of pots. "What's your name?"

She wrapped her arms around herself. "Zoey...Zoey Mills."

"I'm sorry about your friend."

He handed her a cup of coffee, and when she reached for it, a tingling sensation moved between them again. *Did he feel it, too?*

She clutched the Styrofoam cup like it held liquid courage. "Thanks. Why don't you come with me...to meet her? It's the least you can do after I played along with your little ruse."

He tilted his head and studied her, eyes shuttered. She resisted the urge to tap her feet and instead took a sip of coffee. *Say yes, say yes, say yes.*

"I can't. I am hosting a fundraiser at my house"—he checked his watch—"in less than an hour. I kind of have to be there." He pulled a pen from his bag and nabbed a napkin from the coffee bar, then scribbled his address and handed it to Lillian. "Feel free to come by later if you need a break."

His voice did strange things to her insides, and her pulse raced where their fingers brushed, so she almost dropped the napkin. She couldn't let him leave. Not without first seeing Hannah. "Please, it will only take a minute. You'll have plenty of time to get to your party afterward. I promise."

A flash of puzzlement crossed his face before something buzzed in his pocket, distracting him, and he slipped his hand into his jacket and pulled out his phone. Whatever he read on the screen wasn't good news. His whole demeanor changed, all the light and animation leaving his face at once.

"What is it?"

"An emergency. I have to go." He took off at a fast pace toward the exit.

All Lillian could do was stare after him, clutching the cup of coffee in one hand and the crumpled napkin in the other.

Chapter Three

Tristan drove his car to the Gates Mills community he called home. He was several hours late to his own party, but at least his mom was going to be okay. She'd taken a spill walking to the mailbox and had a golf-ball-sized bump on the back of her head and a concussion but no broken bones this time. *Thank God.*

He stretched his fingers, loosening his white-knuckle grip on the wheel. It'd been quite a scare getting the call about her. Two months ago, she'd tripped over her feet while making coffee in the kitchen and fractured both wrists. Only last week, her casts had been removed. *And now this.*

He drove through the security gate, up the long drive-way and around the stone fountain, passing the paved lot filled with cars where the hired valet had left them. He circled the grand front entrance and parked at the back of the estate, hurrying through the private side entrance. The decorators and caterers had been hard at work since this morning, and the hostess he'd hired for the occasion would have greeted his guests and explained his tardiness. He had only to slip on his tuxedo and join the party.

He took the stairs two at a time until he reached the master bedroom on the second floor and switched on the light. His outfit for the evening lay across the monstrous king-size bed as instructed. Black slacks and jacket, crisp white button-down shirt, shiny Italian leather loafers. He fingered the sleek material, a reflection of the wealth he'd received after selling his computer software company—was it only a little over a year ago? While he enjoyed the perks that came with money, he still hadn't quite gotten used to the dramatic shift in his finances.

He straightened, crossing to the master bathroom and flicking on the light. His entire childhood bedroom could have fit in the cavernous space at least twice over. Glistening marble tile covered the walls and floor, and a massive whirlpool tub with shiny gold fixtures sat in the center of the large room, courtesy of a recent six-figure renovation. No expense had been spared to achieve perfection. But tonight, his gut twisted at the opulence.

If only his money could transform his mother from the faded ghost she now was into the bright, vibrant woman he remembered. If only the research firms he gave millions to could find a cure for Huntington's, the disease slowly killing his mom. If only he believed in miracles.

He ripped his shirt off, tossed it on the floor, and stared at his face in the mirror above the sink. Same features he'd always had. Same dark whiskers. Same stubborn jawline. Nothing had changed. And yet his reflection seemed different tonight. He *felt* different.

He found his electric razor and plugged it in. It was the encounter with Angelina that had him so off-kilter. A year and a half ago, they'd been in love. He'd given her a diamond ring and the promise of his name and fidelity for the rest of his life. The engagement lasted nearly a month before she broke it off. She said she didn't want a man who couldn't give her children.

He ran the razor across the stubble on his chin, wishing he didn't still feel the biting pain of her dismissal as if it were yesterday. He had tried everything to convince her to change her mind, even agreeing to adopt a child one day. None of it mattered.

He made a face at his grave reflection, but it didn't stop him from remembering. She had gotten engaged to another man, a neurologist who worked at the hospital, a few days after their breakup. For a while, it seemed everywhere he went, Angelina and her doctor fiancé were likely to appear. The sight chipped away at Tristan's sanity.

He ducked his head, wanting to avoid the starkness in his reflection. But he couldn't stop the memories.

Not long ago, Angelina cornered him at a party. She said she'd made a terrible mistake and ended her engagement. She begged Tristan for another chance. He'd refused. He had his pride, and it didn't escape his notice she returned only after he'd become wealthy. He wanted her back, but he'd be damned if he'd make it easy for her.

He dropped the razor but managed to catch it before it hit the floor and turn it off. He had no idea how much longer he could resist her advances. Tonight's party was only a warm-up. Tomorrow, the hospital was hosting its biggest fundraiser of the year, and he would be the primary benefactor. There would be no avoiding Angelina.

He turned the razor on again and eyed his bloodshot eyes in the mirror. If only he had known she was the event coordinator when he had agreed to participate. Too many people were counting on him to back out now.

He brought the razor back up to his face, but his hand shook, and he had to pause and take a moment to breathe. Hell, after the encounter tonight and his mom's concussion, he was more keyed up than the day he'd sold his software company and became the richest man in the state.

I want you back.

Angelina had whispered the words in his ear, and it had been all he could do to keep from responding. If he hadn't had Zoey Mills on his arm, would he have said yes? Thank God, the mystery woman had been available and a quick study, playing the part of his date with ease.

You didn't give me much choice.

No, he hadn't given Zoey a choice. Amazing she'd cooperated when he thought about it.

He managed to move the razor in slow, steady circles over the remaining five o'clock shadow, ignoring the continued heat in his veins. Unlike Angelina, Zoey hadn't wanted his attention. That much was clear when he'd had to chase her down in the elevator. That and whatever prompted her to comfort little Annie Logan, his accountant's daughter.

He unplugged the razor and splashed his cheeks with his favorite aftershave, wincing at the sting. Maybe it would cut through the fog in his brain. The moment Angelina appeared and he'd decided to make her think Zoey was his girlfriend, he'd felt like he'd been sucked into a bottomless whirlpool, and there was no escape.

He smoothed his fingers over his jaw. Despite Angelina's presence—or maybe because of it—he couldn't ignore the feel of Zoey's soft curves pressed against his side. And her smell—like warm strawberries. His fingers had caught in her hair and brushed against her scalp, and he'd discovered something else intriguing.

The mystery woman wore a wig.

He washed his hands, drying them with one of the plush white hand towels the interior decorator had purchased. Zoey's reasons for wearing the wig were probably complicated. And he didn't need any more complications in his life right now. But it was in his nature to solve problems—he couldn't help himself. And the mysterious Zoey provided a welcome diversion from Angelina.

He removed his clothes and then crossed to the bed to put on the fancy outfit. Maybe she wore the wig because she had cancer and lost her hair? But she hadn't looked sick. No, with her rosy cheeks and sun-kissed skin, she had looked vibrantly healthy.

He put on the crisp white shirt, tucking it into his slacks, then sat on the bed, slipping on his socks and the shiny black dress shoes. What other secrets lurked behind Zoey's expressive green eyes? Had she been as shocked as he by their closeness? Was that why, after trying to avoid him, she'd practically begged him to visit her friend?

He scanned the bed until he spied his cell where he'd dropped it, then he pocketed the phone and took a last look around the room. His stomach churned, but he ignored it, flicking off the light and leaving to greet his guests.

He stood in the doorway of the large room and studied the noisy and colorful scene. A jazz band played in one corner, loud enough to be heard from every room but soft enough not to disrupt the buzzing conversations taking place around him. Candles sparkled from centerpieces on the tables, lending the room a romantic look in the dim light. A few couples swayed together on the dance floor. The smell of prime rib caused his stomach to growl, reminding him he hadn't eaten since lunch.

He entered the main room and scanned each face he saw, his gaze passing over prominent government officials, CEOs of companies, sports celebrities, and local news reporters.

No Zoey Mills. More than likely, he'd never see her again.

An odd pang tightened his chest muscles. Had he honestly expected her to show up at his home tonight? An hour ago, they'd been strangers. Strangers who'd shared a poignant moment. Poignant enough to have him considering blowing off his own party until he'd gotten the text from his mom's caregiver, Nancy, telling him his mom was in an ambulance.

He nabbed a drink from a passing server, tossed it down, and tried to squelch the twinge of disappointment in his gut. Why should he care if Zoey showed up at his party? Was he that desperate?

As if in answer, a high-pitched, familiar laugh rose above the din. *Angelina.* His stomach sank. She was chatting with a Cleveland Cavaliers basketball player—a tall, good-looking rookie who was the talk of the fans this year. Tristan gritted his teeth and practically ran to the bar for another drink.

It was going to be one of those evenings.

❦

Lillian parked behind the line of black limousines in Tristan King's wide driveway and sat for a moment to calm her erratic heartbeat. She eyed the sprawling white mansion, which must be on at least ten acres of wooded property. The place looked even bigger than in the photos her Google search turned up. The front porch covered the length of the house, set off by white pillars and a series of dormer windows. Every room in the three-story house was lit up like Christmas.

She rubbed her cold hands together. The thought of looking into Tristan's suspicious blue eyes and pleading with him to visit her sister put a stitch in her side, so she had trouble catching her breath. And she was risking her life coming to such a prominent party, where the press were likely to be present. But what other choice did she have? Sitting in a car, fretting over the coming meeting, was not going to cure Hannah.

She crossed her fingers, stiffened her spine, and whispered a quick prayer that no one recognize her. Then she forced her body into action—shut off the engine, grabbed her purse, and exited the vehicle.

She followed a couple of last-minute party guests toward the entrance. Lanterns lit the paved walkway and the stone steps leading to the massive front porch. The double doors were opened wide in welcome, a waft of warm air greeting her.

Lillian stepped through the door and into the grand entranceway and gave herself a mental shake. *I don't care how nervous he makes me or how it felt to be pressed against his body. I'm here to convince him to save Hannah. Nothing more.*

She paused and marveled at the beautiful curved wooden staircase leading to the upper levels, and the humongous, sparkling crystal chandelier hanging from the high ceiling. A discreet security system blinked green from a corner. Had she ever seen inside a house so grand? Certainly a far cry from her one-bedroom apartment in Boston she'd chosen for its affordable rent. She gazed at the foyer, which led into another massive room, filled with hundreds of chattering guests like penguins in their finest.

Lillian smoothed her hands down the little black dress she had been fortunate to pack and fingered the jewelry she'd hastily purchased at a discount boutique. None of it could compare to the expensive baubles the other women were wearing. She could only hope she fit in enough not to draw attention.

Nabbing a glass of red wine from a passing server, she gazed across the room. Power tingled along her nerve endings, and a flurry of goosebumps shivered down her spine. *Tristan's energy.* He was nearby. She was sure of it.

Lillian searched the room for him, her gaze bouncing from guest to guest, never lingering too long on any one individual. She recognized the mayor of Cleveland and an Olympic ice-skater she'd seen on television. And then she settled on a blond man talking with a tall, slim redhead. *Angelina.* The man's back was to her, but her heartbeat sped up at the military cropped hair and familiar profile.

Party sounds faded into the background as if her ears were stuffed with cotton. The blood chilled in her veins, and she froze in place, unable to think, breathe, move, a terrifying certainty in her gut.

Dominic Raines? The head of Kinetica? What was he doing at Tristan's fundraiser?

Her heartbeat sped up until it thundered in her ears. She reminded herself that she was in disguise, and Dominic was only Kinetica's front man and not one of the doctors who had experimented on her mother. He'd be unlikely to recognize Lillian. Before she could look away, Angelina glanced her direction and their eyes connected. Lillian's heart fluttered, and sweat broke out on her forehead.

She turned fast and plowed into a hard chest, the familiar scent of a cool ocean breeze washing over her. Tristan caught her in his arms, but it was too late. The glass of red wine she held was captured between their bodies. Some of it splashed onto her dress and his pristine white shirt.

A look of surprised pleasure flashed across his face so quickly she wasn't sure if she imagined it. "Steady now. Where are you off to?"

"I'm sorry," she gasped. "I was looking for you." Could Tristan be working with Dominic Raines? Why else would the CEO be at his party?

She drew in air, working to calm her erratic heartbeat and to think instead of panicking. If Tristan worked for

Kinetica he would have kidnapped her from the hospital parking lot earlier instead of inviting her into his home. Besides, lots of prominent people were at his party, and Kinetica was based in Cleveland. It wasn't an unlikely scenario the CEO would be one of Tristan's guests. Dominic and Tristan probably ran in the same social circles.

Tristan plucked the glass from her hands and set it on an empty tray nearby. "Good, I was looking for you, too. "

"You were?"

"Yes, I was hoping you'd show tonight." He smiled, giving her a glimpse of a dimple in one cheek. "How's your friend?"

"Not well." She darted a look behind her. Dominic Raines still spoke to Angelina, who was giving her the evil eye. She had to get out of here. "I...that's why I came, actually. Can we go somewhere private to talk?"

He studied her for a moment, but she couldn't read the glint in his eyes. "Come with me."

She trailed him through the room, winding her way around the other guests. It seemed to take forever to move through the crowd, although Tristan must have sensed her urgency because he never stopped until they reached the opposite side of the room. Every now and then someone would call his name, and he would give a polite nod and keep moving. The entire time she kept her head down to avoid Dominic Raines and Angelina, while the clock ticked on her sister's life.

Eventually, they exited the room, and Tristan led her down a long hallway. She swiped moisture from the back of her neck. Where was he taking her?

"Here we are. My office." He flicked on a light and led her into a large room with a vaulted ceiling. The entire wall on the right was made of glass, which she could only imagine looked out on the wide expanse of lawn and woods she'd seen behind the house. Caramel-colored leather armchairs sat in front of a wide mahogany desk with a desktop computer, and a matching couch and flat screen TV made up the wall on the left. Bookcases filled with books ran floor to ceiling behind the desk. In between the shelves hung a gorgeous painting of the night sky over the lake.

He shut the door and gestured toward the armchairs. "You'll want to clean your dress, I'm sure, and I need to do the same. There's a sink in the garden room next door. But first, have a seat."

She sat on the edge of one of the chairs, picking at the hem of her dress and crossing and uncrossing her ankles. He strolled to a cabinet to the right of the desk and opened shiny doors to reveal bottles of liquor and sparkling glasses.

"Wine, beer, martini?"

"Huh? Oh, yes."

Tristan gave her an odd look. "You want all three?"

"Oh…no, I meant those are all good options." God knows she could use all three.

He poured them each a glass of white wine and handed one to her. He held up his glass, and when she realized he wanted to toast, she clinked her glass with his. "Cheers," he said.

"Cheers," she echoed. She resisted the urge to down the drink but took a small sip.

"Well?" he asked.

"What?"

"You wanted to tell me about your friend?"

She set the glass on a coaster on his desk. "Yes, yes I do." A cold chill passed through her. Maybe she should make an excuse and leave? But what would happen to Hannah if she did?

She fingered her earrings and then the back of her neck. The room was hot. Too hot. According to her research, Tristan was a brilliant technologist and philanthropist and the state's most eligible bachelor. He'd donated millions to medical research to find a cure for his mother's illness, but there was no indication any of the benefactors had been the company she abhorred.

She crossed her fingers, filled her lungs, and prayed she wasn't making a fatal mistake. "My friend is not doing well."

"I'm sorry."

"The thing is…she's fighting for her life. She'll die if she doesn't get help." She wound her arms around her middle.

Tristan moved to her side, pressing a warm hand on her shoulder, like her father had done earlier tonight. The reminder had her fighting tears. He removed his hand and moved away, leaving an aching loss in the hollow of her stomach.

"You said she caught a virus?"

"Yes, it's called Hantavirus Pulmonary Syndrome, or HPS. She got it from hiking with her friends in a national park. There's no known cure. Her dad thought it was a cold at first. But she's in the late stages of the disease. She can barely breathe. I can't stand to see her like this."

"Have you talked to her doctor?"

"He can't help her any more than he already has." She could feel his eyes on her, digging for secrets. "But maybe you can."

He crossed to the bar and filled a glass with what looked like brandy. "How much?"

"Pardon?"

"She doesn't have insurance? You need help with the bills? How much money do you need?"

All the oxygen left the room, strangling her vocal cords. "I'm not after your money."

He turned, pinning her under his intelligent gaze, the bottle stopper still in his hand. "What do you want from me, Zoey? If it's not money, then…what?"

She took a deep breath and met his eyes. She hated the lie she was about to tell, but there was no way she could reveal her healing ability. It was way too risky, and he'd be unlikely to believe her anyway. A man like Tristan believed in ones and zeros—in computer logic—not faith in things unseen. "I'd like you to come with me…tonight…spend time with my friend."

Tristan let out a laugh that sounded both surprised and wary. "How's that going to help? I'm a software developer, not a doctor."

She pushed back her chair and stood, pacing. Lillian never paced. She was the calm one—she had to be. "My friend is a computer geek. She adores you. She's a big fan of your gaming and productivity software and business acumen. She also greatly admires your philanthropy."

"And you think my visiting will miraculously cure her?"

She stopped pacing and faced him. "No, but it would lift her spirits. She has to fight if she wants to live, and meeting you—her hero—might give her the boost she needs to survive."

He didn't answer but turned and put the stopper back on the bottle of brandy and then tossed down the contents of his glass.

She took a couple of steps toward him. "I would never have come here if the situation wasn't desperate." Without thinking, she placed a hand on his arm. The contact burned into her palm. "Listen, I know you have no reason to help me. But there must be something I can do to convince you."

He glanced at her hand and then turned and lifted one dark eyebrow, a question in his gaze. Her stomach, which was already as twisted as a pretzel, quivered.

"What exactly are you offering me, Zoey?"

She withdrew her hand, wild heat flooding her face, but for Hannah's sake, she stayed in place. He was considering her request, and Kinetica's minions hadn't shown up to grab her…yet. For the first time since she'd concocted this crazy scheme, she felt a twinge of hope. "I'm a talented nurse. I could offer you and your family my services."

He didn't respond so she rushed on, following the mental script she'd prepared to convince him. "I have an outstanding track record. I keep up with the latest procedures and am assigned the hardest cases. I'm great with patients—at easing fears and listening to confidences and consoling their loved ones when they feel all hope is gone." She hadn't worked as a nurse for two years, but she still managed to eke out a living caring for an elderly neighbor in her apartment complex. Hopefully, he'd take her at her word.

Lillian had trouble recognizing all the emotions crossing Tristan's face except for the last one, which looked like cynicism. "I see you've done your homework. You obviously know about my mother."

"Yes." There was no reason to lie.

He sighed and flashed her a look of…what…disappointment? Although why her telling him she was a nurse should be disappointing, she wasn't sure. Maybe he hated nurses?

He turned and strolled to the window, looking out at who knows what. "You equate nursing to a talent, like singing or playing the piano? Let me tell you. You can't help her. No one can. Although maybe you can entertain her with your stethoscope." Sarcasm dripped from his voice.

She didn't care if he thought this was an elaborate scheme to get his attention as long as he agreed to help. She crossed to his side. She could see their full reflections in the long windowpane. His face looked harsh and tired; her eyes wide and lost. A gust of wind blew a tree branch against the window, making a *tap-tap-tapping* sound.

"Why not let me try? What do you have to lose?"

His expression grew grimmer—if that were possible. "I've already tried everything. She has maybe a year or two if I'm lucky." The words were guttural and sharp, as if they were ripped from some well-guarded part of himself.

Lillian turned toward him. She had a feeling whatever she said now would decide Hannah's fate, but she wouldn't offer false hope or make promises she couldn't keep. "I don't know if I can help your mom, Tristan. But I swear if you come with me now, I'll do what I can. In return, I'm only asking you to visit with Hannah for an hour or so. She thinks the world of you and might not live long enough to meet you otherwise."

His dark gaze met hers in the window. Silence stretched between them, broken only by the faint murmur of party noises and the tapping of the tree branch. She'd lost. He didn't believe her story and wasn't going to help.

She couldn't control the tremble on her lips, a small sob escaping before she could stop it. "You might save her life. Don't you care?"

Hot tears rushed to her eyes, blinding her, but she turned her head, refusing to blink. Of course, he wouldn't help her. Why would he? He was a suspicious and busy man who clearly didn't trust easily and had his own mother to worry about. She'd have to find another way to save Hannah.

She retrieved her purse from the chair. If Hannah were well, she could tell Lillian exactly what emotions were happening behind Tristan's well-guarded expression. But Hannah was dying, which was why Lillian was in this predicament to begin with.

She tightened her hand around her purse and moved toward the door. She couldn't fall apart; she was running out of precious time to cure her sister.

"I'm…I'm leaving now. I need to get back to the hospital." Her voice only fluctuated a little.

She reached for the doorknob, but a soft touch on her shoulder stopped her. She hadn't heard him move.

"Zoey, wait. I'll help."

CHAPTER FOUR

"I'll help you, but I highly doubt my presence will have any effect on your friend's health." Tristan led her back inside the office, her arm tingling where he held it. "And there's little you or anyone can do for my mom, short of a miracle." His jaw tightened, hinting at deeper emotions. "But I'm sympathetic to your friend's situation, so I'll make you a deal."

"Deal?"

What deal? She'd already offered him the only item she could think to bargain with, and he'd rejected it out of hand. What more could he possibly want, unless…was he about to pounce on her, demanding a roll in the sack?

She clutched her purse, imagining herself slapping his arrogant face and storming out of the room, dignity intact. Except she couldn't—her sister's life depended on his cooperation.

He gestured to the couch, for her to sit no doubt. She complied—what other choice did she have? The hair on her arms stiffened like a small army ready for battle.

He obviously had no idea of her thoughts because he sat next to her, flooding her nostrils with his clean, masculine scent. Only thirty minutes in his company, and Lillian's body quivered, stimulated by his unusual energy level, no doubt. She adjusted her rear end on the couch cushion and avoided looking at his grim profile.

"I have another fundraiser tomorrow night, and…I could use a date."

"A date?" Alarm sharpened her voice more than she intended. Now she did look up to see his razor-sharp eyes locked on hers. "Are you joking?"

He smiled, and she supposed he meant it to be reassuring, but it came off looking like the Grim Reaper and did nothing to settle her nerves. "I'm quite serious. I need a date for Saturday evening—a large charity event the hospital is hosting, and I'm obligated to attend. You need me to visit your friend tonight. Seems like an even trade."

"I'm sure you know dozens of women who would enjoy being your date. Why do you need me?"

"The women I know would all expect a second date. And a third. I have no interest in romantic entanglements. I need someone who has no expectations of anything further. Someone who can dress the part and look convincing by my side. Someone I won't have to run into and make awkward conversation with at similar parties a month or a year from now. Someone who lives out of state, so I'm unlikely to see them again."

She sniffed, trying not to take offense at his description, which made her sound like…what exactly? An actress, a nobody, an unimportant speck of dust who didn't matter? "What exactly would I have to do?"

Something flashed in his eyes…triumph, regret, boredom? He shrugged as if he hadn't thought through the details fully. "Dress in your finest, hang on my arm, pretend like you admire me—whatever you might normally do on a similar date."

She adjusted the grip on her purse. What did a girl normally do on a date? She couldn't remember it had been so long. What harm would it do to attend a single party with him? Even if she managed to cure Hannah tonight, she couldn't leave until she was certain her sister had recovered. "If I do this, be your date tomorrow, you'll come with me, tonight, to visit my friend?"

"Yes."

"I'll do it, then."

"Great." A ghost of a smile formed on his hard features, and now she recognized the gleam for what it was—satisfaction. This was a man used to getting his way.

"I do have a few other requirements, though."

Ah, now the pouncing would commence. Her tongue stuck to the roof of her mouth, and it took her several seconds to make her lips form intelligible words. "What… what requirements?"

"I want more information. What's your friend's name, for starters?

"Hannah. Hannah Milano."

"I'll need access to Hannah's medical records and will want to talk to her doctor. You'll need to have her family sign the necessary paperwork to make it possible."

Lillian would never let Tristan know it, but he intimidated her. The power he generated pierced her mind, bending her to his will like a tree branch blown about in a strong wind. He oozed confidence, wealth, command. She would have to watch, or he'd run roughshod over her.

She lifted her chin, keeping her gaze on his. "Why do you need all of that? What do you hope to do?"

He gave her a cool look. "I think I can offer more than just a Make-A-Wish style meet and greet. You seem to forget I have a great deal of resources. I want to understand what her condition is and to see what, if anything, I can do to help."

She raised her chin a notch. "All right. But I want you to consult with me before you do anything."

"Fair enough." He nodded easily. Too easily. She got the feeling he was testing her.

He stood and faced her, hands on lean hips, dark hair tousled, every inch a billionaire tycoon. "Where are you staying while you're in town?"

"At the hospital. There hasn't been time to get a hotel room. I'll worry about that when Hannah's well."

"You'll need to shower and sleep. No sense booking a hotel room. You can stay here. I've plenty of space, and it's not far from the hospital. I'll see that you get back and forth safely."

A shiver started at the nape of her neck and tingled down her spine. Was this a trap? An elaborate plan to hand her over to Kinetica? "That won't be necessary. I'm sure I can find a hotel."

"Nonsense. This place is big enough to accommodate a large crowd. If the situation is as desperate as you say, then you don't have time to waste searching for a hotel."

He was right. Besides, if Kinetica were watching Hannah, they'd most likely look for Lillian at the hospital or her dad's house. They'd never expect her to be at Tristan's. She'd be safer from discovery there.

She stood and moved toward the door. "You win. I'll stay at your place. Can we go now?" Hannah would be dead by morning if they didn't hurry.

He pointed to the wine stain on his shirt. "Give me a second to change my shirt. I'll be quick."

He turned and moved past her with all the grace of a tiger stalking its prey. The image lodged in her brain, refusing to remove itself.

"Wait here," he flung back over his shoulder, as if he thought she'd disappear.

And then he was gone, and she was left to tap her feet and study his orderly desk. She reached for the wineglass, bumping the mouse. A large white K appeared in the center of the computer monitor. She almost dropped the glass before she realized the K was for King and not Kinetica. A cold heaviness filled her lungs. Had she made a mistake agreeing to his bargain? Could she trust Tristan? But what other choice did she have?

Her hands went to her cheeks, which were hot to the touch, and her heart tapped out an erratic rhythm. What had she gotten herself into?

She need only spend time with Tristan for a short while. Until she healed Hannah. This was only a brief interlude born out of necessity. A day or so—the promised date—and she'd be gone, and Tristan would be doing Tristan things.

So, why did she feel like she'd wandered into a hungry tiger's den and was about to be eaten for his dinner?

༄

What the hell was he thinking? Agreeing to leave his own party to accompany Zoey because of some crazy-ass fantasy she had that his presence would help her friend.

Tristan tugged off his shirt, pulling it over his head and throwing it on the bed. More than likely this was a sympathy ploy to get him to pay her hospital bills. It wouldn't be the first time. The last time he'd listened to a woman's sob story, he'd been duped into giving a large sum to a charity that didn't exist. He cringed at the memory. He'd be a fool to make a mistake like that again.

He grabbed a replacement shirt from the walk-in closet and slipped it on, gritting his teeth until his jaw hurt. He knew the answer to why he'd agreed to Zoey's request. Tomorrow night's charity bash promised to be excruciating. He needed a partner—someone Angelina might actually *believe* he liked and who wouldn't expect anything more from him. He needed someone like the calm, elusive Zoey.

He straightened his collar, studying his grim expression in the mirror above the dresser. As much as he hated to acknowledge it, he wasn't immune to Angelina's advances, and she knew it. Every time she flirted with other men, she chipped away at his resolve.

He grabbed a comb from his nightstand and ran it through his hair. Resisting Angelina was only part of the reason he'd agreed to Zoey Mills's request, though. How could he—or any decent human being—not feel for Zoey or her friend? There had been sincere desperation in her voice tonight. He knew the feeling well. He wrestled with it every day as he watched his mom slowly slipping away. Slipping into someone he didn't recognize. Someone who couldn't possibly be the smart, independent woman who'd raised him on her own.

He tried to flatten the hair that insisted on curling on one side, but it wouldn't stay down. He couldn't slow the monster stealing his only living relative from him, but if he could find a way to save Zoey's friend, it would give him immense satisfaction.

He slipped into the bathroom and ran water over the comb, tugging it through his hair and letting out a satisfied growl when it finally stayed in place. He would do what he could to aid in Hannah Milano's recovery—arrange for top doctors, see that she had the best treatment. If his position and wealth could make a difference, Hannah would survive.

Tristan gripped the marble sink, considering his reflection. Looking himself in the eye, he could not avoid an important truth. It wasn't only Angelina and an attack of conscience that had him agreeing to help—it was Zoey herself.

He opened a drawer, pulled out his toothbrush and toothpaste, applied a small amount to his brush. Zoey was different than the women who threw themselves in his path on a regular basis.

He began brushing, slowly, methodically, first one side, then the other. She didn't seem interested in him romantically and didn't seem to want his attention. Of course, she could be pretending disinterest, but he didn't think so. This intrigued him.

He wiped his mouth on the plush white towel, then tossed it into the hamper, where he wished he could toss the remainder of his restless thoughts. He would do what he could to help Hannah, and in the process, figure out what Zoey was hiding. Maybe his efforts would keep him from succumbing to Angelina's charms for a while longer.

He gathered his phone and his keys from the sleek mahogany dresser. As unlikely and slim as he knew it was, if by some miracle his visit helped Zoey's friend, maybe the universe held a similar miracle cure for his mother. His heart refused to give up on the possibility, although, logically, he recognized its foolishness.

Tristan made a quick phone call, took a last look around his bedroom, and headed down the hall to find Zoey, his logical mind already analyzing the situation from every angle. His pulse raced along with his thoughts, which was a bit puzzling. It had to be the result of the intrigue surrounding his guest and the fact Angelina was at the party.

Chapter Five

Lillian moved back and forth from the office window to Tristan's desk, refusing to look at his computer monitor. Her stomach shimmied, the overdone grilled cheese not sitting well.

She frowned at the dark mark on her chest from her earlier collision with the glass of red wine. The stain had probably set, but to calm her nerves, she'd see if she could find a bathroom and try to clean it.

Lillian tried the room next door and found a series of tall glass windows and what looked like a workstation used for potting plants, next to a sink. She opened some cupboard doors and spotted a sponge, which she wet to scrub at the stain. After a few minutes with some success, she ditched the sponge. She turned to leave, pausing before the windows to check out the view.

She drew in a breath and let it out slow. If fairies walked the earth, they most certainly lived outside Tristan's window. Winterberry shrubs sporting twinkling solar lights dotted the landscape, reflecting the sparkling stars in the velvet night sky. Lillian slipped off her high heels and leaned toward the cold glass, her breath making it fog.

"What has you so fascinated?"

She flinched, nearly bumping into the windowpane at the sound of Tristan's deep voice coming directly behind her. "Nothing important." Could the man be any lighter on his feet? If she could, she'd hang a bell around his neck. She bent to slip into her heels, avoiding his gaze. "Sorry, I wasn't snooping. I was cleaning the wine from my dress." She gestured at the wet spot. "I'm glad the dress is black. Are you ready?"

He smiled and surprised her by reaching out a hand and brushing what must have been a water droplet from her shoulder. "Yes, are you?"

She frowned at the goosebumps racing up her arm at his touch but managed to nod.

He gestured toward the door, indicating she should go in front of him. "If your friend was well, I'd show you the garden. It's one of my favorite parts of the estate."

She suspected when Hannah had recovered, Lillian wouldn't *be* in Cleveland to see Tristan's garden, but she managed to nod and smile, which he could interpret however he liked.

She followed him downstairs but almost plowed into his back when he paused to point to a shiny silver dish on a nearby table. "Leave your keys. I'll have someone move your car into the drive. We'll take mine."

Her stomach reacted at his authoritarian tone by turning over. It should be no big deal to hand over the car keys. But it was. She shook her head. "This isn't my car—it's Hannah's dad's. I'll need to get it back to him. I took him home earlier and left my rental at the hospital. Besides, you'll need to get to your party afterward, won't you? I'm not leaving the hospital. Why don't you follow me in your car?"

He turned. "I'm not worried about the party. I *am* concerned about your safety driving late at night after what has to be a long day. If you give me your address, I'll have someone drive your car to your friend's dad's house. You can leave your rental at the hospital, and I'll take you back and forth…please." He added the last in what seemed like an afterthought, as if he wasn't used to having his decisions questioned, and held out his hand for the keys.

She studied his outstretched hand. He'd agreed to help Hannah. He'd be spending time with Lillian in Hannah's hospital room. Like it or not, Lillian would have to trust Tristan—at least for tonight. She placed the keys in his palm, but as soon as they left her hand, she itched to pluck them from the dish where he deposited them.

He put his hand under her elbow to guide her along, and she suppressed another shiver. How was it a simple touch had her skin tingling again? She couldn't be shivering every time he touched her, or he'd get the wrong impression.

"This way," he said, leading her through the garage and out to his car, which beeped, the sound reassuring in the quiet night. A breeze cooled her hot cheeks. Nothing stirred in the driveway.

"Are you okay, Zoey?"

Their gazes locked. Heat overpowered her senses, and she shrugged, trying to distance herself from his wild energy. "I'm fine."

Strange how her whole body seemed to come alive with his slightest touch. Strange how her heart thumped at his nearness. Well, not so strange…he was a burner, after all. It would be stranger if she *didn't* sense and absorb his energy.

Power pricked her nerve endings, stirring her healing talent. She reached for the door and jumped when it popped open on its own.

Tristan laughed at her surprise. "I'd suggest you buckle up."

She did as he requested, getting into the car and staring at what looked like a giant computer tablet on the dash and the biggest backup display she'd ever seen. "What kind of car is this?"

"It's a solar-powered prototype I'm testing for a business acquaintance. I should warn you—it's fast."

He flashed her a wide grin from the driver's side, which did nothing to settle Lillian's nerves.

She bit her lip. *Good.* She shouldn't let herself get too comfortable. She was in this fancy car for one purpose—to save Hannah's life. Every moment she spent with Tristan was dangerous for them both.

The car hardly made a sound but moved fast and smooth, like an expensive car should, as he pulled out of the drive and onto the street.

"I know you're worried about Hannah, but you did the right thing coming to me. I'll do what I can to help your friend."

Lillian realized she gripped the seat and put her hands in her lap. "Thank you, Tristan. I'm grateful for your help."

He nodded but didn't say anything. Silence reigned unbroken only by the sounds of the road and her own breathing. She placed her hands under her legs to keep them from moving. Her gaze, however, would not stay still, drifting to Tristan's confident hands on the wheel. She searched for something to say. "What was the emergency you had earlier?"

His gaze flicked to hers and then back to the road. "My mother fell and hit her head. She has a concussion, but she'll be fine." His words were clipped, like he was trying to convince himself.

"She's in the hospital?"

He turned onto the street that ran by the clinic. "No, she's at her home with her caretaker. Nancy will watch her overnight, but she'll go back in the hospital tomorrow for some tests."

"What about your family?"

He cast her an odd look. "What about them?"

"Can't they help?"

"No."

"Why not?"

"You ask a lot of questions."

She bit her lip. Why was she asking so many questions? *Nerves.* She felt like she had to fill the silence, and asking questions was better than answering them herself. "I'm sorry. I'm just making conversation. You're entitled to your privacy."

She turned to look out the window, oddly chastened. Silence was better than conversation, anyway.

Tristan cleared his throat. "There is no one else. My father left my mom when I was a toddler—I haven't seen him since."

She looked at him, but he was staring at the road. "No siblings?"

"No. I…I had a stepdad once upon a time, an alcoholic. It's been years since I've seen him.

"I'm sorry. It's good you have a caretaker, then. What was her name…Nancy, you said?"

"Yes."

"I'm sure Nancy will take good care of your mom." So, he was an only child who didn't have a father or any other family in his life—no wonder he was so attached to his mom. At least Lillian had a sister and a dad and plenty of aunts and uncles and cousins she used to see around the holidays.

She searched for something else to say to break the awkward silence. "No girlfriends to ruin your most-eligible-bachelor status?" She managed a smile, even though inside she cringed at the question. Was that the only thing she could come up with? If he had a girlfriend, wouldn't he be taking her to the fundraiser instead of railroading Lillian to be his date?

"Not really."

Not really? Their gazes collided for a millisecond, tripling her heartbeat, before he looked back at the road. Lillian's stomach squirmed, but she refused to analyze the sensation, putting it down to the fear and panic occupying her brain for the past twenty-four hours.

She busied herself digging in her purse for a canister of mints and popping one in her mouth. She offered him a mint, which he took. It shouldn't be any surprise Tristan had a someone…maybe a few someones. He was a virile male. And he was successful and rich. It was naïve to think he wouldn't have one or more women in his life. Probably that Angelina chick, although Tristan seemed to want to avoid her.

She stilled her hands in her lap. What would those someones think of her and Tristan's current arrangement? For the second time tonight, she found herself reaching to touch him.

"Tristan, when I asked for your help, I didn't think how this might complicate your life. I didn't mean to put you in an awkward position with…anyone."

He had pulled into the hospital parking lot, hitting what looked like a turn signal to put the car in park. He shifted toward her, his intense blue eyes reflecting sincerity and something more. Something that sent a strange tingle through her. Power flooded her senses, shooting a chill up her arms.

"You didn't make me do anything I didn't want to do. I'm glad you asked for my help. Those important to me will understand."

He piqued her curiosity. Who were these important girlfriends? Were they models, actresses, neighbors…fellow billionaires?

"Are you certain? I wouldn't think any girlfriends would be happy at the thought of you shacking up with a strange woman."

One side of his mouth lifted in a half-smile. "Ah, but we're not strangers anymore, are we, Zoey? I hope we can be friends."

Her heart stuttered, stopping and then resuming its frantic beating in her chest. A few words from Tristan and a simple touch had her longing for something she could never have. *Get a grip, Lillian.* She wasn't here to make friends. Not if she hoped to save Hannah and keep all of them safe.

She pulled her hand from his. "We're...we're acquaintances." She unlatched her seatbelt and grabbed for the door handle.

His fingers grazed her arm, and she turned to look at him. It was happening again—the mesmerizing feeling of being trapped in a fairy tale. The temperature rose a notch, and her skin prickled. The rich scent of his breezy cologne filled the space between them.

"You're shivering. Are you cold?"

"Yes," she lied.

He removed his leather jacket and handed it to her. "Here, wear this."

She didn't need the jacket, but she took it anyway. She busied herself putting it on under his watchful gaze, wrapping herself in the warm leather and breathing in his scent like he'd wrapped her in his arms. She swallowed and clutched her purse. "Are you ready?"

He smiled, and the heat in his gaze could have softened diamonds. "Yes." He leaned toward her and unhooked her seatbelt, his warm breath carrying a hint of wintergreen mint.

She fumbled for the button on the door and managed to push it open and stumble out of the car. Then she strode toward the hospital entrance, not waiting to see if he followed.

What the hell had just happened in there? Why was she trembling? And dammit, why had she asked him if he had a girlfriend or not? It was none of her business. The date they would have tomorrow was a pretend date—meant to repay a debt, nothing more.

She could hear Tristan's footsteps close behind. A shiver coursed through her, starting at her scalp and ending in her toes.

Oh, for the love of God, she was attracted to him. She could admit it to herself even though it pained her. She was worried for Hannah, and she was lonely. It had been two long years since she'd had an extended conversation with any person, let alone a man as dynamic and handsome as Tristan. That could be the only explanation for her loose lips and sudden heart palpitations.

She stopped at the sliding glass doors, waiting for him to catch up. Loneliness was no excuse for stupidity. She would not allow the momentary lapse in judgment to repeat itself. A single mistake could harm everyone she'd worked so hard to protect over the last two years. And it could get Tristan killed.

She just had to keep reminding herself.

Chapter Six

O*h, Lordy.*

Lillian avoided looking at Tristan as they entered Hannah's room. What madness had she unleashed when she'd asked for his help to save her sister?

"How is she? Any change?" Lillian asked the night nurse on duty.

"Pretty much the same," the nurse said, eyes widening when she spied Tristan. "She seems to have adjusted as well as can be expected. Her body can focus on healing. We'll evaluate her for the next forty-eight hours to watch for improvement. If so, the doctor will make a decision about whether we can remove the ventilator. My shift is ending, but the next nurse is taking over. Maryanne. She's great."

"Okay, thanks…this is Tristan," Lillian added when she noticed the nurse's gaze pointed his way. "Tristan, this is Dani, one of Hannah's nurses."

Tristan held out a hand to Dani, who shook it as if she were in a trance.

"Are you Tristan King? My son loves your video games. *Gladstone* is his favorite."

Tristan nodded. "That's a great game. Listen, is there a doctor on duty? I'd like to speak with them."

Lillian appreciated how he didn't make a fuss but stayed focused on Hannah.

"Oh, yes. Dr. Beyton should be here soon. I'll be sure to tell him."

He nodded, seeming to take the nurse's admiration in stride, and followed Lillian to the single bed where Hannah lay propped against a pillow, eyes closed, her dark hair spread around her oval face. Tubes and cords ran from her mouth to the large machine at her bedside, which breathed for her. A small bandage covered her nose.

Blood thrummed through Lillian's veins, pounding at the gates of her heart.

Thump. Thump. Thump.

She avoided looking at Tristan, who stood next to her, and curled her fingers into her palms to keep herself from nervous chatter. She'd already talked to him more than she'd talked to anyone in a long while. Less than twenty-four hours in his company, and she'd run a gamut of emotions, from fear to sorrow to embarrassment to… to attraction.

Mercy. Was it hot in here or what?

She forced her fingers open one by one. She'd never be able to cure Hannah while wound tight like this. She drew in air and let it out—another desperate bid to relax. It wasn't working.

She should have kept quiet on the way to the hospital. Talking with Tristan had only increased her curiosity and reminded her of all she was missing in her life. And his close proximity had her so on edge, she was unable to think clearly or even breathe. He was all warm musky male and mint and power.

She trembled, barely managing to conceal it by grabbing her purse and pretending to search for something. Her hand tightened around the tin of mints at the same time Tristan spoke, breaking the silence.

"What now?"

She pulled the tin from her purse, popped it open, and ate a mint before tilting the box toward Tristan, who refused. She put the box back in her purse. Tristan tossed her a puzzled look. "Do you want to try and wake her so she knows I'm here?"

She dug in her purse for a tissue. "Yes, in a moment."

"What's the matter?"

"I'm thinking."

"You're stalling. What do you need me to do? I thought you would let her know I'm here at least. How will this work otherwise?"

She avoided his penetrating gaze. If she had any hope of curing Hannah, then she needed to distance herself from him for a moment. Because she certainly couldn't absorb his energy all keyed up like she was.

"Stand over there." She pointed across the room.

"By the door?"

He made a sound of disbelief, but when she nodded, he sighed and strode to the opposite side of the room as she'd asked. *Thank God.*

He crossed his arms and waited, a look of tired impatience on his face. "Well?"

She wiped her hands on her dress, but it didn't wipe her anxiety away. "Sorry, I can't concentrate with you right next to me."

His lips tilted up in a smirk. "You're kidding, right?

The amusement in his tone stung. He had no idea the difficulty of the task in front of her. How she'd need to focus so that she didn't hurt him. How she risked her own health.

She dropped her gaze to Hannah. What Tristan thought of her didn't matter. All that mattered was saving her sister. She reached for Hannah's hand, smoothing her fingers across her wrist, feeling for a pulse. "I need a minute."

"Go right ahead. Don't mind me. I'll just be right here…waiting."

She closed her eyes on the sight of Tristan propped against the wall like he posed for a painting.

One, two, three…breathe.

It took her a full ten minutes to get her brain into the proper mental state needed for healing.

❧

From across the room, Tristan studied Zoey where she leaned against the bed, head bowed over her friend. An ache of sympathy filled his heart. Was she praying?

He shifted his weight against the wall. With her face smooth of the tension it held earlier, she was quite beautiful. He reminded himself of the gravity of the situation. What did it matter what she looked like? He was only here to help her friend.

He ran a hand across the back of his neck, but it didn't release the hard knot that had formed there. How was he to accomplish anything when she'd relegated him to a corner like a child who'd misbehaved?

After what seemed like an eternity, Zoey grasped Hannah's hand and called to her, but her friend remained unconscious. Long seconds passed with the rhythmic rasp of the ventilator, the beep of the heart monitor, and his own breathing the only sounds breaking the silence.

He pressed his lips together and shifted his feet. "Zoey…"

She motioned for him to come closer. When he neared the bed, she closed her eyes and swayed back and forth, trance-like. Was it his imagination, or did Hannah's face look brighter, more animated? Tristan stilled.

As if she heard his thoughts, Hannah turned in the hospital bed, the first movement Tristan had seen her make since he entered the room. Zoey still held Hannah's hands, her eyes closed, reminding him of how she'd held little Annie Logan's hands.

Zoey opened her eyes and shot Tristan a look of what? Desperation? Panic? He caught the anxiety reflected there before her gaze flew back to Hannah's.

To hell with standing by while she prayed for her friend or whatever she was doing. He was supposed to be helping. He moved to her side and placed a hand on her shoulder. "Let me talk to the doctor. I'll see what we can do to improve Hannah's care."

Lillian made a small noise and pressed her hand over his. Her fingers were cool and curled around his, causing a strange warmth to unfurl in his belly.

"I can't lose her."

"Shh. You won't. Hannah's tough. She'll make it." He entwined their fingers to offer her comfort.

Lillian's grip tightened.

He kept up a steady stream of words, calming words, he hoped. "I have a friend who's one of the top respiratory doctors in the nation. Doctor Melanie Harris. You may have heard of her. She's a regular correspondent on CNN. I called her before we left my house. Mel has agreed to look into Hannah's case."

Tristan waited for some response—a word of thanks, perhaps—but none came. Motion from the bed caught and held his attention. Hannah's eyes fluttered, then opened.

CHAPTER SEVEN

Lillian let out her remaining breath in a whoosh. She tugged her hands from Tristan's and hovered over Hannah. A familiar focus descended, even though her heart lurched in her chest and a dull headache pounded behind her left temple.

She'd overused her talent. She'd been so intent on saving Hannah without harming Tristan, she'd ignored her personal boundaries. Used too much of her own energy. If Tristan hadn't placed his hands on hers when he did, she'd have passed out. Who knows if she would have regained consciousness.

She tossed her hair over her shoulder. Though she'd have to suffer her body's painful reaction, this was an insignificant price to pay if her efforts cured Hannah. She bit her lip. Pain radiated down her spine and settled in her hips. She would not be able to stay on her feet for much longer.

Absorbing Tristan's enormous energy had been difficult. Not that it was hard to access. He oozed power like a leaky hose. But he also caused her pulse to race and sent her system into overdrive, which made it challenging to channel. It took tremendous control to ignore his charismatic presence and focus on the task of healing her sister.

"Hannah, I'm here," she managed. "Can you hear me?"

Hannah nodded, her eyes wide with fear, but with the tubes in her mouth she couldn't speak.

Lillian fought the urge to touch her sister. If she did, the energy she'd transferred would return to Lillian. "You're gonna be okay. Thank God you're awake. I was beginning to worry. I'll get the nurse."

"No," Tristan said. "Stay with Hannah." He pulled out a chair, frowning, and motioned Lillian to sit. "You look like you should be the one in the hospital bed."

She wanted to say something smart, but her legs were about to collapse from under her, so she murmured her thanks and sat.

Tristan left to fetch the nurse, while Lillian's gaze returned to Hannah's. She rubbed her temples. *Think, Lillian, think.* Thank goodness Hannah couldn't speak yet. If she could, there's no telling what would come out of her mouth. And Lillian wasn't in any shape to deal with one of Tristan's interrogations.

As if he sensed her thoughts, Tristan returned with the nurse, his gaze going straight to Lillian's. She could feel his eyes on her, dissecting…analyzing. She angled her face toward Hannah, trying to ignore the fire truck that had taken up residence in her skull. It blasted its alarm, sending tiny trembles of exhaustion through her body.

She clasped her hands and attempted to slow her racing heart. Two years ago, Lillian had made the difficult decision to fake her death, change her identity, and limit communication with her family to protect them. The plan had worked out well, considering she'd remained hidden from Kinetica, and her family had been left in peace.

She flicked a glance at Tristan, who was still staring at her. She couldn't fall apart now. No matter if Tristan thought her strange. No matter if she collapsed in this spot.

Maryanne checked the machine and took Hannah's vitals. When she finished, she shook her head, mumbling under her breath. "It's incredible she's awake. She's made a remarkable turn for the better. I'll be right back." She left in a hurry.

Hannah's gaze latched onto Lillian's. She brought one hand up and wrote in the air.

"You want to write?" Lillian asked. "Are you sure?"

Hannah gave a short nod.

Lillian fumbled in her purse and came up with a pen and a small notebook, which she opened and laid on the bed next to Hannah. "How are you feeling?" She offered Hannah the pen.

Like I was hit by a truck. Hannah scratched the pen against the paper. *Who's this?*

Lillian glanced in Tristan's direction. She cleared her throat. "It's Tristan King, can you believe it? I met him earlier tonight when he was visiting the patient next door. I asked him to stop in since I know how much you admire him."

Did Tristan suspect she'd lied about Hannah being an admirer?

If he did, he didn't show it. He smiled at Hannah—a genuine smile, all warm and sincere and concerned. Lillian's breath caught in her throat. Would he ever smile at her that way? All she noticed whenever she was brave or frustrated enough to look his way was a calculated gleam. As if he suspected she was keeping secrets and was determined to uncover the reason.

"Nice to meet you, Hannah," he said.

Hannah pointed at the tubes in her mouth at the same time Dr. Beyton came through the doorway, Maryanne close on his heels.

"Well, I'll be," the doctor said. "This is a very good sign." He gestured at Hannah. "Looks like our patient has turned a corner."

The doctor's gaze landed on Tristan, his eyes widening, before moving to Lillian. "Are you all right?"

No. She was not all right. She hadn't been all right since she'd gotten the call from her dad, and she'd made the panicked decision to come to Cleveland. The room wavered before her eyes like some kind of drug-induced mirage. Fatigue hit her hard, and she put her head in her hands and struggled to catch a breath.

"She's exhausted." Tristan commanded Dr. Beyton's attention. His hand settled on her shoulder, solid and protective. Warmth traveled from her shoulder to her heart, giving her the strength to remain standing. "Is there somewhere she can lie down?"

"Of course." Dr. Beyton cast her a clinical stare. "The chair over in the corner reclines." He pointed to a blue armchair. "I'll get the nurse to help you."

"I'm okay. It's just lack of sleep," she heard herself mumble from some distant universe. *As well as a massive transfer of energy.* "Take care of Hannah."

Tristan leaned toward her. "Come lie down."

Lillian sniffed the rich scent of soap mixed with cologne that was Tristan. The smell dazzled her senses, opening a longing in her heart she thought she'd sealed long ago. "But you…Hannah…"

"Will be fine. You, I'm not so sure. Your friend doesn't need you collapsing on her." His tone softened. "Relax, Zoey. Let me help you."

"I can manage…"

Strong arms pulled her up and into his side. She clung to him to prevent herself from passing out. The room swung madly, like a thousand colorful horses spun on a possessed carousel. Candles burned behind her eyelids.

And then her mother was there.

"Lillian," she said. "Listen to the man, sweetheart."

CHAPTER EIGHT

"Mama? How did you get here? We all thought you were…"

"Dead? Oh, baby. I'm not dead, I just haven't visited in a while."

Her mother stood in the doorway, a bouquet of daisies in her hand. Lillian gazed at the familiar pink rose wallpaper of her bedroom at her dad's house. Her mother loved flowers. How had she gotten here? She felt the sheets to make sure they were real. The crisp white cotton creased under her fingertips.

Her mom had on her favorite turquoise dress, her dark hair straight and shiny and pulled into a bun. Her cheeks were pink, like she'd been out in her flower garden and had come inside to check on Lillian. Her lips tilted up in quiet delight.

Lillian pulled one hand from under the sheets to beckon her mother to her side. "I'm so glad you're here, Mom. I've missed you. My head hurts. I think I overdid it."

Her mother leaned over her bed and placed a cool hand on her forehead. She smelled like lemon verbena. "You're not running a temperature." She smoothed Lillian's hair, brushing a stray piece from her cheek. "Listen closely, honey. I've something important to tell you."

"Sure, Mom. What is it?" Her mother's touch soothed the jackhammer pounding at her temple.

"You will not be able to run from Kinetica forever."

Her breath caught in her lungs. "They will catch me?"

Cool fingers stroked her cheek in a soothing swirl. "They will steal your happiness if you let them. It's not your job to cure everyone."

Lillian frowned. "Hannah's not everyone. Do you want me to let her die?"

Her mother's eyes took on a faraway expression, as if she saw sights Lillian could not hope to understand. Then she shook her head, giving Lillian a soft smile. It radiated love and concern and motherly wisdom. "You're merely an instrument, Lily. Whether Hannah lives or dies is not your decision."

"What are you saying? This virus will kill her?" Lillian could not disguise the trembling fear in her own voice.

"No, honey. Your sister is strong. But death comes to us all eventually. You won't be able to save the ones you love every time. I couldn't."

"But you sacrificed your life to warn me about Kinetica. You knew they'd kill you, but you managed to write me a letter. After you died, I found it tucked inside the secret compartment in your suitcase. That's how I learned the car accident was a setup—that they'd murdered you and made it look like an accident. That they infected people with deadly viruses and made you try to heal them. That they were using your DNA to create super healers. If I hadn't received your letter, they would have captured me, too, and who knows what they would have done to Hannah and Dad."

"I did what a mother must do. But my fate does not have to be yours." She bent, kissed Lillian's forehead, and whispered. "Feel better, sweetheart."

"No, wait." She stretched her arms in the air, but her mother evaded them. "What should I do to save Hannah?"

"Follow your heart, my Lily."

Strong hands gripped her shoulders, giving her a slight shake. "Zoey, Zoey, can you hear me? Wake up."

Pain crashed into her skull, robbing her of breath. Lillian opened her eyes and squinted at Tristan's face, trying to make sense of his wide pupils and the creased lines indenting his brow. A low moan tumbled from her lips. She was in the hospital, of course. She must have passed out after attempting to cure Hannah.

"Hannah…" She tried to rise, but Tristan held her down.

"Is off the ventilator and resting. No need to worry. The doctor thinks she is past the worst. The nursing staff is keeping a careful eye on her. There's nothing you need to do or worry about. When's the last time you had something to eat?" Tristan raised one eyebrow, demanding the truth.

Lillian wrinkled her nose, trying to remember. She'd had a snack on the airplane. But that had been many hours ago. She'd been so keyed up about her plans to go to Tristan's home and her fear of Kinetica, she'd only eaten a bit of her grilled cheese sandwich.

"I had a small bite before I came to your party."

Tristan turned to Maryanne, who'd entered the room. "Can we get a meal?"

"Absolutely. I'll take care of it." Maryanne smiled at Lillian, her manner confident and efficient. "The cafeteria's closed this late in the evening but we keep meals in the fridge. How does breakfast sound?"

"Fine. Thank you."

Maryanne left to get the food, leaving Tristan by Lillian's recliner. "You need to take better care of yourself."

Lillian sighed. No use arguing. He was right. "I know. It's been difficult. Is Hannah truly okay?"

Tristan glanced toward Hannah's bed. "Yes, she's sound asleep. Honestly, I'm more concerned about you right now. You're far too thin."

"You sound like my…like Hannah's dad. He thinks food solves all life's problems."

"He's a smart man. You should listen to him."

Lillian's lips twitched. The thumping in her head faded to a dull ache. "If I ate what he wanted me to eat, I'd gain fifty pounds."

Tristan found a chair and placed it next to her, gifting her with his unreadable smile and causing a strange excitement inside Lillian. She bit her lip, her smile fading. Why did a simple look from the man have her all jumpy inside?

"That wouldn't be a bad outcome. Has this happened before?"

Lillian dropped her gaze to the blanket covering her. "Passing out? Not often."

"But it has happened before. When?"

Lillian shrugged. "A year ago. Maybe less."

Tristan lifted a finger and raised her chin until their eyes met. Intelligence and something more lurked in his shadowy blue depths.

"Care to elaborate?"

If she told him the truth, he wouldn't believe her. She crossed her fingers under the blanket. "I work in an ER. We're always short-staffed. More often than not, I work twelve-hour shifts. Taking care of patients can be exhausting."

"But you do more than just take care of your patients, don't you?"

Adrenaline pulsed through her veins, but she schooled her features into what she hoped was a calm expression. Now that the sweeping pain had receded, she found she couldn't look away from the directness in Tristan's gaze. "What...what do you mean?"

"You pray over them or whatever you call what you did with Hannah just now and with Annie yesterday."

"Sometimes. What of it?" She held her breath. He'd witnessed her gift in action. Did he understand what he'd seen?

"You spend time and mental energy worrying about your patients. No wonder it makes you ill."

She brushed his hand away. "Usually, I'm pretty good but this situation...it's difficult when my emotions are involved." Knowing Kinetica could show up any moment and steal her away—not to mention the tension between Tristan and her—drained her energy.

"You don't need to convince me." Tristan's tone was reasonable, but Lillian knew if she hadn't just passed out in the recliner, he'd say much more.

Maryanne entered with a container, a bowl, a carton of milk, and plastic utensils and set them on a table, which she rolled to the recliner. Tristan lifted the plastic cover, opened the paper napkin, and spread it on Lillian's lap with a flourish.

"Let's see what gourmet items are on today's menu. Hmm, the special is scrambled eggs, wheat toast, an assortment of fruit—" he poked around with his fork, "—including at least one strawberry, and my personal favorite and the choice of preschoolers everywhere, Cheerios. What would you like?"

She smiled and held out her hand for the fork. "The fruit."

"Excellent choice." He speared a piece of melon with the fork and held it to her lips.

"I'm not an invalid. You don't have to—"

He shoved the melon in her mouth and winked at Maryanne. "Amazing how well this works, isn't it?"

Maryanne laughed, clearly charmed. "I see you know how to handle her. She's in good hands. I'll check on my other patients and will be back in a bit."

Tristan nodded, and Maryanne left in a flurry of uniform. He turned back to Lillian with an exaggerated growl. "All right, my pretty. You are now solely in my clutches. Eat your breakfast, or I'll lock you in the dungeon."

"Tristan, this is silly. I said I can serve myself—"

In went a strawberry. Tristan sighed as if she were the greatest burden in the world. She had no choice but to chew and swallow. When she finished the fruit, he started on the scrambled eggs.

"Really, Tristan, I'm much better now. I'll take over from here." She reached for the fork, but he held it away from her hands.

"And ruin my fun?" His eyes twinkled, laughter in their depths. "Why didn't I think of this earlier? You can't argue with your mouth full of food. Brilliant."

He brought the fork of egg toward her mouth. She tightened her lips and frowned. "Give me the fork, mister."

He laughed but didn't budge when she put her hands on the end of the fork and tried to wrest it from him.

"What, so you can stab me to death? I don't think so. Open up."

"Tristan, I swear—" In went the egg.

"You must be feeling better if you're back to swearing."

Laughter choked her, but she found herself dutifully chewing and swallowing. "Enough." She held her palm out, effectively blocking his path. "I'm much better now, thank you. Will you please hand over the fork?"

He let out an exaggerated sigh, but he gave her the utensil. "A bossy one, aren't you?" He flashed a glimmer of a smile, so she'd know he wasn't serious.

She blinked and took calming breaths. The Grim Reaper had disappeared, and in his place was a charming, attractive male. Lillian could admit it, even if she had no intention of sticking around after their so-called date tomorrow night. She busied herself with the food, trying not to notice the way his dark hair fell across his forehead, contrasting with the sparkle in his navy-blue eyes.

Tristan's cell phone buzzed, and he excused himself to answer it, strolling to the window overlooking the parking lot. He tugged a hand through his hair. His energy shifted, diminished. Whatever the call was about, it wasn't good.

She finished her scrambled eggs and took a sip of milk. The light-headed feeling vanished. Being around Tristan, she'd absorbed more of his energy already.

Lillian pushed the table away and pulled back the cover. She wasn't a patient. She couldn't risk sleeping in the hospital. And once Hannah improved, she'd need to leave as soon as possible, no matter how much she longed to stay. Time to get up and see for herself how her sister fared.

The movement caught Tristan's attention, who turned and frowned at her, shaking his head like she was his to order around. Just because he'd agreed to help her with Hannah didn't mean he could dictate if she stayed resting or not. It was dangerous for her to sleep in the hospital, where anyone could walk in and find her.

She slipped her feet off the side of the chair and headed toward the bathroom. When she came back, he'd finished his call and was prowling the room.

"I have to go visit my mom. Stay here and rest."

She stopped at the foot of the bed and studied her sister. "I don't need rest. What I need is to keep an eye on Hannah."

"Your friend is sleeping. You can't help her right now. You would do well to catch up on your sleep so you *can* help when she's awake again."

Lillian nodded. What Tristan said made sense, but she'd be better off catching up on sleep at Tristan's house where at least he had an alarm system. Kinetica could already be spying on her, waiting for an opportunity to get her alone—to drug her and force her to go with them.

He pulled the blanket from the recliner and held it up with a grin. "Hop in, then. I'll tuck you in."

She rolled her eyes but couldn't contain a glimmer of a smile as she returned to the recliner. She had to admit, it felt good to have someone looking out for her, even if she had no intention of staying on the makeshift bed after he left the room.

He tucked the blanket around her and then whipped out his cell phone and snapped her picture before she knew what he was about.

Cold fear tightened her belly. "Why did you do that?" She tried to grab his phone and delete the photo, but he held it out of reach.

He smirked. "I believe that was the first real smile you've given me since I met you. I thought I'd better capture it so I don't forget."

Fear turned the blood in her veins to ice. "I didn't say you could take my picture. Delete it."

He narrowed his gaze and frowned, and Lillian realized her strong reaction to being photographed had made him suspicious.

"Why do I have the feeling the minute my back is turned, you'll give me the slip? Remember our deal. You promised to be my date for the fundraiser tomorrow evening." The Grim Reaper had returned.

Lillian took a breath. There was no sense drawing further attention to herself and feeding his suspicions. She wasn't going anywhere at the moment, and if she stayed calm, perhaps she could convince Tristan to delete the photo later.

"I haven't forgotten."

He brushed the hair from her eyes and his tone softened. "Good."

She grabbed his arm. "Tristan, I…"

He turned, and his gaze held hers. "What is it?"

"If anything happens to…to Hannah's dad, please keep an eye on Hannah—at least until she's well."

Hard muscles clenched under her hand, and his forehead creased. "Nothing's going to happen to Hannah's dad."

"I worry for them."

He paused, a considering expression on his face. "Hannah is vastly improved. What exactly do you think is going to happen to her dad?"

"Nothing." She couldn't very well tell him about Kinetica, could she? He'd start poking around, asking questions. They'd come after her and kill him if he stood in their way. Kill her family. "I'm afraid for Hannah when I'm not around. She only has her dad to look after her, and he's exhausted."

"I promise I won't let anything happen to either of them. But you must make me a promise, too."

Her heartbeat stuttered, then fluttered against the walls of her chest cavity like a trapped bird. "What?"

"Stay here and sleep until I get back."

She dropped his hand. "That's silly."

His eyes bore into hers, all trace of laughter removed from their icy-blue depths. "Is it?"

She swallowed. "What do you mean?"

"I mean, I won't be a pawn in any games. You asked for my help, and I've given it, but if there's something you're not telling me, spill."

She swallowed hard and prayed her expression appeared innocent. "There's nothing."

Tristan searched her eyes but must have been satisfied by what he saw because he gave her one last nod and then walked to the door. "Rest. I'll be back in a couple of hours."

Lillian flopped her head against the recliner. She took deep, calming breaths—anything to still the butterflies wreaking havoc in her stomach.

Tristan didn't know anything. She didn't have to listen to him, and he'd probably forget about the photo he'd snapped after she'd returned to Boston. At least, she hoped he would.

She tried to slow her breathing. Sure, she'd asked for Tristan's help, but that didn't mean he was entitled to take her picture and order her to sleep. Lillian didn't care how angry that made him. He didn't comprehend the danger of her situation.

She closed her eyes. She'd just lay here for a few minutes until she calmed her racing heart, then she'd get up to keep watch by Hannah's bedside.

❧

"Tristan, Tristan, wait up." Angelina's familiar voice carried down the hospital corridor.

Tristan paused, holding his breath before turning around. She'd pulled her long, red hair behind her ears, which emphasized her slender neck. A small pair of diamond studs he'd given her one Christmas glittered in her ears.

A familiar ache formed in his chest. "What is it?" The words came out gruffer than he'd intended.

"I never got to say goodbye last night after you left the party so quickly. Is your mom getting her usual treatment?"

He nodded. "I'm on my way to see her now."

"I'll walk with you."

His heart pounded, which was annoying enough to make him frown. Would he ever not react this way in her presence? "Don't you have more important things to do?"

"I can't think of anything more important than keeping you company." She looped her arm in his, blinding him with her smile. "I know how hard this is for you."

He swallowed a lump in his throat. "Yes." But he wasn't only talking about his mom's condition.

They walked in silence for a minute before she got to what was really on her mind, as he knew she would. "Have you thought about what we talked about?"

"What was that?" He refused to make it easy for her.

"You remember…about getting back together. You said you'd think about it. Well, it's been a few weeks, so I was wondering…"

"I have thought about it." He'd been thinking about nothing else until Zoey's arrival.

"And…are you going to forgive me or keep punishing me?"

Punishing himself was more like it. He stopped walking, dropping his arm and stepping away from the warm invitation of her body. "I…I don't know yet."

She blinked up at him with wide, knowing eyes, causing his heartbeat to accelerate. "I love you, Tristan. And I'm pretty sure you still love me. I've apologized for what I did and asked for your forgiveness. If you still want me, you need to let me know that."

"I…I know."

"Good. Because I won't wait around forever." She leaned forward, the powdery scent of her perfume permeating his senses. "I have to run, but I'll see you at the party later. I'll be waiting for your answer."

CHAPTER NINE

"How long has she been sleeping?"

Lillian's eyes fluttered, but some sixth sense made her keep them closed when she recognized Tristan's deep voice. He was talking to someone. *Dad?*

"She was asleep when I got here at nine."

"It's eleven now," Tristan murmured. He sounded satisfied that she'd obeyed his command to rest, which was annoying.

"Thank you for checking on her," her dad said.

"It was nothing. But I'd like to ask you another question. Do you mind?" Tristan asked.

"Not at all. What is it?"

"Is Zoey in some kind of trouble?"

"Not that I'm aware of. We don't see or hear from her much. She works a lot. What makes you think she's in trouble?" Her father sounded wary, and with good reason. If Tristan started fishing around, asking questions, he'd blow her cover and put them all in danger.

"I don't know. She seems nervous. Before I left the room earlier, she made me promise I'd take care of Hannah if something happened to you."

Her dad grunted. "It can't be easy seeing her best friend in a hospital bed."

Enough. Lillian cleared her throat and coughed.

"She's awake."

Lillian stirred and opened her eyes to see two pairs gazing back at her, one set a worried brown, the other a suspicious blue. "How's Hannah?"

"Talking and eating, both good signs," Tristan said.

"You were supposed to wake me up, mister. I want to see her."

"And now that you're rested you can see her."

She narrowed her gaze. "I don't need your permission to visit my friend."

His eyes glittered like the tanzanite in her favorite ring. "I never said you did."

"Good." She sat up and pulled the covers off her. "I'm glad we got that straight."

She didn't wait for a response but stretched and stood, pushing past the curtain and striding toward Hannah's bedside. Her sister's eyes were closed, the ventilator removed. Her chest rose and fell, and her pale skin had taken on a bit of color. *Thank goodness.* Once Lillian was sure Hannah had fully recovered, she'd be on the next flight to Boston.

"I told you she was sleeping."

Tristan's deep voice vibrated her hair, causing her to jump.

How had she not heard him move? "I...I know. I just needed to see for myself."

The door opened, and she startled. It was just the nurse to check vitals. Lillian didn't look at Tristan, but she didn't kid herself he hadn't noticed her reaction.

Her dad came to the rescue. "Why don't you two grab lunch? I'll stay with Hannah."

Lillian frowned, exchanging a silent communication with her dad, whose expression indicated it was the only idea he could think of to distract Tristan. She hoped her dad correctly interpreted her answering frown as saying she shouldn't be leaving the hospital.

She flicked a quick glance at Tristan, who nodded, his blue eyes piercing. "Good idea." He motioned for Lillian to proceed in front of him.

She ran her fingers through her hair, fluffing it, and forced a smile. Objecting would only put Tristan on full alert, and she had to eat at some point. "Call or text me when she's awake, okay?" she told her dad. "I'll come *right* back."

Her father had already taken the chair next to her sister's bedside. He nodded and waved her off. "Don't worry. I will." She hoped he caught her emphasis on the word "right" and understood she wanted him to summon her to return as soon as possible. She didn't need to be hanging out with Tristan any longer than necessary.

Then she was heading toward the stairs, Tristan's warm breath on her back. He placed a hand on her shoulder, directing her to the nurse's station. A wave of heat traveled over her skin and lightened her step. How easily his presence calmed and energized her.

"Let's stop at the front desk. Hannah's father told me you're authorized to request her medical records. I want to look them over and share them with the doctor I was telling you about—Melanie Harris. She'll check into Hannah's treatment."

He guided her toward the desk where two nurses sat.

"My friend is feeling better now. Is it really necessary to involve another doctor in her care?"

"Mel—Dr. Harris is the best respiratory doctor around."

She wanted to argue that Tristan's fancy doctor friend couldn't do anything more for Hannah than Lillian already had. But he wouldn't believe her, so she might as well save her breath. Besides, she'd agreed to let Tristan have access to Hannah's records, and it wouldn't hurt Hannah to have Tristan's doctor friend look over them, would it?

"Hello, Tristan," a familiar female voice purred, interrupting their conversation. "How did it go with your mom?"

Tristan stiffened, and Lillian had a strange sense of déjà vu when he draped an arm around her shoulder and pulled her into his side. Every place where her body touched Tristan came alive, and she had to work hard to keep from shivering.

"Hello, Angelina. She's recuperating. Have I introduced you to my friend?"

She peered at Lillian and nodded her head, not missing a beat. "Oh, yes, the other night. And you brought her to yesterday's little shindig." She turned to Lillian, offering her a limp hand and a fake smile. "I'm Angelina Ramos."

"Zoey Mills." Lillian knew the smile she mustered up was also fake.

"Did you enjoy the little party?"

Enjoy it? "Yes, yes it was nice," Lillian said, hoping she sounded enthusiastic enough for Angelina.

But as it turned out, Angelina was only being polite and had already turned her attention to Tristan. "I'm looking forward to talking with you at the event tonight. Why don't we ride together? I can pick you up at six."

"I can't. Zoey will be coming with me."

"Oh." Angelina's smile faded, but she shrugged and gave a sad little pout that Lillian wondered if she practiced because it somehow looked cute and not all that sad. It seemed to work on Tristan, though, because he hadn't taken his eyes off Angelina, even though he had Lillian tucked into his side like a life preserver.

"I'll look forward to seeing you there, then. We have a lot to catch up on, don't we?"

She smiled and walked away, and Tristan's gaze followed her swishing hips all the way down the hall until she disappeared around a corner.

Lillian managed to detach herself from his side.

"How do you know her?" she asked to break the awkward silence.

"Sorry?" He finally seemed to realize he was still staring at Angelina's backside. "We met at a charity fundraiser a few years ago. She's the coordinator for tonight's event. Listen, I have to use the restroom. You go ahead. I'll be right back."

She frowned and watched as he hurried away. Was he really going to the restroom, or was he chasing after Angelina? Why did she care? It gave Lillian a breather, didn't it?

❧

Tristan followed Angelina down the hall, his blood pumping in his veins. Who was he fooling by playing hard to get? He still had the hots for her, and she'd made it clear she still wanted him. They had been good in bed together, hadn't they? And she knew how to please him. What the hell was he waiting for then?

She stopped to talk to a young, handsome medical student, laughing at something he said. Tristan strained to hear but was too far away to make sense of the conversation. He could see the man's gaze checking out her perfectly proportioned body as she pointed at something down the hall.

Tristan took a step forward. Maybe it was high time he put an end to this foolish charade. Angelina was a beautiful, confident woman, and she was his if he set aside his pride. But would it solve the issues between them? She wanted children and he didn't. If they married, wouldn't that eventually cause resentment between them? The truth of the logic didn't ease the tightness in his chest.

She turned and saw him, raising her brows in surprise before heading in his direction. She stopped when she was directly in front of him, her blue-eyed gaze wide and perceptive. "Did you need something?"

You. He wanted to shout, but he cleared his throat instead. "Just the restroom," he croaked.

She tipped her head back and laughed, then leaned forward and whispered in his ear, her cool lips grazing his cheek. "The restroom is that way." She pointed in the direction he'd come from.

Warmth flooded his cheeks. She gave him a jaunty wave and continued down the hallway, her throaty voice drifting back to him. "See you tonight, Tristan."

He stood there like a fool, watching until she rounded the next corner.

❧

After Tristan disappeared in the same direction as Angelina, Lillian turned to the desk, where a nurse she had not seen before greeted her with a friendly smile. The nurse had a thin face, close-cropped black hair, and was partly hidden by a large vase of yellow tulips.

Lillian peeked around the flowers. "Excuse me. I'd like to request a copy of Hannah Milano's medical records. I'm her personal representative and here's my power of attorney." She handed the nurse the form she kept in her purse.

The nurse scanned the document then Lillian, and she must have passed inspection because she handed her a piece of paper on a clipboard and said in a bored tone, "I'll need you to complete a HIPAA release form and sign it at the bottom. I'll need to see your driver's license, too. Will you want a printed copy or electronic?"

"Can I get them both ways?"

The nurse nodded. Lillian took the clipboard and began filling out the form. She glanced at the flowers and paused in the act of signing the document. She squinted at the signature on the card stuck in the vase, a strange feeling gripping her belly. *Frank Milano?* It wasn't her dad's signature, and when would he have had time to order flowers, anyway? A frisson of fear pricked her nerve endings.

The nurse caught her gaze.

"Beautiful flowers," Lillian said, injecting a casual note in her voice.

"Aren't they? A patient's father sent them this morning."

"I recognize the name on the card. That's my friend's father. I'm surprised he would have had time to send flowers, though. His daughter's pretty sick."

The nurse glanced at the card. "Oh, we've been giving him regular updates on his daughter's condition. He sent these as a thank you."

Why would her dad call looking for updates when he was at Hannah's bedside most of the time?

Lillian dropped the clipboard in the act of handing it to the nurse. It clattered against the counter and onto the floor, nearly hitting her in the process. She scooped it up, placing it on the counter and flattening her sweaty palms against her legs. She managed to take a breath.

"How long before I can get a copy of her records?"

"Shouldn't be long, maybe an hour or so. If you leave me your telephone number, I can text you when they're ready."

Lillian nodded. "Yes, okay."

The nurse handed her a piece of paper and a pen, and she took them and scribbled her phone number at the same moment Tristan returned, flashing her his confident smile. Was that a trace of lipstick on his cheek?

"All set?"

Lillian nodded, hoping he wouldn't notice the increased fragile state of her already fragile nerves.

"I thought we'd go to a deli nearby. It will taste much better than hospital food. Is that okay?"

"Yes," she said, thankful he'd not witnessed her distress over the flowers her father had supposedly sent. She suspected he would hound her until he had answers.

They stepped through the automatic doors into the sunlight almost in tandem, her blood slinging through her veins. She scanned the parking lot, alert to any sign of danger.

Tristan's hand settled on her elbow. "What is it?"

"Nothing."

"You have been on edge since the moment I first spotted you at the hospital." Tristan managed to sound both conversational and dangerous at the same time, which increased her anxiety.

"Of course, I'm tense. Who wouldn't be? My friend is ill."

"There's that."

They had reached his car and the door handles popped out. She flinched as if to prove his point. Why couldn't she get used to the way his techno vehicle worked? She ignored looking at him and the suspicious expression on his face and slid into the passenger seat.

He donned a pair of aviator sunglasses and put the car in gear. It glided from the lot. "You have a stalker?"

"A...what? No...of course not."

"You act as if you think someone is going to grab you when you're not looking."

"That's ridiculous."

"Is it? Who or what are you afraid of, Zoey?"

Lillian tightened her fingers against the edge of the seat and cleared her throat. "I'm not afraid, but even if I were, it's not your concern."

"You made it my concern when you asked for my help."

Fear settled in her chest, a hard mass pressing against her lungs so she could barely breathe. She couldn't tell Tristan the truth—couldn't knowingly drag him into a dangerous situation that could take his life. She had to convince him there was nothing to worry about. But how? She focused on the flashing scenery outside her window to give herself time to think.

He sighed. "Zoey, if you're in some kind of trouble, I need you to tell me. I want to help."

She risked a glance. He stared at the road and not at her, but she could sense his stubbornness in the way his hands gripped the wheel and the hard lines of his profile. Tristan would not give up until she told him the truth, which meant she needed to lie, and it needed to be convincing.

She kept her gaze trained on his and forced a lightness to her tone. "I can't imagine what you are going on about. I'm fine. I'm just worried about Hannah." She threw in a sigh for good measure. "It's been a long couple of days."

Tristan pulled into the parking lot of a delicatessen and put the car in park. He took off his dark sunglasses.

She didn't waste any time unfastening her seatbelt and finding the button on the top of the door handle, but before she could open the door, Tristan touched her knee. "Zoey, wait."

She turned toward him. "Wh… What?"

Sunlight caught his perceptive blue eyes, making them sparkle. A flop of dark curly hair lay across his forehead, taunting her with an insane desire to brush it away. Why hadn't her mom told her the impact being near a burner would have on her libido? She sniffed the cool, minty scent of his cologne, which filled the space between them, hitting her senses like a powerful punch to the gut. Goosebumps chased up and down her leg as her body absorbed his potent energy.

"You're afraid, and it's not just for Hannah. Is someone threatening you?"

Adrenaline surged through her veins, urging her to flee, but she'd learned a thing or two about keeping cool in tense situations over the past couple of years. She clasped her purse in her lap and stole a breath. She kept her voice even, as if she had everything under control, as if she hadn't spent the last two years terrified of every movement and shadow, as if she never double-locked the doors or assumed a separate identity or kept a loaded pistol in her purse.

She laughed and hoped it sounded light-hearted. "I think you've spent too much time inventing video game scenarios, Tristan. I'm fine. Really."

She didn't wait for him to argue but pressed the button on the door and scrambled from the vehicle.

CHAPTER TEN

Tristan clenched his jaw and watched Zoey flee his car. What had her so afraid? Maybe a disgruntled ex-boyfriend or husband? The thought of Zoey with an abusive man caused a strange ache in his belly. How was it he felt so protective of her after they'd only known each other a day?

He got out of the car and followed Zoey into the restaurant, a Jewish deli he ate lunch at regularly whenever his mom visited the clinic. The woman at the counter—Cassie—favored him with a bright-pink-lipstick smile, smacking her gum. He pushed the sunglasses up on his head and nodded hello.

"Your usual ham and cheese on rye?"

"That's right, and whatever my friend would like."

He gestured to Zoey, who studied the menu over the counter. She avoided his gaze, which for some reason frustrated him.

"I'll have the tuna salad on wheat, please."

"To go," he added.

Now she did finally look at him, her jade-green eyes wary and nervous at once, like a skittish kitten.

He tried on a smile he hoped was reassuring. It didn't work—at least, she didn't smile back. "I thought we'd take this back to the house—you can grab a shower."

"I need to return to the hospital. I want to be there when Hannah wakes up."

"Her dad's with her, and she's sleeping. There's nothing you can do for Hannah right now. This is the perfect opportunity to get a shower and put on clean clothes."

She hesitated and then huffed. "Fine, but as soon as we're done, I'd like to return to the hospital."

"Good." If she thought humoring him by agreeing to come to his house would stop him from discovering whatever she was hiding, she was in for a surprise. Tristan had the resources to hire the best detective agency if that's what it took to learn her secrets. And learn them he would.

He pulled out his wallet. He wasn't sure why tackling the mystery of Zoey had become so important to him. Maybe because he'd been lied to one too many times by a pretty face? If there was a single personality trait he despised more than any other, it was dishonesty.

Zoey opened her purse, but he reached across her to hand Cassie his credit card. "This one's on me."

"You don't need to—"

"I know. I want to, though." He offered her a smile, and in return, she gripped her purse tighter, like he might snatch it from her and spill the contents. "Consider this a pre-date to our official date."

She opened her mouth—he suspected to deny his claim of a pre-date—but was interrupted by Cassie, who chuckled.

"Honey, if a good-looking man wants to buy you lunch, I'd take him up on it. Especially this one." She offered him a playful wink. "He's one of the nice ones." She rang up the bill and shoved his card in the reader.

Zoey's cheeks flushed, but she seemed to realize she appeared ungrateful because she inclined her head slightly, and her eyes met his for once. "Thank you."

Warmth circled his heart and entered, thawing some of the ice he'd built around it. "It's nothing." He felt absurdly happy, like he'd won a major victory by buying her lunch. Why he should feel this way was hard to decipher. Most women he knew would be clamoring for him to buy them a meal. Was Zoey being deliberately difficult to capture his attention? If so, it was working.

He returned his card to his wallet and pulled out a twenty, shoving it in the tip jar.

"Such a generous fellow you have here, sweetie," Cassie said with a wink at Tristan, making him smile.

He'd known Cassie for five years now with all the trips he had to make back and forth to the hospital with his mom. When he'd heard about her struggles to pay for her daughter's college, he'd chipped in with a little scholarship of his own. She'd been a loyal friend ever since.

"Here you are. Tuna salad and ham and cheese. I added in some cinnamon muffins on the house. Enjoy." Cassie handed him a large brown bag. "How's your mom these days? Isn't she participating in another clinical trial?"

"That's right. She took a spill recently but is doing well enough. Thanks for asking. Bye, Cassie."

"Bye, hon."

Tristan grinned and gestured Zoey to proceed him to the door, sliding his sunglasses on.

Zoey hesitated then complied, but as soon as they stepped out into the bright parking lot, she whirled to face him. "Why did you let her think we're a couple?"

"We are a couple, at least through tonight." Why he enjoyed baiting her was beyond him.

"You know what I mean," she huffed. "You let her believe we're dating seriously."

She walked ahead of him, and he lengthened his stride until he caught up to her. He had enjoyed watching Zoey squirm at the insinuation they might be together. And he supposed it had been refreshing not to be chased for once.

"What did she mean, clinical trial?"

He'd known it might come up sooner or later. But for some reason, the simple question sent a rush of emotion through him. Thank the good Lord he'd put on his sunglasses. He waited until they reached the car and were seated inside to answer.

"How much do you know about Huntington's?"

"A little. It's a genetic condition, which impacts muscle control and cognitive function."

"That's right. My mom's participating in what's called a gene silencing treatment. She's been getting shots every eight weeks. The treatment is supposed to decrease the protein in her brain, which will reduce her symptoms."

"Has her condition improved?"

"Not enough to make a noticeable difference. Her recent fall is proof of that. Unfortunately, the study ends in two weeks."

He pressed Start and backed the car out of the parking lot without looking at her.

She touched his arm. It was only a light touch—nothing to get excited about. Still, for some reason his pulse shot to the moon and back. He frowned at the steering wheel. Must be lack of sleep causing him to react this way.

"Tristan, I'm sorry."

"It's okay." He detested pity—it didn't solve a damn thing.

"A disease like that is difficult to cure."

Anger, hot and furious, erupted inside him like a festering blister. "There is no *cure*. As a nurse, you must know that."

She shrank in her seat, her hand falling from his shoulder.

He dragged a hand through his hair. It wasn't fair to take his frustration out on Zoey. She didn't understand how hard he'd been working to find a cure and how difficult it had been to watch his mom's declining health. His mom had been the only constant in his life, the only one who loved him without expecting anything in return.

"I've tried everything to find a cure. It doesn't exist. This is not the first time my mom and I have been through this rodeo."

"How bad is she?"

He stole a breath, and the fierce pressure in his chest eased a little. "She has trouble speaking and walking. She can't remember simple things, like what day it is."

Zoey hesitated, probably afraid to say anything more after his outburst. "You're fortunate to be so close to your mom. I'm sure that makes it difficult to watch her decline. It's a helpless feeling."

"Yes." He tightened his lips. There was no one else. His father abandoned Tristan when he was five. His stepfather was an abusive alcoholic who came damn near to killing his mom until the day Tristan was old enough to fight back. That was the day he and his mom had packed their bags and fled. That was the day they'd made a pact to always look out for one another. That was the day he'd sworn always to protect her.

"Huntington's is genetic. Have you been tested for the disease?"

Tristan pulled onto the road toward home. Why hadn't he changed the subject? That's what he normally did with strangers. But seeing Zoey's struggle with her friend's illness, he had the urge to confide his own. "No. What's the point? No effective cure or treatment currently exists. After watching the hell my mom's been through, I'd rather not know."

"I'm truly sorry."

He nodded, but he didn't say anything. He'd already said too much. She was quiet, too.

He turned on the radio to fill the silence. The Beatles were singing "Help." *How fitting.* Worry had been his relentless companion the past ten years. When his mom first complained of clumsiness and not being able to think clearly. When she couldn't remember how to get to the grocery store and said her joints hurt. When he'd taken her to one specialist and then another and another.

He got off the exit and turned right toward home. Huntington's cursed its victims with a relentless and slow death. The disease was slowly killing the nerves in his mom's brain and stealing her personality with it. She rarely smiled or laughed these days. The best he could hope for was to prolong her life.

He drove the car up to the entrance. The guard recognized him and opened the gate. A few minutes later, he pulled into the driveway and turned off the car. Silence settled between them, broken only by the click of Zoey unlocking her seatbelt.

She opened the door and got out, and he followed suit. They were almost to the front entrance when he noticed the footprints. The landscapers had been told to keep to the sidewalk.

"What's the matter?" Zoey turned, giving him a puzzled look.

"I recently had grass seed planted, and someone's stepped in it." He pointed to the footprints, which stretched around the perimeter of the house.

She stared at the tracks in the mud, her face draining of all color. "We'd…better get inside."

He touched her arm. "What is it, Zoey?"

She frowned and stepped back, holding the brown paper bag with their lunches like a shield in front of her. "Nothing. I'm dizzy…from hunger, probably."

Her nervousness was so thick he could cut it with a knife. He tapped in the code to unarm the security system and unlocked the door, and she scurried inside. She turned to frown at him.

"Aren't you coming?"

"You go. The kitchen is straight ahead. I'll be just a second."

He thought she might argue, as she'd been doing since he'd met her in Annie Logan's room, but she clutched the bag and stared at him, her wide eyes shining like green jewels.

"Okay. But…what are you going to do?"

Why did a few footprints have her so alarmed? He shrugged. "I just want to see where they go."

"Be…be careful."

He nodded, and she took off into the house.

He shut the door and peered at the muddy tracks, following them to the back patio, where they ended at the door leading into the garden room. His heart thumped loud in his ears. There were a few scratches on the door, which hadn't been there before. It looked as if someone had scraped it with a metal tool of some kind.

He turned to stare at the yard, which led to acres of woods behind the house, the footsteps fading into the muddy grass. They did not belong to the landscaper. Whoever had done this might have been here when they pulled up and had taken off into the woods. The footprints looked fresh and certainly hadn't been there yesterday.

His stilled, his gut clenching, a cool breeze chilling the hair on the back of his neck and every instinct screaming danger. Someone had attempted to break into his house. He whipped out his cell phone and called his security firm.

CHAPTER ELEVEN

Lillian stumbled her way into the massive, open kitchen and dropped the lunch sack onto the counter. She leaned against the sleek, dark granite to catch her breath. Her gaze took in the flecks of orange and the warmth of the complementary glass trio of hanging lights above the counter, before passing over the stainless steel appliances. A chef's dream—not a smudge dulled their bright surface. Outside the glass patio doors, she caught a glimpse of an in-ground pool.

Her heart beat loud in her ears, and she couldn't seem to take in enough oxygen. Had she run out of time? Had she led Kinetica to Tristan's doorstep? Should she grab her things and return to Boston despite the promised date? But what if Hannah hadn't fully recovered?

Her cell phone buzzed, and she checked her messages—the hospital notifying her Hannah's records were ready. She pocketed the phone and scooted onto the nearest barstool, contemplating the bag of food and fighting the queasy feeling in her stomach.

"Why are you staring into space?"

Tristan's sudden appearance had her jolting. "I was thinking about Hannah." Which wasn't a lie. "Is everything okay?"

"Yes." He crossed to the tall cupboards and pulled out a couple of plates and glasses. "What would you like to drink? I can offer you milk, water, soda…something stronger?"

"Water's fine."

He filled a tall, clear glass with filtered ice water from the fridge and handed it to her. She held her breath when their fingers brushed, but it didn't seem to faze him. He opened the bag and placed her tuna sandwich and a cinnamon muffin on the plate, then added some large purple grapes from the fridge. All the while his face remained a closed mask.

She managed to chew and swallow half the sandwich, but it seemed to stick in her throat. The domestic scene didn't dull the thumping of her heart in her ears, which roared to life when Tristan placed both of his hands on the counter and leaned toward her, his expression serious.

"You're worried about the footprints, aren't you?"

Lillian's pulse thrummed, and her neck tingled as if it were attempting to denounce the lie she was about to tell. She looked him in the eyes. "Concerned, not worried. You have the funds to replant."

She took a bite of the tuna and managed to chew and swallow despite her pounding heart. Kinetica could be watching the house right now, preparing to kill Tristan so they could grab her. The less he knew of her life in Boston, the less he knew of *her*, the better.

"Replanting the grass is the least of my worries. It appears I'm the victim of an attempted break-in."

She turned, the blood draining from her face and her voice scratching like she'd swallowed sandpaper. "You saw something? I thought you said everything was okay?"

"Relax. Everything is okay. But someone took a chisel to the door to the garden room. They nicked it up pretty well, but they didn't get in, which is why the alarm wasn't triggered."

She managed to breathe, but it didn't slow her thumping heart. "Did you call the police?"

"My security company is investigating. Unfortunately, they tell me the outdoor camera malfunctioned, and there's no video of the incident. Who is it, Zoey? An ex-boyfriend? A jilted lover?"

Her heart stopped and started again. Tristan's mouth moved, but it took a full five seconds before his words made it past the dull curtains in her mind. His eyes caught hers, trapping them within their steely confines. Game over.

She set the sandwich on her plate and wiped her mouth with a napkin. When telling a lie, it was always best to stick close to the truth.

"No one I know."

She thought he might say something after he'd stared her down, but he didn't. Instead, he opened the sack, put his food on a plate, pulled out a stool, and sat next to her. She managed to take another small bite of her sandwich.

"Why do you wear a wig?"

She coughed, almost choking on the mouthful of sandwich, but managed to swallow. She took a drink of water. She had wondered if he'd noticed the wig. It was safer for him if she didn't explain her reasons.

"You're not going to tell me, are you?"

"I promised you a single date, not an inquisition." Lillian set her plate aside and stood. "Where can I take a shower? I'd like to get back to the hospital."

"You haven't finished your lunch."

"I had a big breakfast in the middle of the night, remember? I'm not hungry."

His eyes labeled her a liar, but he polished off his sandwich and stood, pointing her toward the grand staircase to the floor above. "You room is the first bedroom on the left. I put your suitcase there, and there are plenty of towels and washcloths in the bathroom."

She brushed by him, pretending to be oblivious to the heat of his hard body and the annoying scent of his minty cologne. But she couldn't control a shiver at his next words, which seemed to chase her up the stairs.

"I will learn what has you so frightened, Zoey, whether you decide to tell me or not."

☙

The minute Zoey was out of sight, Tristan grabbed his cell phone and made his way to his office, kicking the door shut behind him. He found the number in his recents for Brian Townsend, a high school buddy who ran the security firm he hired, and called it. Then he paced back and forth in front of the window until Brian picked up.

"Any leads on the attempted break-in?"

"None yet, but I've tightened security." Brian's raspy baritone managed to sound both confident and surprised. "You have more evidence?"

"No, but I have another assignment for you."

"Sure, my man. What is it?"

"I'd like you to do a thorough investigation of a woman I recently met. Her name is Zoey Mills."

"What can you tell me about her?"

"Not much. She's a nurse who lives in Denver and works in an emergency room. She's in Cleveland because her childhood friend, Hannah Milano—is ill. I have a hunch she's gotten herself into some difficult circumstances. I need to know what or who is causing her problems."

"I'm on it. M-I-L-L-S?"

"Yes."

"How old is she?"

"I'd say she's in her late twenties."

"What does she look like?"

"She's petite, slim, about five-four, with green eyes and long blonde hair. Her hair and eye color may not be natural—she wears a wig. I have a photo of her…I'll text it to you. I want daily reports. And I'll pay double if you can get this information to me fast. There's some urgency."

"Gotcha."

He ended the call and studied the photo he'd snapped of Zoey. Her eyes looked too big in her thin, pale face. She couldn't be older than thirty. What was she hiding behind her calm façade?

He sent Brian the photo, then stared out the window without really seeing anything. Townsend Security was the best in the business. He'd be surprised if Brian didn't have everything he wanted to know in a report to him tomorrow morning. And then he and Zoey were going to have a little heart-to-heart about the importance of trust and honesty between them.

❧

Lillian looked around the spare bedroom, which in her opinion seemed more like the primary, and stole a breath. A large queen bed, covered in a cranberry-and-white quilt and an assortment of pillows, was flanked by two large windows on either side and a striking oil painting of a gold vase with multi-colored flowers that hung in between. The shiny wood floor was covered in a lovely faded gray-and-pink Oriental rug, and Lillian's suitcase had been placed on an antique luggage rack in front of the bed.

She turned and locked the bedroom door, testing the knob to make sure it was secure, and then strode forward to study the painting. It looked like it had last been displayed in an art museum. A matching gold vase sat in the center of the nightstand with an assortment of pale pink and white flowers, which coordinated with the bedspread and the painting. *Perfection.*

The room had a soft, feminine air and smelled like lavender. It was the kind of room that made Lillian want to curl up and take a nap. But of course, there was no time for napping.

She removed her wig and undressed, putting on a plush white bathrobe she found in the room's massive closet. Then she took the hottest and fastest shower she'd taken in some time. Her pulse thrummed, and she couldn't stop from peeking behind the shower curtain, fearing Kinetica's soldiers had raided the premises and would catch her while she was naked and vulnerable and unable to fight.

Thankfully, her fears were unfounded, and within a short time, she had dried her hair, put on the wig, changed into clean clothes and was heading down the winding staircase to find Tristan and let him know it was time to return to the hospital. As soon as Hannah was recovered, Lillian would be on an airplane home. The attempted break-in was a clear warning she'd be foolish to ignore.

She made her way into the kitchen, where Tristan was seated at the table with his computer, looking cool and elegant in a navy-blue polo almost the exact shade of his eyes. By the look of his slightly damp hair, he'd changed his shirt and taken a shower. She sniffed the air around him, which smelled like a cool, refreshing waterfall.

"Working?"

He gave a slight shrug and closed the laptop. "Playing online chess. Keeps the brain sharp. Feeling better?"

"Yes." She did feel better now that she was clean, and he had stopped asking pointed questions. "I need to get back to Hannah. I can drive myself if you're busy."

"No, I can take you, but first I want to mention I've heard from Mel, the doctor I was telling you about. She's talked to Hannah's doctors. She's amazed at the turnaround. Called it a miracle."

Ding-dong.

The chime of the doorbell interrupted their conversation and sent adrenaline spiking through Lillian's veins. "Are you expecting someone?"

He stood, shooting her an apologetic look. "Yes. A business acquaintance whom I couldn't put off. I'll be quick."

Her heartbeat settled, and he disappeared, presumably to greet his visitor. She was in the act of pulling out a chair at the table when he came back into the kitchen followed by his guest.

Dominic Raines, holy crap!

All the blood froze in her veins, and she lost her balance, lurching to the side like a drunk crab. The chair she held toppled to the ground with a loud bang.

"I'll get it," Tristan said, reaching out a strong arm to steady her. "Are you okay?"

She nodded because she couldn't trust herself to speak.

"Sit," Tristan said, righting the chair and ushering her into it, his brow creased.

Lillian sat, when all she wanted to do was run screaming from the room. Although he hadn't been the doctor who had experimented on her mother, the man standing across from her, this horrible, evil man, was ultimately responsible for her mother's murder.

"Zoey, this is Dominic Raines," Tristan said. "Dominic's company conducts research on emergency cell and gene therapy."

Oh, she knew all about how Kinetica conducted cell and gene therapy. That's why her mother had been so valuable to them. She'd had a rare mutation in her DNA that made her extra special. They planned to use her cells to create their own super healers. But her mother had escaped, and they murdered her before she could go to the police. With her mother gone, they now needed to find someone else with the gene. Someone like Lillian.

"Zoey is a friend of mine." Tristan's deep voice cut into her horrified thoughts.

"You look familiar." Dominic held out a hand with a flash of white teeth and glassy, gray eyes that showed no emotion. "Have we met?"

Acid reflux burned her throat, fear tightened her muscles. Zoey could not bring herself to shake the asshole's hand, but for her own safety, she needed to put on a convincing act. She shook her head. "I don't think so." She cupped a hand over her mouth to keep from losing her lunch in front of him.

Tristan touched her shoulder. "You okay?"

She forced her lips in an upward tilt. "I've been better."

"Zoey's friend is sick," Tristan said to Dominic. "She's had a hard time of it. Why don't you and I go into my office and leave her some quiet time." To Lillian he said, "We'll be quick."

"Of course," Dominic said, flashing her a dentured smile. "I'm sorry about your friend. I do hope she recovers quickly."

Goosebumps rolled down Lillian's spine like cold little marbles. The words of sympathy sounded ominous coming from Dominic. Had he come here to verify her identity?

She waited until the men vanished from sight, and then she pulled herself together and hurried after them without making a sound. She would discover what Tristan's dealings were with Kinetica and then get the hell out of his house.

Lillian crept upstairs and tiptoed down the long hallway, pressing her ear against the office door to hear what they were saying. They spoke so quietly, she had trouble picking up anything but murmurs. But then Dominic must have passed by the closed door because she heard him say, "…five million."

There were some more murmurs, and she was about ready to give up, in case they opened the door and caught her eavesdropping, when she heard Tristan say, "…heal her," and Dominic respond with what sounded like, "We're running out of time."

The doorknob started to turn, and she jumped, racing through the long hallway and down the stairs until she reached the kitchen, out of breath. She had only a minute to park herself at the table before Dominic and Tristan re-entered the room.

She busied herself picking up her glass and taking a sip of water. Was Tristan planning to fund Kinetica's research in exchange for a cure for his mother? It seemed the most likely reason for the two men to have struck up a business relationship. Did he have any idea what he was funding?

"You wouldn't have something to drink before I head out? My throat is parched," Dominic said to Tristan.

"Sure. Water or something stronger?"

"Water's fine." Dominic turned toward Lillian. "So, Zoey, what do you do for a living?" He pulled out the chair across from her and sat like he had all the time in the world.

Lillian clutched her glass, her heartbeat drumming in her ears. She had to consciously slow her breathing so she wouldn't hyperventilate. "Not much."

Tristan came and stood beside her with a puzzled frown. "She's being modest—she's a nurse."

Lillian set her glass down and rose. "Not to be rude, but Tristan, I really must get back to the hospital. It's after two. I can drive myself. You two can finish your business discussion."

"Zoey, you're not feeling well. I'll drive you wherever you need to go."

"There's no need…" she started to say, but Tristan wasn't listening. He was talking to Dominic again. "Sorry to rush you out, but can we do this another time?"

"Certainly." Dominic rose from his seat and held out his hand to Tristan, who shook it.

"About our conversation, if you want in, don't wait too long."

"Right," Tristan nodded. "I'll be in touch."

Dominic turned to Lillian, his watery eyes like shards of ice. "I hope to get the opportunity to talk to you again, when you're feeling better, Zoey."

Lillian murmured something nonsensical, but it must have been sufficient because Tristan walked him to the door. Dominic was gone, and she could breathe again.

She put her head in her hands and rubbed her sinuses, which had begun to throb. Was Tristan already invested in Kinetica or was he just considering it, as the conversation she'd overheard seemed to indicate? Did it matter? Either scenario had Tristan consorting with the enemy.

She had to get out of here. *Now.* Unfortunately, Tristan was right about her stress level and not feeling well. She was in no condition to drive.

"He's gone. Mind telling me what that was all about?" Tristan stood in front of her again, his brow creased in concern.

"I have a headache."

He crouched until they were eye level. "Try again."

"What do you mean?" She avoided his gaze.

"I mean something has you so terrified you're about to collapse. That would be the second time today. What is it, Zoey?"

She took a breath, and then another. Thankfully, the spinning room slowed, and she was able to hold his gaze. "I'm really worried about Hannah. Thanks for everything, but you've done enough. I'd like to stay at the hospital from here on out. No need to put yourself out any longer. I'll call an Uber."

His lips thinned. "Why do I have the feeling you're planning to forfeit your part of our bargain?"

Bargain? How had she forgotten about it?

"This is a fancy event, and I'll need you to dress the part. How will you accomplish that from the hospital?"

"I…"

"That's what I thought. You don't have a plan. Will it really kill you to stay a little longer?"

It might. And him as well.

The pressure increased behind her eyelids. She pressed her fingers against her sinuses, a poor attempt to stop the pain. She really didn't have the strength to argue with him. She just wanted to get back to her sister.

"Fine. I'll stay one more day. Just take me back to the hospital. Please."

He stood and held out a hand to assist her. "Of course. And I'll get you an aspirin."

Lillian blinked up at him. "Thank you." She took a breath and placed her hand in Tristan's.

The room finally stopped spinning.

Chapter Twelve

Tristan kept to his own thoughts on the way to the hospital, mostly because he'd didn't want to upset Zoey further, but he wasn't fooled by her innocent act. She'd been so frightened of Dominic she'd been physically ill, which meant…what?

He pulled onto the street and headed west toward the hospital before glancing her way again. She sat clutching her purse, seemingly lost in thought. What exactly did she have in there?

He pressed on the accelerator and moved into the left lane to pass a semi-truck. Something didn't add up about Zoey. She was on the run from someone or something. And he still hadn't fully digested the conversation he'd had with Mel while Zoey had been taking a shower.

"I've talked to Hannah Milano's doctor, and he says the patient has had an amazing turnaround," Mel had told him.

He'd agreed. Hannah had made a remarkable recovery.

"It's more than remarkable, Tristan," Mel continued. "From what the doctor told me, the patient has gone from her lungs and organs shutting down last night to sitting up in bed this morning talking and laughing. You know how rare that is? One in a million. It's incredible. She's a walking miracle."

It was incredible, wasn't it? Impossible his visit had any impact on Hannah. He hadn't even attempted to talk to her.

Tristan flicked another glance at Zoey. Annie Logan's recovery had also happened overnight after Zoey had paid her a visit. One minute the little girl had been deathly sick, and the next day she was sent home symptom-free. If he didn't know any better, he'd think Zoey had slipped the child a miracle drug or something.

His heartbeat sped up, and he tightened his grip on the wheel.

I'm a talented nurse.

Did her talent run to healing patients overnight?

I have an outstanding track record.

What exactly was her track record?

I'm great with patients—at easing fears and listening to confidences and consoling their loved ones when they feel all hope is gone. I could offer you or your family my services.

He rubbed the back of his neck with one hand. Did her services include miracle cures? If this were true, why had she asked him to visit Hannah?

He pulled into the hospital and parked in the visitor lot. He had so many questions buzzing around in his brain with no place to land. Because what he'd just entertained in his thoughts wasn't possible...was it?

Nah. He'd watched her the whole time with Hannah, and she'd done nothing but hold the woman's hands.

The minute he shut the car off, Zoey unfastened her seatbelt and opened the door. She scurried toward the entrance, hunching as if she didn't want to be noticed. Who was she hiding from?

He scrambled from the vehicle and hurried after her. He was letting his imagination overrule his logic. People couldn't miraculously cure other people of fatal illnesses simply by touching them. But what if Zoey had slipped Hannah a shot of a powerful drug?

"You're awake," Zoey said to Hannah when they entered her room. Her friend lay propped against the pillows in the hospital bed. A large ball of blue yarn lay next to her, and she held a pair of knitting needles, which she put to good use. Her dad still sat in a chair by her bedside.

Zoey placed a hand on Hannah's forehead and brushed a stray hair from her face. "You must be feeling better if you're knitting. Whatcha making?"

"I'm not sure yet." Hannah turned to him, smiling. "Hi, Tristan." Her dark-brown hair had been pulled back with a bright-blue headband, her skin no longer flushed and pale.

Tristan nodded. "Hi, Hannah, Mr. Milano."

"Call me Frank." Hannah's dad stood and stretched out his hand. "I've been meaning to thank you for leaving your fundraiser to visit Hannah last night. I'm grateful."

"A small thing." Tristan shook Frank's hand then turned to Hannah with a smile. "It's good to see you feeling so much better."

Frank wrapped an arm around Zoey, giving her a squeeze. "Thank you, dear, for everything."

Zoey laid her cheek against Frank's shoulder. "It was nothing."

"We both know it was more than nothing," Frank said, patting her back before turning to Tristan. "We're grateful to both of you."

"I wish I could say I had a hand in Hannah's recovery," Tristan said, nodding toward Zoey, "but it was all Zoey."

She flashed a glance his way. Their eyes locked, his pulse sped up, and the universe seemed to take a giant pause. She looked away first, the expression in her wide eyes appearing almost guilty. She bent her head and checked her phone.

"I want to talk to the nurses. I'll be right back." She hurried from the room.

He wanted to follow and demand answers, but Frank was talking to him and to leave in the middle of their conversation would be rude.

"Please, grab a seat and tell us how you met Zoey." Frank rubbed a hand over his chin and nodded, motioning to an empty chair next to Hannah's bedside.

Tristan did as he asked. "We met last night in the patient's room next door—a little girl with a severe case of pneumonia, who happens to be my accountant's daughter."

"How is the little girl?" Hannah asked, knitting needles flashing in and out of the blue yarn.

"She's doing remarkably well. Her parents told me she was able to go home this morning. Zoey's visit must have done her some good." He might have missed the swift look father and daughter exchanged with one another if he hadn't been looking for it. They knew something he didn't, Tristan felt sure of it.

"Zoey is a fantastic nurse," Hannah said, setting her knitting aside.

"After seeing your turnaround, I have no doubt."

She wrinkled her nose and tilted her head, reminding him of Zoey. Heat seemed to radiate from her wide, amber eyes. "But you do doubt her skill, don't you?"

"My mother is dying. The doctors and nurses haven't been able to cure her. Why would Zoey be any different?" The words spilled out of him, as if she'd tugged on an invisible cord and opened a hidden corner in his heart.

Hannah held out a hand, and he got up and leaned over her bed to take it like it was the most natural thing in the world to do. A warm feeling moved through him. *Contentment.* He had trouble recognizing the sensation, it had been so long since he'd felt it.

"It breaks your heart to see your mom suffer."

"I don't want to lose her. It's been the two of us for as long as I can remember."

"Until now. I can see it when you look at Zoey. You feel a strong connection with her."

Hannah understood his feelings for Zoey better than he did. He couldn't take his gaze off her. "Yes, but it's all one-sided. I don't think she's interested."

She laughed, and the sound was both musical and jarring at the same time, as if by laughing, she harmonized the notes until they reached a flawless pitch. "You won't let a small thing like that stand in your way, will you? You're perfect for one another. You just don't know it yet."

She let go of his hand, and for a second, his vision wavered in and out before settling again. What had just happened?

"Are you okay?" Frank peered at him like he thought he would pass out, which was plain ridiculous. Tristan had never fainted a moment in his life.

He stood and was happy when he stayed on his feet. "I'd better check on Zoey."

Now who was the one running away?

His cell phone buzzed as he left the room, and he checked it to see a text from Brian.

Have some information. Call me in twenty.

❧

Lillian was on her way back to Hannah's room when she almost plowed into Tristan coming from the opposite direction. He gripped her shoulders to keep her upright, the strength in his hands causing a ripple of excitement to slither down her sensitive skin and settle in her chest. Lillian's heart fluttered like a frightened butterfly.

His energy was stronger than normal and flowing outward, his chakras wide open, which could only mean one thing: Hannah had used her talent on him.

The large white envelope Lillian held lay trapped between them.

He drew back. "What's this?"

She handed him the envelope. "Hannah's medical records. I don't suppose you'll need them now. The nurses tell me she may be released as early as tomorrow."

"That's great news."

"It is."

Tristan stilled; his blue eyes searched hers, a question in them. "You're upset."

She frowned and shook her head. "I'm just relieved, that's all." As if in protest, a tear trembled at the corner of her eye. *Dammit.* She couldn't afford tears.

"Zoey, whatever this is, whatever sorrow you're holding, please tell me."

She didn't answer, but he used the pad of his thumb to brush the wetness from her eye and then pulled her into his arms as if holding her was an everyday occurrence. She couldn't resist resting her cheek against the reassuring strength in his hard chest and listening to the steady *thump-thump-thump* of his heart. His breath brushed the top of her head, heat exploding across her senses.

"Trust me," he urged, his tone soothing.

Power flowed into every part of her. "I do trust you." It was true. Despite the conversation she'd overheard, despite his association with Dominic, despite their short acquaintance, she trusted him. But it wasn't fair to expose him to further danger.

She swallowed the dryness in her mouth. She couldn't keep Tristan by her side, even though every particle of energy inside vibrated at their rightness together. "I'm leaving."

He pulled far enough away so he could see her face, his intelligent eyes boring into hers. "When?"

"Don't worry, I'll uphold my end of our bargain tonight. But I've booked an early morning flight for tomorrow. Now I need to…to say goodbye to Hannah and her…her dad, and then if you'll take me back to your house, I'll change and get my rental. If you give me the address, I'll meet you at the fundraiser…"

He placed two fingers on her lips, silencing her. "I'm not letting you drive by yourself in your condition. Besides, we need to get a few things straight between us."

He was so handsome telling her the way it was going to be, he took her breath away. And the power emanating from his tall form could light a forest fire. An intense longing gripped her in its clutches, shaking her to her core. A longing for a dream she could never have. A longing so deep and wide and vast, her heart ached for her own little happily ever after.

He must have sensed her feelings because twin flames leaped in his eyes, setting her body on fire. He dropped his chin, and she tilted her face, and somehow their lips met in the middle.

She hadn't known a kiss could be so soft and firm at the same time, not tentative at all, but not in a hurry, either. He brushed against her lips once, twice, three times until she opened her mouth and took him inside. And then his tongue and teeth were exploring her in a way she'd never experienced before, like he would learn every one of her secrets by kissing her.

And God help her, now that she'd started, she liked the sensation of kissing Tristan way too much to tell him to stop.

"Zoey," he muttered when they came up for air. He framed her face with his large hands. "You've cast a spell on me."

A stranger brushed by too close and bumped against them, startling her and bringing her to their surroundings faster than if he'd dumped a bucket of cold water on her head. *I'm standing in the middle of a hospital kissing a man I only met yesterday. Have I lost my mind?*

She took a step backward and dodged the guy dressed in a blue uniform, who was pushing a cart of cleaning supplies. She blew out a breath. Just an ordinary maintenance man, but it easily could have been someone who recognized her or a member of Kinetica in disguise.

"Someone you know?"

"No…it's…I…this is unexpected. I didn't mean… I'm sorry. It's a mistake." She curled her hands at her sides to keep from reaching for him. It was more than raw attraction she fought. She fought the need to protect him from her own selfish desire. She fought the need for someone to share her worries and fears and triumphs, for someone to care for and who cared for her.

For someone to love.

"It's not a mistake. I've been wanting to kiss you since we first met."

She took another step away from him. "Tristan…this can't happen."

He frowned, and she could almost see the tycoon walls go up. "It's because of what I told you—that I could have Huntington's."

"No." Tristan had not inherited Huntington's—a burner's extraordinary energy level made them virtually immune to most illness, even genetic ones. But if she told him he was safe from the disease, would he believe her?

"So, you do have someone in Denver. Which is it? An ex-boyfriend, or"—his frown deepened—"a husband?"

She couldn't bring herself to lie outright, but she wouldn't bother denying his accusation. It was easiest if he believed she was taken. "I'm not free to start a relationship."

"I see." His voice sounded clipped and cold. His expression chilled and then froze.

"I do appreciate everything you've done for me."

His demeanor didn't lighten, but something changed in it—grew more intense, like his logical mind was analyzing the problem from all angles, determined to find a loophole. And the crazy thing was, she wanted him to discover the truth and convince her to stay, which was dangerous.

"Say your goodbyes, then, and I'll take you back to the house. I have a call to make first. I'll come back and get you in, say, twenty minutes? Is that enough time?"

She nodded, and without another word, he turned and left her, his long strides eating up the hallway. All she could do was stare after him, swallowing the hard knot in her throat, which felt a lot like heartache.

Chapter Thirteen

Tristan found a seat on a blue swivel chair in a private lounge he sometimes frequented when he accompanied his mom on one of her routine hospital visits. Tall glass windows let in the sun but were frosted to offer privacy. A thrill of nervous anticipation moved through his veins as he found Brian's number in his favorites.

"What do you have for me?" he asked as soon as Brian answered.

"Hang onto your hat. Or in your case, your computer," Brian joked, but there was a gritty edge to his voice. He'd been in the military before leaving to start his own security firm, and he was always calm, always in control, and always joking. Tristan suspected he used humor as a way of coping with a mighty stressful job. "You were right to be suspicious of the woman."

Tristan straightened, pulse leaping. "Why? What have you discovered?"

"I can't find a Zoey Mills who is a registered nurse working in Denver that fits your description."

She'd lied to him. Hadn't he known it? A doomed feeling settled in his stomach, and he rested his head in one hand, his other still clutching the phone by his ear. "She's not a nurse?"

"We ran a computer program that matches Social Security Numbers with nurses in the United States who go by the name Zoey Mills and matched those with the photo you sent. Your girl is not among them."

Tristan thought of Zoey as he'd last seen her—denying any attraction between them. Who was she? His instincts had been right. She was on the run, obviously desperate and alone, lying to him about her identity and occupation and yet…and yet, she'd come to Cleveland for her sick friend.

"Still there?" Brian interrupted his thoughts.

"Yes."

"Good, because there's more."

Tristan waited. What more could there be? Was she an escaped felon dodging law enforcement? Perhaps she'd had a run of bad luck and ditched her name along with a pile of debt?

"I did some checking on the friend…Hannah Milano, you said."

He gripped the phone tighter if that were possible. "What about her?"

"Don't worry. She appears to be legitimate. But her family has had more than their share of tragedy. The mother was killed in a car crash a few years ago, and an older sister died in a freak boating accident shortly afterward."

"That's unfortunate."

"It is. But something told me it was a little too much of a coincidence, so I dug a little deeper."

Tristan held the phone closer to his ear. This was what made Brian Townsend one of the best investigators in the country. And Tristan knew him well enough to know, when he got a certain ring in his voice, a bombshell was about to drop. "You found something."

"Let's call them odd coincidences. Hannah Milano's mother was a nurse. She'd been away from home, volunteering on a mission trip in the Appalachian Mountains in West Virginia when she died. The older sister was also a nurse."

"How old was the sister when she died?"

"Almost twenty-five. Just a few years into her career, when she took the family sailboat out on Lake Erie and got caught in a freak storm. The body was never recovered. The boat was later found washed up on shore. The death certificate lists drowning as the probable cause of death."

"What's this have to do with Zoey Mills?"

"I believe the woman you know as Zoey Mills is actually Lillian Abigail Milano."

A rush of what...fear, excitement...thrummed in his veins. "Are you certain of this?"

"Yes. I've compared pictures I found online with the one you sent. It's the same woman. She's disguised her looks and eye color, but there's no disguising the face."

Tristan's heart lurched like a broken engine before roaring to life. All the clues he'd been holding onto suddenly came together, like he'd plugged in the missing digit in a complicated computer code. Zoey and Hannah were sisters, which explained the facial resemblance between the two. And Zoey—or Lillian, as he needed to think of her—wore a wig and contacts, so her hair and eye color could be more like Hannah's. "Why the alias?"

"We don't know yet. From what we've uncovered, Lillian led a pretty normal life until she faked her death. No jail time, no record of criminal offenses, not even a traffic ticket. She had a student loan and was paying down a car loan, but no other large debts."

"Where did she work?"

"In the emergency room at a major Cleveland hospital called the Pullman Clinic."

"I'm familiar with the Pullman Clinic. My mother once participated in a study there."

"We talked to someone who worked with Lillian. From all accounts, she showed up on time, did her job well, didn't take time off. And the patients loved her."

"Was she married?"

"No marriage license. No children…lived in a small apartment in North Royalton at the time of her supposed death. I'll include the address in the report I send you."

"Any threats on her life?"

"None that we've discovered."

"What about miracle cures for her patients?"

"That I don't know. No one we talked to mentioned it. But I've got staff checking into her mother's death. Give me a little more time, and I'll see what I can find."

"Okay, great work, Brian. See if you can find any connection with the family and Dominic Raines, the CEO of a genetic research company called Kinetica. Lillian seemed frightened when she met him today. Perhaps there's a link. I'll pay double if you call me with new information within the next couple of hours. Send me your bill."

Tristan ended the call and stuffed his cell phone in his pocket. Zoey was not Zoey at all but Hannah's missing sister, Lillian. And Frank was their father.

He stood and crossed to the window, even though he couldn't see through the frosted glass. It would take some getting used to thinking of Zoey as Lillian. He pictured her as he saw her earlier, sea-colored eyes filled with fear and sadness as she told him she had to leave, hinting there was someone else. *A lie.* She wasn't married. And her eyes probably weren't green—colored contacts were likely part of her disguise.

He pressed his fingertips against the cool glass, creating a fog handprint on the window. Lillian *was* a nurse—this, at least, she hadn't lied about.

If he was smart, he'd let her leave and run like hell the other direction. But what if Lillian were in danger? He didn't want to see her hurt. Whatever Lillian hid from was so terrifying she'd faked her own death and left her family.

He scrolled through his favorites until he found his housekeeper's number. Before Lillian left, he needed to convince her to trust him with the truth of her situation. Once he understood the threat, he would find a way to protect her.

“Did you see Tristan? I think Hannah spooked him.” Her dad craned his neck the moment Lillian reentered Hannah's hospital room, as if she hid Tristan behind her back.

“Yes, we ran into each other…literally. Said he needed to make a phone call, and he'd be back in a little while. You guys know who he is, don't you?”

Hannah's eyes widened. “Are you kidding? The Video Game King? Everyone in Cleveland knows him. He told us how you met. So romantic.” Hannah batted her eyelashes.

Lillian narrowed her gaze. “Hannah Milano. I'm not happy about what you did. You're barely recovered from near death. Why would you attempt to read him?”

“He was growing suspicious of you, and I couldn't stop myself. The heat is so high when you guys are together, it could melt steel. I needed to know how he felt about my sister.” She widened her eyes. “Did something happen between you just now?”

Lillian grimaced. “Quit the innocent act. He's a burner. He gives off an extraordinary amount of energy, which is why I asked him to visit you in the hospital last night. I was desperate. It was the only thing I could think of to save your life. Imagine my surprise when he agreed.”

Hannah laughed, which turned into a cough, reminding Lillian her sister was still recovering. “Of course, he agreed. He likes you. A whole heck of a lot.”

Lillian pulled a chair next to the bed and sat, eyeing the ball of yarn and knitting needles. “Don't go getting any harebrained ideas. I only met him yesterday, and it's dangerous my being here. Did you decide what you're making?"

Hannah grinned, and to Lillian, the sight was worth all the worry and fear she'd experienced since returning to Cleveland.

"Socks—you can never have enough…" She wove the needle through the yarn. "Plus, they make great gifts."

Lillian cleared her throat, hating to break the light-hearted moment. "I'm leaving first thing tomorrow morning."

Her dad lowered his voice. "Does he know?"

She shook her head. "I didn't tell him anything. But he's a smart man. He suspects something's wrong with me."

"You're worried they're on to you," Hannah whispered. "What happened?"

Lillian folded her hands in her lap. She didn't want to alarm her family, but she'd told enough lies for today. She kept her voice soft. "Dad, have you been calling the nurses multiple times to ask after Hannah?"

Her father shot her a puzzled frown. "No, I've been here. Why?"

"Did you send the nurses flowers?"

"No, but that's not a bad idea."

"Too late. Someone else already thought of it. They signed the card from you."

The puzzled look on her dad's face morphed into alarm.

"There's more. This afternoon, someone tried to break into Tristan's home. They weren't successful. He thinks we scared them off when we pulled in."

Hannah's face lost color. "Did Tristan call the cops?"

"No, he called his security firm. They told him his video camera malfunctioned."

"There's more, though, isn't there?" Hannah reached for Lillian's hand and squeezed it between her palms. Her sister's empathic gift clued her in on Lillian's emotions before she could relay the rest of the details.

"While we were there, Kinetica's CEO showed up. I suspect Tristan is considering a large investment in the company, hoping they can develop a cure for his mom's disease—a disease he worries he may have inherited."

Hannah raised her eyebrows. "I thought he was a burner?"

"He is. He won't develop Huntington's. But I can't tell him that. He's already suspicious of me, and he wouldn't understand."

"Did the CEO recognize you?" her dad asked, his dear face creased in alarm.

Lillian shook her head. "He didn't seem to, but unfortunately, his presence caught me off-guard, and Tristan told him I'm a nurse, which piqued his interest. And it's too much of a coincidence for me to stay and jeopardize everyone's safety. It breaks my heart to leave you both again, but I booked an early morning flight to Boston."

"So this is goodbye?" her dad asked, his expression grim.

Lillian nodded, afraid to speak.

"Are you sure you have to go so soon?" Hannah sniffed, her eyes glittering with unshed tears.

"Yes, Mom warned us what would happen if they catch me. How they'll force me to kill innocent people to perform their 'tests.' How they'll torture me until I agree. As long as I stay hidden, they won't find me, and you'll all be safe."

"But they haven't found you for two years. Are you sure you have to keep hiding?"

"They haven't found me because I've kept a low profile. I don't work unless I'm paid under the table, and I use the cash I earn and what Dad sends to pay the bills. No credit cards or bank accounts mean no paper trails. But now Kinetica's looking at your medical records; they must suspect I'm still alive. Your turnaround is the evidence they're looking for. I've run out of time."

"Tristan has the resources to keep you safe. And he has feelings for you." Hannah's big brown eyes radiated worry.

Lillian dug her nails into her palms. "Yeah, angry feelings. He's sharp…he knows I'm not telling the truth."

"It's more than that, Lillian. I felt it when I first woke up, and he was here. And when I held his hand a moment ago, I knew. He cares for you. Feels protective. I believe he'd understand if you told him the truth."

Lillian pushed her chair out and stumbled to the window. "You know I can't ever do that."

"Why not?" Hannah's voice followed her. "He's a billionaire. I think he would spend quite a bit to ensure your safety. And he's drawn to you—he won't let go easily."

"He doesn't need to be saddled with this. No one does. Being with me is dangerous. What if they kill him? Because that's what they'll do if they find me."

"You don't know that."

"Yes, I do. Mom told us in her letter. Kinetica will stop at nothing to get what they want. Don't you remember?" She held up a finger as she ticked off the facts.

"They want healers like me, and there's not that many of us. Only twenty-five women were part of the original study before the government shut it down, and they're all dead. Only about a quarter of their female offspring inherited the gene, and only a few of us have the special DNA which allows us to heal others. They need me and the others to conduct their experiments. As long as they believe I'm dead, we're safe. But if they discover I'm alive, they'll find me. And when they do, they'll kill you, Dad, and anyone else who gets in their way."

She paced from the window to the bed. "I shouldn't even be staying with Tristan now. If this hadn't been an emergency, I'd never have involved him."

Hannah sniffed. "He's not keeping secrets. I'd know it if he was."

"He asked me a few questions," her dad said.

"What do you mean?"

He shrugged. "When you were sleeping earlier, he wanted to know where you lived in Denver. I told him I didn't know, you moved around so much. Then he wanted to know what I thought of your nursing skills."

Lillian stopped pacing. "What did you tell him?"

"I told him you were well-trained..."

"And...?"

Her father passed a hand through his hair and smiled. "Your nursing skills are better than your cooking skills."

She laughed, and suddenly they were all laughing. She felt almost normal, being with her family again. By the time Dr. Beyton walked through the doorway and approached Hannah, Lillian had almost forgotten the danger of her situation. *Almost.* Worry always hovered nearby, waiting to squelch her joy.

"I see having your loved ones around is doing you some good," the doctor said to Hannah. "How are you feeling?"

"Much better."

The doctor looked over her chart. "Your recovery is incredible. Your vitals are greatly improved. The nurses tell me your appetite has returned."

"Does this mean I can go home?"

He placed a stethoscope on Hannah's chest and listened closely before dropping it and offering another wide smile. "Your lungs sound much better, but there's still a bit of congestion on the latest chest X-ray. We'll see about releasing you tomorrow, but I'd like to keep you here for a little while longer, just to be safe. If you continue with this remarkable recovery, though, it seems likely. In the meantime, enjoy your visit. I'm off to see another patient."

The doctor waved a hand at the three of them and left the room as one of the nurses entered, carrying a large vase with an assortment of brightly colored pink, purple, and white flowers. She placed the vase on the table next to Hannah. "These are for you."

Hannah smiled. "They're gorgeous. Read the card, Lillian."

Lillian reached for the card and read the printed black handwriting. *"Celebration flowers — Tristan."*

"How thoughtful of him."

"Yes." Lillian tucked the card back among the flowers, a familiar tingle racing down her spine.

"Speak of the devil," Hannah mumbled.

Lillian's blood heated in her veins, and she tried not to look at the attractive picture Tristan made where he stood in the doorway. He carried a gift bag, which he presented to Hannah with a flourish.

"A small gift to go with the flowers. But the nurse told me the doctor thinks you can go home tomorrow, so maybe I should take it back?"

"No way, mister." Hannah took the gift bag. "I love the flowers, too. Thank you. They're beautiful."

Tristan smiled. "You've been through quite an ordeal. It's the least I can do."

But he'd already done so much for Hannah—for her—just by being there, although he didn't know it. Lillian's skin prickled, and she raised her gaze until she met his. He looked at her as if he knew the truth. A shiver chased across her skin, leaving goosebumps in its wake. She crossed her arms.

"This is fantastic." Hannah held up a roll of soft, gray yarn. "I'll make some more socks. I was just telling Zoey a girl can never have too many." She reached into the bag and pulled out a hardback book and gushed. "And the newest Tom Grady mystery. I'm so excited to read this. How did you know? Oh, I told the nurse…she must have told you."

Tristan nodded and brushed aside Hannah's thanks with a shrug. He hadn't taken his gaze off Lillian. Now he crossed to her side. "You look exhausted. Why don't we head out so you can rest before the event tonight."

Her muscles tensed—this was it, her final moments with her family. "I need just a little longer to say goodbye."

Tristan nodded. "I'll wait outside."

Her dad's concerned gaze met hers after Tristan departed, and he lowered his voice so they wouldn't be overheard. "You're going back to his house? Is that wise?"

"Probably not. But my car and suitcase are there, and I made a deal with him."

"What deal?"

"In exchange for him going to the hospital with me last night, I promised to attend a fundraiser with him tonight. That was the only way he'd agree to help Hannah. I won't stay long, though. I'll be on a flight first thing tomorrow morning."

Hannah offered a mischievous smile. "He obviously likes you if he's bargaining for a date with you."

"That's not why he did it. He needed a partner and asked me because he felt I wouldn't get attached. I think there is...a woman he's trying to avoid."

"And you believed that? Heck, if I realized getting sick was the way to get you to come visit *and* you'd meet the love of your life, I'd have done it ages ago," Hannah teased.

"He's just an acquaintance." Lillian's eyes burned, but she refused to let the tears fall. There'd be plenty of time for crying when she was back in her apartment in Boston. "Don't you dare get sick again. My heart can't take it. And I might not be able to cure you next time."

She reached for their hands, and the three of them stayed unmoving for a moment.

"I love you both," she said. "I promise I'll come home again when it's safe."

"It's okay, Lillian. Really. I'll miss you, but I understand why you have to go."

"Hannah will be fine now," her dad said. "You only need to worry about yourself."

"Stay well, sweetheart," Lillian whispered.

The sisters hugged and cried and eventually parted.

"I'll walk you to the door," her dad said and followed her there. He placed a wad of cash in her hand. "This should last you for a little while until I can send more."

"Thanks, Dad."

"What about a ride to the airport?"

"I have the car you rented for me, remember? You stay here and make sure Hannah gets home okay tomorrow."

"I wish to God your mother never participated in that damn study. I still wonder if we should have gone to the police after we discovered the truth."

She gripped his arm. "You read Mom's letter. She warned us not to do that unless we had concrete proof— that it would only alert Kinetica to my existence."

Her dad sighed and wrapped her in his arms, squeezing the oxygen from her lungs. "I love you, Lou-Lou. I won't rest a minute until you're safe in your apartment. Make sure to let me know as soon as you're home. And keep a low profile at that party. I have a bad feeling about this."

"I'll be careful. I promise. I'll call you just as soon as I can."

And then she was heading out the door, swiping at the tears that wouldn't stop flowing, and she suspected, looking a complete and utter wreck.

Tristan was waiting outside when she stepped into the hallway. He took one look at her face and reached for her hands, his warm breath parting her hair. "What is it? Is Hannah okay?"

Lillian struggled to remember all the reasons she shouldn't let Tristan get close but couldn't recall a single one. She felt protected, cared for, safe. "Yes. She's wonderful. I'm just missing her already. It's…hard to say goodbye."

She sniffed and somehow found the strength to let go of his hands, swiping at the tears that wouldn't stop. "I'm sorry. I'm crying all over you." She searched inside her purse and found a pack of tissues, her fingers trembling as she struggled to open it.

"I don't care about that. I care about you. Here, let me." Tristan took the package from her hands and pulled out a tissue. Then he tipped her chin and wiped the corners of her eyes. "Better?"

She hiccupped and nodded, and he shoved the tissue in his back pocket and pulled out another, which he handed to her.

She took it and blew her nose, then crumpled the used tissue and stuffed it in her purse, along with the package of unused tissues Tristan returned to her.

He smiled and reached again for her cold hand, which he held between his warm ones. "How are you feeling?"

She tried to smile, but she suspected it looked pitiful. "Okay." Ignoring the fluttering in her chest, Lillian kept her hand in his. Energy flowed between them, heating her from the inside out.

"Before we leave, there's someone I'd like to introduce you to."

"Tristan, I…"

"Please." He held up a hand. "I promise it will take no more than twenty minutes. It would mean a great deal to me if you would meet my mother while you're both here."

She hesitated, then nodded. It was a small favor she could do in return for his help saving Hannah.

He led her down the hallway, and by the time they reached their destination—in a totally different section of the hospital—she was out of breath and her skin tingled all over. He knocked on a door and then opened it, gesturing Lillian inside.

A thin woman lay in a hospital bed—Tristan's mom, Lillian presumed. She was a lot like Tristan—dark curly hair, blue eyes fringed by dark eyelashes, straight nose. But that's where the similarities ended. Dark circles shadowed her eyes, and her skin had a pale-yellow tone.

"Mom, this is the friend I was telling you about… Zoey. Zoey, I'd like you to meet my Mom, Brenda."

"So nice to meet you." Lillian breathed through her nose, careful not to disturb Brenda's energy level, which flickered like a candle with a short wick—one wrong move on Lillian's part could snuff it from existence.

She gave Brenda a warm smile and sat in one of the chairs near the bed.

Tristan bent his tall frame and hugged his mom. "Feeling better?"

"My head still hurts. What did you say your friend's name was again?"

"Zoey. Remember, she's the nurse who's staying with me while her friend is ill." Tristan's tone soothed.

"She's pretty." Brenda smiled at Lillian like a child who'd spotted a long-awaited toy.

Blood heated Lillian's cheeks, and she pressed cool fingers against them. "Kind of you to say so."

"Tristan's never brought any of his girlfriends to see me before." She glanced at Tristan. "Have you?"

Tristan smiled. "No, Mom."

"We're just friends," Lillian said. She cast a quick glance at Tristan, but his face didn't change expression, so she had no idea what he thought of his mom referring to Lillian as his girlfriend.

"Zoey is a talented nurse."

Lillian tucked her hands under her legs. If she thought she could cure his mom now, she would skip the fundraiser, knowing her debt had been paid. But the moment she sat next to Tristan's mom, she understood it would prove challenging. Brenda's body chemistry was vastly different from Lillian's, making it impossible to attempt a cure in Lillian's exhausted state.

She pulled in air and held it in her lungs so she wouldn't harm Brenda and gave her a warm smile. "It's lovely to meet you." Lillian ignored the glimmer of light in her mind's eye. A dark shadow covered most of it, indicating the extent the disease had taken over Brenda King's body. Her health was declining fast.

Brenda's expression changed, going from calm and serene to annoyed in an instant. "You're not the nurse I had this morning."

"Zoey isn't your nurse, Mom. She's my friend."

Brenda's glare intensified, and she raised her voice, becoming agitated. "Why would you bring a stranger here," she said to Tristan. "You know I'm not feeling well. What were you thinking?"

Tristan gentled his voice and clasped his mom's hands in both of his. "Zoey has become an important friend in a short space of time. I wanted you to meet her before she has to leave."

Lillian couldn't seem to catch her breath—his mother hated her, but Tristan had just admitted Lillian was important to him. Was he exaggerating? She bit her lip. What difference did it make what he confessed. Lillian couldn't let their friendship interfere with her plans to leave Cleveland tomorrow.

"You shouldn't have brought her here. I don't like her."

"Mom." Tristan sighed and motioned Lillian to follow him. "I'll be back, Mom."

He lowered his voice an octave when they stepped out of the room. "I'm sorry, Lillian. She doesn't know what she's saying. This is not a good day for her."

"It's okay. I'll leave you two alone."

"Thanks for understanding. Wait for me outside. I'll be just a minute, and then I'll drive you back to the house."

Chapter Fourteen

Lillian found a seat in a nearby lounge empty of other visitors and tapped her foot on the floor while she waited. It shouldn't matter if Tristan's mom disliked her, she'd be out of his life after tomorrow anyway. The reminder didn't offer much relief.

She pulled out her cell phone and checked her flight, which appeared to be on time. A shadow fell across her lap, and she half-rose from her seat before she realized it was Tristan. He hadn't exaggerated when he said he'd be just a minute.

A knowing awareness flickered in his gaze. "Thank you for meeting my mom."

She shouldered her purse and stood. "It was nothing. Do you need to stay with her? I can take an Uber to your house if there's someone who could leave my suitcase on the porch and the keys to the rental."

His gaze sought hers out, stubbornness carved in the hard lines of his face. "She was only here for a treatment. My mom's caretaker is with her and will take her home and get her settled, so I can drive you. We're still on for the fundraiser tonight, right?"

"Of course."

"Good." He gestured for her to go in front of him.

They walked side by side until they reached the elevator and then rode in tense silence to the lobby. She shoved her hands in her pockets, doing her best to ignore her thundering heartbeat. She wished he'd speak and tell her what he was thinking, but they were halfway to the exit before he obliged.

"I'm sorry I put you through that."

"Don't be sorry. I'm glad I got to meet your mom. I know how important she is to you."

"She's not always that difficult. I wish…"

She waited for him to finish, but he didn't, and after a minute of silence, she couldn't resist prompting. "What do you wish, Tristan?"

He shook his head and sighed, gravel in his voice. "I wish you could have met my mom in normal times, before Huntington's. She was warm and funny and good with people. All my friends loved her. I loved her. The woman I introduced you to isn't anything like the woman who raised me. Huntington's has stripped her personality until I hardly recognize her. This is all I have left."

His voice hitched on the last word, and she automatically reached for his hand. Their fingers entwined, his palm warm and sturdy and right in hers. She never wanted to let go. But she must.

The exit doors slid open, and they stepped outside together.

Even with his solid strength, she paid attention to their surroundings, alert to danger. The March sky was overcast, and it was breezy, but the late-afternoon sun managed to peek out from behind the clouds, casting flickering shadows on the pavement.

They paused as if they'd made an agreement.

"The crazy thing is, I thought she would be in a good mood. She usually is after she's finished a treatment and knows she'll be going home," he murmured, his thumb sliding against hers. "Zoey, I want you to know I'm here for you…at any time…if you need me."

Never had she been more tempted to tell all, to bring him into her world and lean on his considerable strength. But if she did that, she'd be risking his life without giving him a choice. And she cared too much to put him in danger. She moved forward, and he came with her.

"I appreciate the offer, but I'm fine. You have enough to worry about with your mom."

They had reached his car, and the doors popped open. She pulled her hands from his and climbed inside. She fastened her seatbelt, and he did the same, but he made no effort to start the car.

"Are you sure you have to leave tomorrow?"

She didn't hesitate. "Yes."

Zoey lay her head back on the seat and closed her eyes and said a silent prayer of relief when Tristan didn't argue. He started the car and drove out of the hospital lot and toward home.

❧

Tristan put on his sunglasses and stepped on the accelerator, passing a line of cars on the right. Zoey—or Lillian
rather—was determined to leave. He could feel her deter-
mination from where she sat next to him, eyes closed to
shut him out. She would continue her stubborn refusal to
confide in him.

On some level, he understood it. They'd only known
each other a short time—why should she trust him? He
clenched his teeth until his jaw ached. Because whatever
her issues, he wanted to help her, dammit. The more she
pushed him away, the more Tristan vowed to slip through
her defenses.

As if she heard his thoughts, Lillian stirred, opening
her eyes and clutching the purse that was never far from
her body—it either sat in her lap like now, or it hung
from her shoulder. He turned at the light and headed east
toward home. It wouldn't be long before Brian would figure out the rest of her story. Why wasn't he more satisfied
by the thought?

Lillian stared out the window, avoiding his gaze.
When he'd kissed her, she'd kissed him back, which meant
the attraction he felt for her was not all one-sided. And
yet, she'd refused to acknowledge it, refused to confide in
him, refused to let him into her world. Although he didn't
understand why it was so, her continued refusals hurt.

He tightened his grip on the wheel and sped up, easing his car into the right lane. Perhaps it was only his ego
she'd damaged. It didn't feel like it, though. It felt like
she'd reached a hand inside his chest and squeezed his

heart. His gut twisted at the thought of saying goodbye tomorrow. He couldn't shake the frightening feeling he might never see her again.

If this was their final evening together, then he would use the opportunity to convince Lillian to confide in him. Maybe there was still a chance to earn her trust.

∽

Lillian avoided looking at Tristan as she got out of his car and made her way to the door. There was no reason to interact with him any more than required—it would only make it harder for her to leave later. She'd go to her room, lay her outfit out for tonight, and freshen up.

Unfortunately, she had to wait for Tristan to unlock the door for her to enact her plan. It seemed to take a millennium as he disarmed the security system.

Her pulse pounded, but whether she feared Kinetica's soldiers would be inside waiting or how her body responded to Tristan's tall form, she wasn't sure. All she knew was her skin tingled when he touched her arm, and the breezy scent of him could be bottled and sold for profit.

She took a whiff and held it in her lungs, avoiding his sharp gaze by pretending to check out the gleaming kitchen appliances—microwave, Keurig, dishwasher. Her eyes landed on the kitchen table. A centerpiece of pink tulips was perched in the middle between two ivory candlesticks, gold place settings, and a bottle of champagne in a bucket of ice.

Her stomach turned over. "You're expecting company?"

"Yes."

A pain settled in her chest. Was it with that glamorous hospital administrator, Angelina? Had he finally given in to her flirting? "I'll just get my things and go then."

"That would be a shame." He removed his jacket and tossed it on a barstool. Then he moved toward her, accelerating her heartbeat. "The table is set for you and me, Zoey. I thought we could celebrate Hannah's recovery with an early dinner."

"Dinner?" Her pulse quickened, and her voice sounded breathless.

He stopped in front of her, causing her heart to beat harder if it were possible. His breath warmed her hair, and the temperature rose a notch. She couldn't take her eyes off his broad shoulders and the few dark chest hairs that peeked from the vee in his shirt.

"Yes, dinner. There will only be appetizers and drinks at the fundraiser, and it has been a while since lunch. I don't want you passing out. You have to eat, don't you? Unless you were expecting something else?" He raised his eyebrows.

Something else? She stared at his hard chest and fought the devil on her shoulder that tempted her to enjoy his company. Would it be a horrible mistake? It was only four thirty—the event didn't start until seven. Tonight might be the last time she'd ever see him in person again.

"Well…" Her stomach chose that moment to make itself known with a rumble.

He laughed. "Have dinner with me, Zoey." His eyes were deeper than the ocean, a hint of magic swimming in their navy depths.

She sniffed. She really should find a way to bottle that smell. *Oh, hell.* What was one last meal together? Tristan was right, she couldn't afford more fainting spells, and she had to eat, didn't she?

"What's on the menu?"

He smiled, giving her poor heart palpitations. "Eggplant Florentine with fire-roasted tomato sauce and toasted ciabatta."

"Seriously?"

He laughed, and she felt the joyful sound in her heart. Now that she'd made up her mind to stay for dinner, the atmosphere between them took on a festive note.

"Seriously. I have a fabulous chef."

"You have your own chef?"

"For special occasions like this…yes. I'm not much of a cook."

He pulled the padded chair out from the table and motioned for her to sit. "I just have to heat up the meal. I promise, it will only take a minute."

"Can I help?"

He smiled, revealing a glimpse of the dimple that only seemed to come out to play in moments like these. "To use the microwave and oven? I've got it. You sit and rest and talk to me."

Talk to him? What safe topics could they talk about they hadn't already covered?

He opened the fridge and proceeded to pull out an assortment of covered dishes, which turned out to be a tossed salad, butter, and a white casserole dish, which he put in the microwave.

"Will Angelina be at the hospital fundraiser tonight?" The minute the words came out of her mouth, she regretted them. *Of all the questions to ask.* That was not a safe topic. Besides, what business was it of hers?

"Yes, she organized it. It's the largest fundraiser the hospital puts on. She's been planning it for more than a year." He pressed a button on the microwave until it beeped and hummed, then set the salad on the table along with the butter and turned to look at her, all trace of laughter removed from his expression. Tension vibrated on an invisible cord between them. "Are you married?"

The unexpectedness of the question had her skin tightening. *Tit for tat, obviously.* The heat in the room rose another notch, and she didn't answer but took off her jacket and draped it around the back of her chair.

He stilled, his gaze never wavering, waiting for her response.

She pressed her lips together. Despite the way she'd evaded the topic earlier, she couldn't outright lie now. "No, I'm not married. What about you?"

The tension in his expression vanished. "Nope, too busy working."

Of course, developing the software that made him a billionaire. "You're not working now." Her stomach cringed. She really should change the subject.

"I've been a bit preoccupied with my mom."

"Of course."

He straightened a tulip in the vase. "Besides, I doubt I'll ever tie the knot."

He said it casually, as if they were discussing the weather, but the admission was meant as a warning. He could save himself the trouble—the last thing she wanted was commitment.

She dropped her gaze to the gold placemat in front of her, sliding moist palms down her lap. The earlier light camaraderie between them had faded and been replaced with…what? Fear? Curiosity? Her throat scratched.

"How can you be sure?" She meant the words to be teasing, but they came out breathless.

His eyes met hers. "Because I don't want children."

She frowned and wrinkled her nose. "Why not?"

He grimaced. "Any child of mine could inherit Huntington's. I won't consign an innocent child to that fate."

He turned away to check the oven, and she fingered the fancy cloth napkin. How sad a man as vital as him would never have children of his own, especially knowing he did not have Huntington's. But she understood his dilemma all too well. If she ever made the mistake of having children, they would have a 50 percent chance of either inheriting the healing gene or some other mutation, like the gene that allowed Hannah to know the secrets of the heart. And any children who could cure the sick would have a target on their back.

"Have I shocked you?"

His deep voice interrupted her musings, and she realized he'd returned to the table, while she'd been preoccupied. She cleared her throat. "I'm sure there's a lady out there who doesn't want children also."

"Do you?"

Her gaze flew to his, and it came to her then, someone had wounded him deeply—someone who had wanted children. He turned away, picking up the champagne bottle and pouring the sparkling liquid into their glasses. He handed her a glass and waited for an answer, his eyes challenging.

"Want children?" She took a gulp of champagne, the sweet taste dulling the ache in her chest at the thought of never having babies of her own. Yes, she wanted children, and a husband, and a white picket fence. Foolish dreams she had been forced to relinquish when she'd fled Cleveland. "No, I'm too into my job." Which was as close as she'd allow herself to get to the truth.

He raised his glass, clinking it with hers. "To workaholics."

He flashed a smile, pulling her from her sad thoughts, and the atmosphere magically lightened again. He tipped his drink and swallowed, and she found herself mesmerized by the way his Adam's apple moved in his throat.

He refilled their glasses and offered her the salad. Pieces of tomato, cucumber, and black olive peeked out from under romaine lettuce drizzled with some kind of homemade dressing. She took a bite and chewed and swallowed, the combination of flavors bursting on her tongue.

"This is fantastic."

"Thanks. I'll let Chef Batz know."

He had put on a pair of gray oven mitts with white writing on them. She squinted—one had a whisk and said, "Whip it good;" the other had kitchen tools and said, "Choose your weapon."

She giggled, and he glanced over his shoulder.

"I like your oven mitts."

He held them up and grinned. "A gift from my mother when I bought this place. Wait until you see the dish towels."

He carried the steaming casserole to the table and set it on another hot pad in front of her. The smell alone had her drooling. The bread toasted in the oven came a few minutes later with melted garlic butter. My God, she'd forgotten how good home-cooked food could taste. Living alone, she didn't make elaborate meals, and she rarely ate at restaurants.

She'd eaten most of the serving on her plate before she realized he wasn't eating but watching her. Heat rushed to her cheeks, and she grabbed for the champagne.

"Aren't you hungry?"

He laughed. "I'm having too much fun watching you eat. I like a girl with an appetite. You have a bit of tomato sauce on your face."

She grabbed the cloth napkin and wiped. "Better?"

"Not quite."

He got up and came toward her. What was he doing?

"Let me." He took the napkin from her hands and wiped her nose. His hands were gentle and strong and for a mad moment she wanted to melt into their solidness. Then he set the napkin down and pulled her up and into his arms.

And God help her, she let him.

Chapter Fifteen

She shouldn't let Tristan hold her. But she had to admit, it felt incredible.

"Aren't you hungry?" Lillian whispered, which had the satisfying effect of giving her a flash of Tristan's dimple.

"Ravenous," he said and dipped his chin until his mouth found hers.

He didn't lie. His mouth stripped away any lingering resistance, nipping at her lips until she opened and he plunged inside. His tongue swept her teeth and the roof of her mouth, tasting of champagne and magic.

She threaded her hands through his thick, dark hair like she'd itched to do ever since they'd first kissed. She moved her hands around his neck, enjoying the feel of corded muscles and the cool mint and leather scent of him. His arms smashed her breasts against his hard chest, and he groaned into her mouth, his breath raspy.

They may have only remained locked together for minutes, but it felt like forever. Eventually, they had to come up for air, but he didn't let her go, and she didn't object. He rested his forehead against hers, his breathing labored.

"Don't leave after the party. Stay for at least another day. I promised you a tour of the garden."

"I can't."

"Why not?"

She sighed and pulled herself from his arms. "I have a job. My life is…complicated."

"Too complicated to delay your departure by a single day?"

She took a breath and tried to pretend her pulse wasn't racing. "Yes."

His expression grew challenging, which did nothing to calm her nerves. When he looked like that, she wasn't at all sure what he'd do next.

"Tell me you don't feel this…pull between us."

"I…I have to get ready now." She stood and grabbed her jacket from the back of the chair. "Thank you for dinner." She headed toward the stairs.

"Zoey, wait."

She turned to look at him.

"Is it because of what I said earlier? About not having children?"

She swallowed the dryness in her mouth and was grateful she didn't have to look him in the eyes.

"Yeah," she lied. "That's it."

In truth, the mutation in her genes would override any other inherited diseases. If they had babies together, he'd have to worry about their children inheriting super-natural diseases, not neurological ones.

She left the room, but not before she caught the flash of hurt in his expression. One more reason she shouldn't linger in Cleveland. The longer she remained, the more likely she would leave a permanent scar.

She navigated the stairs by focusing on each individual step. Why hadn't her mother warned her how attracted she would be to a burner? She'd only mentioned their rarity and the power they generated. Not that she'd want to rip his clothes off every time she got too close.

She twisted the doorknob with slick palms and entered her room, her stomach doing a series of flip turns. How would she ever manage to stand by Tristan's side and play the role of his date tonight when every molecule in her wanted it to be true?

A long, slow shiver slithered down her spine. And what if Dominic Raines had figured out her identity and arranged for her capture?

She moved to her suitcase and unzipped it, pulling out the party dress and shaking it in front of her, looking for wrinkles. Thankfully, the wine stain wasn't noticeable. Was it only yesterday she'd worn this dress at Tristan's home? What if she were recognized tonight by someone who knew her? It would be impossible to relax until the evening was over, and she was on the early morning flight to Boston.

Satisfied her outfit was in good shape, she undressed and tugged the garment over her head, eyeing herself in the full-length mirror in the humongous bathroom. The cut made her appear sleek and sophisticated even though she knew she was neither.

Her hands trembled as she added the sparkling costume jewelry to the ensemble. How would she be able to keep a low profile at the party when all eyes would be on her as Tristan's date? Would Kinetica's spies be present, waiting for the right moment to grab her?

She studied her reflection in the mirror, noticing the tiredness in her eyes and the apprehension on her face. A stranger stared back at her—red lips, pale skin, sad green eyes, and the blonde wig so different from her thick dark hair. Who was this person she'd become, flinching at shadows and unable to respond when a handsome man paid her attention? If only she were an ordinary girl living an ordinary life.

She stuck her tongue out, defying her troubled thoughts, then slipped into her heels and grabbed her purse. She took a parting look around the cheerful bedroom, knowing she'd never see it again once she left here. Someone had made the bed—a visiting maid perhaps? She hadn't seen evidence of hired help, but Tristan was bound to have a cleaning service for this big house. She only needed to get through this one last evening, and she'd be back in the safety of her apartment in Boston.

When she entered the great room, Tristan stood in front of the fireplace, peering into the flames, his profile somber. He looked tall and confident in a black tuxedo, which was probably tailor-made to fit. He had tucked one hand into his pocket, the other clenched by his side.

Lillian shivered, and the movement must have alerted him to her presence because he turned to look.

Energy rushed between them, sending tiny tremors of excitement through her. If only this were a real date and not a forced outing for some murky reason of Tristan's. If only she were just a girl who was free to fall in love. If only…

"You look beautiful tonight," he said, scattering her thoughts to the four winds.

She blushed and fingered her dress like a child of thirteen and not a grown women of twenty-seven who knew better.

"So do you."

His eyes glittered, and it was in that moment she understood the concept of "playing with fire." She flirted with him at her own peril. He moved toward Lillian, stopping only when he stood directly in front of her, blotting out the light from the fire and looking every inch the billionaire computer genius.

"Zoey, look me in the eyes and tell me you don't feel this chemistry between us."

She wet lips dry as a desert and blinked to avoid his hot gaze, which blazed into hers.

"I…" she faltered, and a silence fraught with tension stretched between them.

He moved, crushing her to him and devouring her lips, his large hands framing her face.

Run, Lillian, run. Run fast. Run far.

Lillian didn't want to listen to the warning in her head—not with the delicious heat of Tristan's hard body surrounding her and the power in his kiss, which stripped her of every defense. Her body opened to him, unfolding like a hot-house flower sensing the right combination of temperature and sunlight. Her legs buckled, but it didn't matter because he held her so close, he'd never let her fall.

She snaked her arms around him, and God help her, she didn't want the moment to end.

But even as she had the thought, he was stopping, pulling away from her and setting her aside while they both breathed hard.

"What was that for?" she gasped.

"Proving a point. I can't ignore what is happening between us any more than you can. We need to sort this out, but we're short on time. We have a party to get to, remember? If we leave now, we'll be fashionably late."

The party! How could she have let him distract her to the point she'd completely wiped it from her mind. Warmth flooded her face, setting her cheeks on fire.

"C'mon." He snagged her hand and pulled her along until they reached the door, where he paused to look down, his blue eyes locking with hers. "Promise me you won't leave until we've had a chance to talk after the party."

His eyes flashed a challenge in their depths, and another long shiver chased down her spine.

Lillian crossed her fingers behind her back because this was a promise she might not be able to keep. "I promise."

She managed to hold herself together during the short car ride to the fundraiser, which was held at a fancy party center not far from the hospital. As Tristan predicted, they arrived a little late and were the only guests entering the building.

He tucked her hand in his and pulled her close as they walked into the large banquet room. She imagined all eyes turned to stare at them. Well-dressed couples stood at tables scattered around the room, each covered with black tablecloths and glowing crystal centerpieces. They ate petite appetizers from gold trays carried by wait staff in black and white uniforms. Others moved together on the dance floor. She dropped her gaze to the polished wood floor, praying no one recognized her.

Tristan lowered his head to her ear and grunted. "Smile and try to at least look as if you're happy to be with me."

She raised her gaze to meet his, then cast another quick glance around the room. No one looked suspicious, but if Kinetica had men here, they wouldn't make their presence known.

Her gaze moved to the far corners, where she spotted little window alcoves partly shielded by gold damask curtains, then settled on the band, who was cranking out tunes from the 1940s. She flicked a glance back at Tristan, who still watched her, and forced her lips into a semblance of a smile.

"How's this?"

Instead of answering, he wrapped an arm around her shoulders, leaned in, and kissed her neck. The move was so unexpected she nearly screamed.

"Act natural," he muttered.

There was nothing natural about what he had just done, so why he'd expect her not to react was beyond Lillian.

A familiar, silky voice greeted them from behind. "Tristan, I've been looking for you. You're the guest of honor tonight. How are you enjoying the party? It's fantastic, isn't it?

"Oh, hello, Angelina." Tristan sounded too polite. "The party's great. You remember Zoey, don't you?"

Angelina passed a brittle smile over Lillian. "Of course." She sized Lillian up and down, taking in her outfit and costume jewelry, no doubt. "Are you enjoying yourself?"

Lillian nodded and cemented her smile in place. "Yes, although we only arrived a few minutes ago. I'm sure you two have a lot to catch up on. Why don't I leave you to it?" She tried to escape, but Tristan pulled her backward, gripping her hand in his, with a look that said he was not happy she was trying to get away. "Zoey is here as my special guest tonight."

Power overwhelmed Lillian's senses, her heart pounding. She could read Tristan's emotions better now. He was bothered by Angelina—not annoyed bothered, but frustrated bothered—like he wasn't sure how to handle her attention. It was like Angelina repelled and attracted him at the same time…like…if her hand had been free, Lillian would have slapped it against her forehead. Could she be any more dense? Angelina had him so on edge because she was the woman who had hurt him in the past, the one who had left him because she'd wanted children.

Angelina shot a thin, cool smile Lillian's way. "Ah, that's right. So, kind of you to bring her along. You were always so thoughtful in this way. I'm happy to see that hasn't changed. Speaking of which, would you be a sweetheart and get me a drink from the bar—you remember what I like, don't you? I'll keep Zoey company until you get back."

Tristan hesitated but nodded and released his grip on Lillian to go after the drink. No sooner was he out of sight than Angelina protracted her claws.

"Tristan and I were engaged once upon a time. Did he tell you?"

Lillian shook her head, her stomach sinking with the knowledge that her instincts had been right. Tristan had feelings for Angelina, which explained why he'd wanted Lillian to come to this event as his date so bad. Someone who wouldn't get attached. He obviously viewed her as a potential bed partner. Well, that was Lillian in a nutshell, wasn't it? Available for a one-night stand and nothing more. She didn't blame Tristan for seeing her that way, since she'd been blowing hot and cold since they'd met.

So why did it feel like Angelina had poked a hole into Lillian's heart and blood was slowly spilling into her chest cavity?

Lillian swallowed. "I haven't known Tristan long."

"Well, so you know, I broke things off with him over a year ago, but it was a mistake. He knows it was a mistake, but he's a proud man, so it will take a little time for him to come around. I'm determined to win him back. I'm not above eating humble pie, either, if that's what it takes."

"Why are you telling me all this?"

Angelina lowered her voice and dropped the fake conversational tone. "You're not the first woman to want Tristan to put a ring on your finger, and you'll likely not be the last. Let me assure you, Tristan is playing some weird game with me by bringing you here tonight. He may act the eligible bachelor, but he's not. His heart belongs to me…always has, always will. You'd be smart to hightail yourself back to wherever it is you came from."

Lillian's headache returned full force and spread to her temples. Negative energy directed her way tended to have that effect.

"Your point?" She held her head high. Regardless of how she felt about Tristan, she'd remain calm and not let Angelina guess her true feelings.

"He'll come back to me eventually, and when he does, I'd hate to see your little heart get broken."

"I'm sure I'll be fine." Lillian managed to force the words out, knowing she told a lie. The thought of Tristan with Angelina knotted her stomach.

"Speaking of being fine, I heard about your friend today—the doctors and nurses were all talking about her. Quite the miracle turnaround."

"Thank you. If you'll excuse me, I see someone I need to talk to." Lillian had enough of Angelina to last a lifetime, and Tristan was returning with Angelina's drink, which had a piece of pineapple sticking out of it.

Lillian turned and hurried in the opposite direction. Behind her, she could hear Angelina saying, "You're looking fine tonight." And Tristan's deep voice answer, "I could say the same for you."

My God, he was still in love with Angelina. How could she have been so blind? Their mutual admiration was sickening.

To think she'd almost given in to her attraction to Tristan. Well, she'd not make that mistake again. She just needed to remember that after tonight, none of what she felt for Tristan would matter. As long as she stayed clear of Kinetica, she'd be on her way home tomorrow and all would be well.

She swiped at the wetness in the corner of her eyes and prayed her mascara didn't smudge. How could she pretend to be happy when all she wanted to do was cry?

Chapter Sixteen

Lillian moved quickly, stopping when she'd put some distance between herself and Tristan and Angelina. She kept her head down to avoid making eye contact or drawing attention to herself.

She spent some time in the restroom, touching up her makeup, but she could not spend the entire party in hiding, so eventually made her way out to the ballroom, where a waiter passed by and offered her a large glass of water. She thanked him and greedily drank, allowing the cool liquid to slide down her throat.

She flicked a glance around the room, careful not to stare too long in any one direction. Her quick scan revealed nothing out of order, so she headed in the direction of the hidden alcove. She was almost there when nausea overcame her. The room swayed left, then right. She would have fallen if she hadn't managed to open the curtain and grasp the back of the divan behind it. She collapsed onto the cushions, putting her head in her hands. What was wrong with her? Why was she so hot?

The curtain parted.

She vaguely recognized the man who entered.

∞

"Where's Zoey?" Tristan asked Angelina, handing her a Mai Tai, her favorite drink. His gaze swept the room, searching for Lillian's familiar shape, but she was nowhere in sight.

Angelina pursed her lips. "I'm not sure. She said she saw someone she knew."

Who? He hadn't thought she knew anyone here. And she was supposed to be by his side, dammit.

Angelina picked up the stirrer from her drink and sucked the piece of pineapple from it. Then she moved toward him, stopping in front of his chest to straighten his bow tie.

"Why don't you ditch her and come home with me tonight?" she whispered.

"I'm sorry, Angelina."

"Oh, come on now, Tristan. Are you deliberately trying to make me jealous? I know I hurt you when I left, and I regret that. At the time I thought I was justified— you could have a serious illness, yet refused to be tested. I wanted children and you couldn't give them to me. But I've come to terms with that now."

A strange heaviness filled his chest. Weren't these the words he'd been longing to hear? "What are you saying?"

"I'm saying, I need you in my life much more than I need my own biological babies. If you don't want to be tested for Huntington's, that's okay. I'm lonely without you—pleasssse put an end to your stubborn pride and give in to what we both want. Come home with me tonight. I promise I'll make it worth your while."

He frowned. "You no longer want to have children?" Why wasn't he more ecstatic?

She took a sip of her drink and licked her lips. "Not if it means I can't have you. Besides as you once told me, we can always adopt, can't we?"

"I'm flattered." She was agreeing to adopt, the solution she'd refused to consider before she'd given him back his ring. This was what he wanted, wasn't it?

He nabbed a glass of wine from a waiter with a passing tray and took a drink. What was he waiting for? He could have it all. He could build a life together with this beautiful, sophisticated woman who was willing to give up having babies just to be with him. A week ago…hell, just yesterday, the news would have had him overjoyed. Now, all he could feel was this damn heaviness in his chest, like he'd arrived at the pot at the end of the rainbow only to find it…empty.

She blinked up at him and placed her hands on his chest, looking both innocent and calculating at once if it were possible. He could smell the sweet scent of her expensive perfume.

"So, you've forgiven me? You'll take me home after?"

"No, Angelina." The words came without conscious thought on his part, but the moment they were spoken, he knew they were right.

"Good God. There's no way you can have strong feelings for a practical stranger so soon—if you feel anything for that gold-digger, it's good old-fashioned lust.

Why complicate your life when you can have me for the asking?"

Angelina did a small pirouette, showing off her body and her long shapely legs.

The move, which ordinarily would have been compelling, couldn't seem to hold his attention. He found his mind wandering, imagining what Lillian was doing and why she'd deserted him when he needed her most.

Angelina made a small sound and pouted. "My offer won't last forever. Tell me to my face you don't want me anymore. Don't you remember how good we were together?"

Another time, he might have found her pout cute, but after spending the last day and a half with Lillian at her sister's bedside, her pout struck him as childish.

"What were you thinking, just now? You have a weird expression on your face."

Angelina waited for his response, but Tristan didn't think she'd like it if he told the truth. Thankfully, his cell phone chose that moment to buzz with an incoming call. *Brian.*

"Sorry, but this is an important call I have to take. Excuse me."

Angelina made a sound of frustration, but he ignored her, making his way outside the ballroom, where he and Brian could be sure to talk undisturbed.

"I have more information." His friend didn't bother with pleasantries. "I'll include everything in my formal report, but I didn't think you'd want to wait."

"You thought right." Tristan found a chair near a small alcove under a window in a corner looking out over the parking lot and hunched over his phone. "Whatcha got?"

"Get a load of this. Pullman Hospital's average patient recovery rate for terminal illness is thirty percent. But the year Lillian Milano worked there, the recovery rate jumped to fifty percent."

Tristan stilled. "Impressive. But do you really think it's because of Lillian?"

"Well, that's the interesting part. The increase could be attributed to many factors outside of Lillian; however, we tracked down a few of her former patients from the year she worked there. Each miraculously recovered from a terminal illness. Each of them recount the same unique experience."

"Which is?"

"I'm working up to that, buddy."

Tristan held the phone tighter to his ear. Brian was clearly drawing the facts out for maximum impact.

"They all told stories about how Lillian held their hands until their symptoms disappeared. One young man told me he got a warm feeling up and down his body. Another described the sensation as being overheated. An older woman and her granddaughter couldn't praise Lillian enough. Called her an angel sent from God to destroy the pancreatic cancer that ravaged the grandmother's body—the doctors had told the family the grandmother had six months to live. That was more than three years ago."

My God. Excitement curled in Tristan's gut so he couldn't sit still any longer. Heat raced up and down his spine. He picked up his phone, strode toward the window, looked out at the night. Hadn't he thought Lillian had some miraculous way to heal the sick? He hadn't believed it at the time, it seemed too fantastical, but he'd witnessed her ability himself. If it were true… He let out the breath he'd been holding.

Lillian might be able to cure his mother. And if he had inherited the disease…

"Still there?" Brian rumbled.

Tristan cradled the phone by his ear and tapped his fingers against the glass. A strange feeling filled his chest. Hope. It had been so long since he'd felt the emotion, he had trouble recognizing it.

"Yeah, sorry, it's quite a lot to take in."

"I told ya."

"Have you learned who might be threatening Lillian?"

"Not yet. But we've got some leads that look promising."

"Well, keep on it."

"Will do."

"And, Brian, I know you know this, but be discreet. I wouldn't want to inadvertently bring more trouble to Lillian's back door."

Brian grunted. "Discreet is my middle name."

Tristan ended the call and shoved his phone in his pants pocket. Then he headed into the ballroom. He was more than eager to finish his duties at the party and find Lillian and take her home to resume their earlier conversation.

⌘

Tristan walked the ballroom, mingling with the other guests, looking for his missing partner, but she was nowhere to be found. His stomach tightened when he caught a glimpse of a waiter stepping behind a curtain in the corner alcove. Something about the swift movement caught his attention, and he hurried after the gentleman, pulling the curtain back to peer inside.

The waiter was bent over a long and narrow couch, blocking his view, but he noticed the arms and legs sticking out, and they definitely belonged to a woman—his woman. Strange how this single adrenaline-heavy moment solidified his feelings.

"What are you doing?"

The waiter rose swiftly and turned to face him. "I think the lady's had a little too much to drink."

Tristan turned his attention to Lillian and saw that it was true. She'd passed out on the couch. "I see that. She's my date—I'll take it from here."

"Very good," the waiter said, and without another word, left.

"Zoey, wake up," he said, patting her cheeks.

Lillian opened her eyes, but they were glazed and unfocused. How had she managed to drink herself into oblivion in the short time she'd been missing?

"Where am I?"

"We're at the hospital fundraiser, which you would know if you were on my arm, where you're supposed to be, and not hiding inside here, getting plastered."

"I'm not…plastered." She stood, nearly tripping over her heels until he caught her. She sniffed his chest, burying her face into his shirt. "Mmmmh. You smell good."

He did his best to ignore the softness of her cheek pressed again him and checked his watch. "It's almost eight. I'm taking you home, but first I need to present the room out there with a sizable check. Can you manage to stay on your feet long enough for me to accomplish the task?"

"I think so." She pushed herself away from him. "You have terrific coloring," she murmured, her voice dreamy.

He tucked her arm in his. "C'mon, my drunk companion, you can admire my coloring while we're walking."

He managed to get her on her feet and tugged her along, leading her into the main ballroom, where Angelina was announcing the five-hundred-thousand-dollar donation he was making to the North Side Clinic in honor of the care given to his mom.

The audience clapped all around. He sat Lillian on a chair off to one side where he could keep an eye on her and made his way to the microphone to hand Angelina his check. They smiled for the cameras, the guests clapped, and his obligation was complete.

"Your date looks like she's about to pass out," Angelina muttered.

He turned in time to see Lillian standing and stumbling toward what appeared to be the direction of the restroom. He moved as quickly as he could without causing a scene and latched onto her arm, pulling her into his side.

"What's wrong with her?" Angelina asked. She must have followed him.

As if in answer, Lillian pressed a hand over her mouth.

"Excuse us," Tristan said, pulling her through the guests as fast as he could, then half-carrying her into the women's restroom and angling her into a stall just in time. What followed wasn't pretty, but he held her hair out of the way while she appeared to lose everything she'd eaten since breakfast.

CHAPTER SEVENTEEN

Lillian groaned and pushed herself away from the commode, wiping her mouth on some toilet paper Tristan handed her.

The bathroom door banged open, and Angelina trounced inside. "What's wrong with her?"

"She's not feeling well. I'm taking her home," Tristan said.

"You can't leave yet—there are several reporters here who want to talk to you. It's fantastic publicity for the hospital and for you. Let me call a cab."

"No," Tristan said. "I've got this."

"But..." Angelina sputtered. "You can't bail on me now. This is an important moment. You know how long I've been working on this event. I promised the reporters a story. It will encourage other wealthy patrons to donate."

"You'll have to talk to the reporters. Excuse us." Tristan helped Lillian to her feet and half-carried, half-dragged her to the door. He paused and turned back to Angelina. "Could you flush the toilet?"

If she didn't feel so lousy, Lillian might have laughed at the strangled sound Angelina made at this request.

Tristan somehow got her out of the party center without too much fanfare and settled her in the passenger seat of his car. The cool air outside of the building helped to restore some of her equilibrium. Guilt set in—she was supposed to be playacting as his date for the night and instead he was taking care of her…again…and now he had to leave the party early.

She huddled in her seat and squeezed her eyes shut, trying to remember how she had landed in this predicament. She didn't remember drinking. She didn't remember much of anything. Her head felt like it was stuffed with cotton, which wasn't her usual reaction to alcohol. It must be the unrelenting stress she'd been under over the past two days—begging a stranger to help her cure Hannah, saying goodbye to her family, watching out for Kinetica's men, and now, witnessing Tristan's feelings for Angelina first-hand. A girl could only take so much.

"Are you feeling any better?"

She cracked her eyes open to find Tristan had gotten in the driver's seat and started the car. "A little."

She no longer felt nauseous, thank God, but a languorous, sleepy feeling had taken root. She yearned for a bed and pillow and this nightmare of an evening to be over.

"Go to sleep then. I'll have you home in no time."

Home. How could a single word be so comforting and so alarming at the same time? If only she were home. But she couldn't ever go back to her dad's house with Kinetica still looking for her. And Tristan's mansion was not home. No, home was an efficiency apartment in Boston, and even that had never felt like home.

The sound of the tires hitting the pavement and the wind resistance lulled her into a semi-conscious state. When she awoke, they were sitting in Tristan's car, and he was staring at her with a strange expression on his face.

She blinked and moaned, covering her mouth, which tasted like moldy bread. "Where am I?"

"In my driveway. You don't recognize it?"

Did she? She looked around, her mind a fog of confusion.

"How are you feeling?"

"I…my head hurts."

"Why did you drink so much?"

"I…I don't know." Why didn't she remember? She didn't realize she was shaking until Tristan pulled her into his strong arms.

"Shh. It's okay. You've been worried about Hannah, and it happens to the best of us. Besides, it was a convenient excuse for me to leave early."

"Hannah?" She latched on to the single word. Had something happened to her sister? "I…I must go."

"You're not going anywhere in your condition except straight to bed." He unlatched his seatbelt and came around to open her door. "C'mon, I'll help you inside."

"What are you doing?"

"Carrying you into the house."

"The house? I don't think…"

But it was too late—he'd reached inside the car and lifted her up and into his arms, with barely a ripple of muscles, placing her over his broad shoulder like a large sack of potatoes. "I'm getting you inside and into bed."

She was too tired and disoriented to protest. Dimly, she was aware he entered the house and carried her up the stairs and laid her on the bed. He began taking off her shoes, first one, then the other.

Wasn't there somewhere she was supposed to be? Her body felt thick and heavy, and it was too much effort to concentrate on the answer, so she closed her eyes and slept.

⌘

Tristan covered Lillian with warm blankets he found in the closet. He figured she needed sleep more than she needed to be out of her party clothes. That could wait until the morning.

For a while he studied her chest, which rose and fell, reassuring himself she still breathed. Why would a woman who was afraid for her life drink so much alcohol she passed out? It didn't make sense. But then again, there were many facets to Lillian he didn't understand.

He brushed a strand of her golden hair from her eyes and allowed his fingers to caress her smooth cheek. At least he didn't need to worry about Lillian fleeing his house in the middle of the night. Which would give him time to convince her to confide in him.

He filled a water glass and placed it and two aspirin on the bedside table. He had a strong suspicion she'd have one hell of a headache in the morning. Then he left the door open a crack in case she needed him while he changed his clothes, and tiptoed to his own bedroom down the wide hallway.

The first thing Lillian noticed when she opened her eyes was daylight streaming through the large window. The next thing was the dark-haired man with high cheekbones and swarthy skin sitting next to her bedside in sweatpants.

She wrinkled her brow. "Tristan? What are you doing in here?"

"Watching you sleep," he said, his deep voice sending shivers down her spine.

"What for?" She started to get up.

"No, don't get up. Take it easy. How are you feeling?"

A fuzzy memory surfaced of Tristan carrying her up the stairs. "You put me to bed last night. What...what happened to me?"

He frowned, but the tone of his voice remained gentle. "I found you last night passed out on a couch in an alcove at the party. I carried you out of the place to get you home and into bed. Don't you remember?"

She rubbed her head, trying to make sense of his words. "Not really. It's all kind of hazy. But I don't drink as a rule, and I don't remember drinking anything but water last night." She rubbed her eyes, her contacts burning. "Were you in here all night? What time is it?"

"Yes, and almost seven."

"Seven?" Adrenaline raced through her system, her heart thumping in her ears. "I missed my flight."

"Yes, and it's a good thing. You were in no condition to fly. Do you remember where you got the water you said you drank?"

She wrinkled her nose, bringing in a fuzzy image of a waiter handing her a glass of water from a tray. "Yes, a waiter was passing by and offered it to me."

"Did he have dark hair and a mustache?"

Lillian rubbed her head and tried to visualize the fuzzy image more clearly. "I didn't look that closely at him…but I think so. Why?"

Tristan stood and whipped out his cell phone. "You may have been drugged."

Drugged? Oh, shit. Kinetica had found her. It felt like an icy hand reached into her heart cavity and squeezed, and for a moment, she couldn't think or move or breathe.

"Brian," Tristan barked into the phone. "A waiter at the party last night may have slipped something into Zoey's water glass. He had dark hair and a mustache—about five ten. Check to see if the facility has video surveillance."

There was a short pause, where Lillian suspected Brian agreed. The room closed in around her, cutting off her oxygen.

"Contact the police if necessary and call me pronto if you find anything."

"I was drugged?" she managed to choke out the second Tristan ended the call.

"If you weren't drinking, then it's likely. How else to explain your symptoms? The only way to know for sure is to have you checked out in a hospital."

"No. No, I can't." A sick feeling of dread settled in Lillian's gut. Kinetica had found her. Every minute she stayed in this house was jeopardizing Tristan's safety and her family's lives. She didn't let herself think further but moved as quickly as she was able in her current state to rise and pack her things.

"Zoey, what do you think you're doing? You need to rest."

"No. No, I…I can't. I need to leave right now. I've already stayed much longer than I should have." Her voice shook. My God, what if Kinetica were outside right now?

She looked down at her outfit, noticing for the first time she was still dressed in her party clothes. Did it matter? She couldn't afford the precious time it would take to change.

Lillian began shoving clothes into her suitcase, not caring if it was neat or not, not caring that tiny hammers were pounding her skull. Although she was still not quite steady on her feet, it didn't take long since she only had the one suitcase, and she'd never fully unpacked.

Tristan placed his hand over hers, where she gripped her suitcase. "Stop this. You don't feel well, and there's no need to panic. I have my security firm checking into the situation and keeping an eye on us. They're top notch. You'll be safe here until we get to the bottom of this. You have my word."

As much as she wanted to believe him, Tristan didn't understand how ruthless Kinetica could be when they wanted something. And they wanted Lillian.

"I appreciate everything you've done for me, but I can't stay here. I'm sorry."

She pulled her suitcase from his grasp and took a step toward the door.

"When you told me yesterday you had a talent for nursing, what you really meant is you have a talent for healing."

Although he didn't raise his voice, his words sliced through her fear, causing a new, more-panicked sensation. Her heart beat furiously, and she stiffened, frozen in place. In the stunned stillness that followed her gaze flew to his. "I'm not sure what you mean." She gave herself credit for trying.

"I think you do." His intense blue eyes captured hers, demanding truth.

A rush of adrenaline sent a shiver up and down her spine, and her stomach tossed and turned and rolled over. She shouldn't be so surprised he knew she could heal—she'd given him enough clues, and he was smart. It was only a matter of time until he'd figure it out.

She couldn't hold his knowing gaze, so she looked at the suitcase in her hands, the unmade bed, the window with the billowing curtains…at anything but his face. All the while, she lectured herself. She shouldn't have prolonged their goodbye. She shouldn't have gone to the party. She shouldn't be falling for him because, although she'd lied to him earlier to protect herself and her family, she didn't want to tell another lie.

"Zoey, look at me. Is it true? Can you cure the sick?"

She took a sharp breath and raised her head until their gazes met. Looking in his eyes, she read stubbornness, knowledge, fear, awe… Looking in his eyes hurt her heart. "It's time for me to go now." She intended to be assertive, but the words came out soft and weak, and she still hadn't moved.

He placed his hands on hers, warming them between his palms. "Please. I need you to be honest with me about this."

"You don't know what you're asking." She shivered and pulled her hand from his, an icy, cold resolve filling her chest. She didn't waste more time thinking, stumbling toward the door.

"My mother is dying."

His voice was quiet, desperate. He didn't try to stop her from fleeing the room, but the anguish in his words pierced her heart and held her in place as if he had. She froze again, unable to move forward but afraid to turn-around and witness his despair.

"If there's a grain of truth to your ability, you could possibly…Zoey, you might be able to save her."

Don't turn around.

If she were smart, she'd listen to the inner voice, urging her to flee…urging her to grab her keys and drive straight to the airport. She'd return the rental and find somewhere to hide until she boarded her flight. She'd go back to her life and forget she'd ever met Tristan or his mother.

She turned.

In matters of the heart, she'd never been smart.

Tristan stood in front of her, hands fisted at his side. His tortured gaze met hers, and whatever resistance she'd been clinging to crumbled, washed away by the anguish in his expression.

She found herself setting the suitcase down and moving toward him, placing one foot in front of the other until they stood facing each other, mere inches apart. She studied the raw emotion in his eyes, compassion warring with her own self-preservation. Even if she agreed to Tristan's request, there was every likelihood she could not cure his mother of Huntington's.

Her eyes burned and teared, clouding her vision. She risked everything by staying in Cleveland. Dominic would have gotten wind of Hannah's miraculous recovery and probably suspected her real identity. Even now, Kinetica's soldiers could be mounting their attack. They would kill Tristan if he tried to prevent them from taking Lillian.

A shiver made a slow circuit down her spine until her toes curled. If she left, she'd be sealing his mother's fate to one of death. Would he ever forgive her? Could she ever forgive herself?

She still looked into his eyes, but now she reached for his hand, her fingers tingling as they curled around his, their energies merging and blending. He'd not abandoned her when she'd begged for his help. How could she do the same now their positions were reversed?

She stole a breath. "It's true. I can heal."

CHAPTER EIGHTEEN

Tristan's pulse sped up, and he had trouble drawing in air. Was this a dream? Did Lillian really just admit she could heal the sick? Or would he wake up disappointed to find it had all been a fantasy?

"You must understand it's highly unlikely I can totally cure your mom of Huntington's."

Lillian's serious gaze caught his, her body demanding his full attention as she paced back and forth in the bedroom. She looked angelic with her golden hair, glossy and long, and her pink cheeks.

She stopped pacing and crossed her arms to fix him with a steely gaze. "I don't want any publicity. Whatever the result, you must swear not to tell anyone, not even your mom."

"I'll keep your secret. You have my word."

She resumed her pacing. At this rate she would wear a hole in the expensive carpet.

His heartbeat matched her footsteps. For the first time in a long while, Tristan dared to hope, not just for his mom, but for his foolish heart. Lillian had stayed to help him when she could have run.

"I'll be tired afterward and may need to rest. If that happens, I'll need a place to recover."

He moved a hand around the room. "Plenty of space here." And he wasn't about to let her out of his sight until he knew she was safe. Last night, he'd ordered additional security to ensure Lillian and her family would be under surveillance at all times.

"I won't stay here longer than necessary. You must promise not to follow or contact me after I leave."

He nodded his head in agreement. "Understood." He would let Lillian leave if she insisted on it, but he had every intention of convincing her to stay.

"There's one more thing you should know. A healing like this is dangerous, not only for the patient and the healer but…for the donor."

"Donor?" He frowned. What donor? "What exactly happens when you heal?"

She finally sat on the bed, twisting her hands in her lap. He settled next to her and waited.

She cleared her throat but didn't look at him, her voice so low he had to strain to hear. She had probably never explained her ability to anyone else before.

"If you remember from high school science class, every living thing contains energy, right?"

He nodded but kept his mouth shut. Now she was finally talking, he didn't want to interrupt for fear she'd quit.

"Albert Einstein said the total amount of energy in the universe remains constant. It cannot be created or destroyed but is converted from one form to another. Energy that's stored in the body is potential energy, but when the energy is set in motion, it becomes kinetic."

She paused and fidgeted, fingering a fold in her dress. He stilled and waited for her to continue.

"When I'm near people, I sense their potential energy—whether it's high, low, or in between. When a person moves, their potential energy becomes kinetic energy. My cells automatically absorb the kinetic energy, which is then stored in my body as potential energy. When I capture enough of this stored energy, I can transfer it to the person I want to heal."

He hardly breathed. "Is the donor aware this is happening—that you've absorbed their energy?"

"Not usually."

"You steal it then."

She turned to him, her wide eyes sparking with indignation. "I don't steal energy—I only absorb and store the energy people give off when they move. It doesn't hurt them. Like I said, they don't even know it's happening."

"You said 'not usually'."

"Yeah." She nodded and returned to looking at her hands, which she still clutched in her lap. "A few rare people produce an extraordinary amount of potential energy. They're called burners. I'd never actually met a burner until…recently."

Secrets hid in her voice. She got to her feet and strolled to the bedroom window. The sun had risen, and there was plenty of light for her to see outside, although he suspected she was not looking at the landscape but considering what to tell him.

She turned, smoothing her hands down her dress, but he noticed she didn't meet his eyes. "Usually, I have to wait until I have enough potential energy stored in my body to heal a patient. But with a burner, it's different. They give off so much energy, I can channel it directly when they're near me, without trying to store it."

She paused, expectant, as if she waited for him to decipher a complicated computer code.

Tristan was beginning to feel like he was trapped in a bizarre sci-fi movie. He moved toward her. Now he was the one who felt like pacing. "What exactly are you trying to tell me?"

She blinked once, twice. "Tristan, you're a burner."

Hadn't he known she was leading up to this? His pulse quickened—his gut clenched and spasmed. "Is that why you begged me to visit your...Hannah the other night?" Had it only been two days ago?

"I had no choice. You were the only one who could save her."

"You should have told me what you were doing." To her credit, she didn't flinch at the bitterness in his voice.

"You wouldn't have believed me, and I couldn't take the chance you'd say no. Hannah would have been dead by morning."

His anger fizzled out like a snuffed flame, leaving him cold. She was right. He wouldn't have believed her. But it still didn't take away the ugly feeling of being used.

"Where are you going?"

"To the entertainment room. I need a drink," he flung over his shoulder, not caring if she followed. He headed down the stairs, the tap of her footsteps echoing behind him.

Since he'd come into wealth, he'd been on the receiving end of more pleas for money than he cared to count, most of them scams. Women propositioned him routinely. Everyone wanted something. Everyone had a price. Did anyone tell the truth?

He reached the room and found the whiskey behind the bar, splashed some into a glass. He didn't trust easily, but for some reason, he'd trusted her. *Hell.* Hadn't he suspected Lillian of having ulterior motives? What other secrets were hiding behind her cool composure Brian had yet to uncover?

He raised the glass and eyed the amber drink as if it held answers, ignoring the woman who stood in the doorway. Lillian hadn't wanted his money. She'd wanted something much more valuable. Something she'd taken from him without his knowledge. He lifted the glass to his lips—he'd welcome the burn.

"I wouldn't do that if I were you." Lillian stepped into the room.

The lady was back to giving orders. Well, he didn't feel much like marching. He narrowed his eyes, tipped the glass, and swallowed the whiskey, then turned and grabbed the bottle.

"Alcohol dulls your energy. We're going to need every bit of it if we hope to cure your mom."

He hesitated, then set the whiskey bottle down with a sigh and faced her. He was being selfish, wasn't he? What did it matter if Lillian used him? She'd agreed to cure his mom, if that were even possible to do. Wasn't that all that mattered?

"Fine. I won't drink, but I've got a few questions for you, and I want the truth." He moved forward until he towered over her.

She nodded. "I will tell you what I can."

He had to give her credit; she didn't back down. "If I'm a burner, as you call it, why didn't I sense when you were siphoning my energy?"

"I was careful not to use too much. I didn't want to hurt you."

Tristan didn't miss the way her fingers clutched her sides. He tightened his brow, his mind locking in on the truth. "You protected me, didn't you? That's why I didn't feel anything. You used your own energy until you passed out."

She shrugged as if it were nothing. "Perils of the job."

He lifted her chin until their gazes clashed, injecting steel into his voice. "I don't want you passing out to heal my mom. You can have as much of my energy as you need. You're not to put yourself in danger."

"Believe me, I try to avoid passing out." She cleared her throat and spoke so low, he had to lean forward to hear. The smell of strawberries filled the air. "Tristan, I never meant to hurt you. But I was desperate to save Hannah, and I can't always control the process."

"You should have trusted me with the truth. What else are you keeping from me?"

She dropped her gaze, her shoulders slumping.

"Zoey, look at me."

She lifted her chin, and he read sorrow, fear, and something that looked a lot like resolve in her eyes.

"What do you see when you use my energy to heal...a glowing light?"

She frowned and played with her dress—a pattern he noticed her doing whenever she felt uncomfortable. He didn't think she'd answer, but she did, her voice low and hesitant and laced with vulnerability.

"Usually, it's more of a dark figure in my mind that I wrap light around."

"How does it work?"

She hesitated, then grabbed his hand. "It will be easier if I show you. Hold my hand and keep your eyes closed."

He did as she asked. He didn't notice any change at first, but gradually, his palm warmed, then his arm, then his whole body. If he didn't know better, he'd think he was standing next to a fire.

Desire hit him hard, the hair on his arms on full alert, his whole body tingling. He basked in Lillian's heat, which seemed to bring new life to his heart and limbs. He might have stood with his eyes closed forever if she hadn't pulled her hand from his.

He opened his eyes and blinked. "Is that what you did to Hannah?"

She didn't look away from his gaze. "Yes, but I didn't mean to have such a dramatic impact. It's easy to get carried away with you."

He did his best to mask the flare of satisfaction at her words. She admitted she got carried away around him… progress.

"I've never given anyone a demonstration like this before. You must understand healing takes extreme concentration, and it can be dangerous for everyone involved."

He frowned. "Why dangerous?"

"I could draw too much energy from donors. I could use too much of my own energy. I could take too much of the patient's energy. It's a delicate balance and easy to make a mistake. That's why I made you stand in the corner when I cured Hannah."

He smiled. "And here I thought you were punishing me."

Her cheeks flushed a rosy pink. "I did what I thought was best at the time. Listen, we should get going. I'll make the attempt to heal your mom, but I can't stay longer. I'll book another flight."

She turned and moved toward the door, but he stopped her with a hand on her shoulder.

"Not before I fix breakfast. Why don't you clean your contacts and get out of those party clothes while I make you something to eat. And don't worry about your flight. I have a private helicopter. It will be much faster and easier than trying to book a commercial flight, I promise. I can have you in Denver in a couple of hours." He wouldn't mention he would be the pilot.

Her face paled, and she nibbled her lip.

"Don't tell me you're afraid to fly in a helicopter?"

"No, of course not."

"Good. The helicopter is at Burke Lakefront, which is a short jaunt. We can turn your rental car in and leave from there."

"I appreciate the offer, but there's no need."

He started to object, but his smart watch chose that moment to vibrate with an incoming message, and he paused to glance at the screen. Brian was back with more information. Adrenaline had him moving toward his office. "Excuse me, but I have to take this call. Use the time to freshen up. I'll return shortly." He left before she could think of another argument.

He dialed Brian's number, and the investigator picked up just as Tristan reached his office door. "What do you have for me?"

"It's big. Are you sitting down?"

Tristan closed the door behind him and grabbed the chair from behind his desk. "What is it?"

"I told you we had some promising leads. We've been sniffing around, asking questions. We looked into Lillian's mother, Emily Milano. Unlike Lillian, Emily Milano's lifeless body was recovered after her car accident, and a death certificate was issued. The cause of death is listed as head trauma and internal injuries."

"That sounds logical."

"We thought so, too."

Brian was warming up. Tristan drummed his fingers on the desk.

"By all accounts she lost control of her vehicle and hit a tree. One of the news articles we read mentioned that Emily had been volunteering as a nurse on a mission trip in the Appalachian Mountains in West Virginia at the time of her death for an organization called Project Green. I checked into Project Green, and that's where this gets weird."

"Go on."

"The organization's stated mission is to raise awareness for immunization and safe births. They sponsor a clinic at a women's crisis center there called Oak Haven. One of my guys got a tip from a former resident who claimed she'd been injected with the Ebola virus and then miraculously cured by Emily Milano."

"No shit." Tristan's pulse pounded. "The former resident never told anyone?"

"No, quite the opposite. She complained to anyone who'd listen, including the police."

"They didn't take her seriously?"

"She's a recovered heroin addict and diagnosed bipolar. Everyone thought she was loony. No one believed her—at least not enough to do a thorough investigation."

"But you did." Tristan couldn't keep the satisfaction from his voice. Brian's agency was the best in the business.

"I did," Brian rasped. "One of my investigators snuck into Oak Haven yesterday, and what she reports is appalling. Cramped quarters, horrible abuse, human experimentation. We think they're injecting these women with deadly viruses and using nurses like Emily Milano to cure them."

Tristan pushed his chair out and stood. "There are others capable of healing?"

"At least one other. They had her under lock and key—probably not there willingly. But my investigator swears she witnessed the healer put her hands on a young mother with pox marks all over her face, and when she removed her hands, they'd vanished."

"My God. No wonder Lillian's terrified. They want to force her to participate in these experiments. Who the hell is funding Project Green?"

"Looks like their major sponsor is the genetic research corporation you mentioned, Kinetica."

Chapter Nineteen

Tristan leaned on the desk to steady himself. Cold drops of sweat trickled down his back.

"Kinetica? Are you certain?"

To think he'd been considering investing a million dollars into the firm. That's why Lillian had been so terrified of Dominic. The final piece of the puzzle snapped into place.

"Yes."

"It makes sense. They're a major player in DNA research."

"We've been looking into them. My instincts tell me they're up to their eyeballs in this mess, although we haven't found any direct evidence."

"We need to get the FBI involved."

"I've already contacted them."

"Good. And I want even more security watching the hospital and my house. If anyone shows up to try and take Lillian or her family, we need to be prepared to stop them."

"I'll take care of it."

"Thanks, Brian. Tell my friends at the FBI I'll offer a sizable reward to anyone willing to come forward and provide evidence that leads to the group's arrest. We need to nail these assholes."

"Gotcha."

Long after he ended the call, Tristan remained standing, staring at his phone, trying not to panic. A shard of icy-cold fear broke free from his control and moved through his veins. What if they had captured Lillian before he understood what was happening?

He gripped the phone with cold fingers. He needed Lillian to trust him with the truth of her situation. If he were missing any details or there were others involved, he needed to know. Not only so he could protect her and any other innocent victims, but because lies and distrust were no way to begin a relationship. Hadn't he been down that road before? If she wouldn't share her past with him, how would they have any hope of a future?

He shoved the phone in his back pocket and went to find Lillian.

❧

Lillian had changed her clothes and returned to the entertainment room, pacing back and forth in front of the stone fireplace, but she stopped as soon as she saw Tristan in the doorway.

"Is everything okay?"

He nodded but didn't say anything, which had the effect of making her heart beat harder if that were possible. "What is it?"

"Nothing alarming, I promise. We can talk over breakfast. C'mon. I won't have you attempt to heal my mom until you have a good meal in you."

She thought about insisting they leave at once, but it was clear he knew something he wasn't telling her, so she followed him into the kitchen. "Can I help?"

He paused in the act of pulling out eggs and milk from the refrigerator. "You can sit and relax and talk to me."

She did as he said, pulling a chair up to the bar and watching him work. "I thought you said you weren't much of a cook?"

"Scrambling eggs isn't cooking."

She searched for something to talk about. "How do you spend your free time? I mean, when I'm not around to complicate things."

He laughed. "I spend a lot of time figuring out how to spend money."

She smiled. "Be serious."

"I am serious. I donate to a lot of causes."

Kinetica among them. She stilled, her pulse throbbing almost painfully "Donations to research firms working on finding a cure for Huntington's, like...like Kinetica? That's why the CEO came to your house yesterday, isn't it?" He would fund the organization that killed her mother.

He turned from the stove. "Not Kinetica. I had considered a donation but changed my mind."

"Why?"

He set a mug in front of her. "I'm not convinced it would be a good investment." He filled the mug with coffee from the pot and handed her cream and sugar, then turned his attention to putting bread in the toaster.

Did Tristan have any idea of just how Kinetica accomplished their research? She couldn't control the long, slow shiver coursing through her nervous system. He seemed to sense her teeming emotions because he scooped egg onto plates, added toast, then set one in front of her. Their gazes caught, and some dark emotion she couldn't name flickered in his eyes.

"Are you cold?"

She shook her head. "No."

The single word seemed to stick on her tongue, and she licked dry lips. Would he kiss her again? Did she want him to?

A longing struck hard, and her heart pounded the truth into her. She wanted Tristan to want her. She didn't want him to have Angelina or any other woman. In fact, the thought made her want to scratch those women's eyes out. The strength of her jealousy was so shocking, it rendered her speechless.

ভও

Tristan focused on taking a bite of egg, when all he wanted to do was go to the woman across from him and pull her into his arms. He would reassure her everything would be okay. He would find a way to keep her safe...as long as she told him the truth.

"What's it like…to have all this?" Lillian swept a hand around the kitchen.

"Lonely." The word popped out before he thought about it, but he realized it was true. He was lonely. Or had been, until Lillian's arrival.

She frowned, her gaze widening. "You're joking."

He flicked a glance around the room, seeing it through her eyes. Wide glistening gray countertops stretched in front of him, and beyond that a large round kitchen table with eight cushioned chairs circled it. The table was surrounded by windows that looked out on the patio and pool. Shiny wood floors covered the massive room.

His gaze returned to meet hers. The house looked warm and inviting, but it had felt empty…until now. In the short time Lillian had been here, his home had come alive. "No, it's true. This is a big house, and I live here by myself. It can be lonely."

She gazed at him, her large eyes questioning and… wistful? She blinked and shrugged and whatever softness he thought he saw vanished under a blank veneer. She dropped her gaze and rubbed at a nonexistent spot on her jeans.

"You don't have to live alone. I'm sure any number of women would be more than willing to move in with you. Your former fiancée An…Angelina, for instance."

She stumbled over the name. Was she jealous? He dropped his gaze to her pink lips but couldn't seem to move past them. A ripple of excitement moved through his veins. If she were jealous, she cared, no matter how hard she fought whatever this thing was that was happening between them.

He presented her with what he hoped was his most attractive smile. "I see you've been busy Googling me again."

She shook her head. "No, this time it came straight from the lion's mouth."

His smile faded. Of course. It would be just like Angelina to stake her territory. If he wasn't enjoying Lillian's company so much, he might have been angry.

Her gaze flicked away and back, her cheeks rosy, and he realized he had been staring at her lips. He raised his head until their eyes met.

She cleared her throat. "Do you still love her?"

"No." He didn't have to think about it, which should have been surprising, but was not.

"Why haven't you told her, then? Why is she so confident you'll get back together?"

He took his time answering, using the opportunity to swallow.

"Because I didn't know I didn't love her until last night."

"Oh."

He felt the instant the knowledge sunk in, and she believed it. In that moment, he hated the task in front of him, hated how he must destroy the easy contentment between them with the truth, hated that he would be the one to cause her fear. But he knew the truth was necessary if there were to be any hope for a future together.

❧

Lillian managed to take a bite of the eggs, but she barely tasted them. Thankfully, Tristan had turned his attention to his own meal, leaving her to her thoughts, which were mostly chaotic. She ate as much as she could, then brought her dish to the sink and scraped the leftovers into the garbage disposal.

He followed with his own empty plate. "That's all you can eat? You've barely made a dent in your eggs."

"I'm afraid I'm still a bit nauseous. Can we go and see your mom now?" she asked after he'd opened the dishwasher, and she'd placed her fork and plate inside. Now that she was feeling better, it was high time to repay her debt and move on.

"Are you sure you're feeling well enough?"

"Yes, since I've been fed. Thanks for making me breakfast."

"Of course." Their gazes caught, and there was that dark emotion in his eyes again. But now she knew it for what it was because an identical feeling filled her. Desire. Tristan wanted her. She could see the struggle in his expression—like he was helpless to resist the pull between them. Like he fought the feeling and failed, as she was doing.

"What is it?" Her voice sounded husky and breathless.

He leaned toward her, and she closed her eyes, waiting for what would come next. Her heartbeat kept up a steady, thumping beat, and she could feel his cool breath and the scent of him, like a fresh mountain rain, covering her. Her skin tingled, her nerves thrumming and muscles tightening in anticipation at the thought of his lips pressed against hers.

He tugged on a strand of her hair. "Zoey."

His deep voice rumbled near her ear, something about his tone setting her body on edge. Her pulse fluttered and jumped, her muscles tightening, and she opened her eyes to see the heat in his gaze.

"What are you hiding under this?"

What did a person say when they were expecting A and got B? She started to deny she hid anything and then clamped her mouth shut. She must have looked ridiculous because his warm gaze softened, and his eyes peered into hers like he'd found the door to her heart and would pry it open. In that moment, it hit her that she'd fallen into some clever web he'd woven—maybe that he'd been weaving since the moment she'd met him—a web that demanded truth. He was far too smart…too much in control of his emotions, while she was…what was she? Naive, silly, foolish?

She pushed at his chest, making space between them until she could breathe. She couldn't do this…reveal her secrets…she couldn't give him what he demanded without putting him in danger. She had been under some hypnotic trance of his making, but now she was painfully aware of what she must do.

"I'm not hiding." She tried to inject a lighter tone to her voice, but the words came out sounding brittle and useless.

Her denial didn't seem to make a dent in his composure, and he leaned toward her, as if he could force the truth from her lips. "If you show me now, I promise I'll never ask again."

She shook her head, crossing her arms. Deny, deny, deny…it was her only defense. "There's nothing to reveal.

Listen, if you want me to attempt to heal your mom, we must go now."

He towered over her, his brawny shoulders and the massive amount of energy he projected, dominating the space between them. "I shouldn't have pressed you. There's no need to show me if you don't want to."

His deep voice soothed frazzled nerves, like a familiar song. She suspected he was deliberate in his efforts to look harmless. He held out his hand, palm up.

Don't hold his hand.

She'd never had an out-of-body experience, but she could imagine this was what it felt like...like watching someone else, a softer version of Lillian...a Lillian who hadn't spent two fear-filled years in hiding, wondering if her safety was a figment of her imagination or if it would last a lifetime...a Lillian who understood love was within her grasp and who yearned to reach for it.

This Lillian placed her hand in his, even with the other wiser, smarter Lillian warning her to be cautious. She curled her fingers in Tristan's warm palm and held on tight, glorying in the familiar tingling as his energy filtered into her body and brushed against her heart.

"I need you."

She raised her gaze to his, and she couldn't look away. Maybe he wasn't as in control as she'd imagined. The desire in his eyes lit up the blue of his irises and set her body on fire.

She blinked and took a step toward him, as if he'd tugged on a string binding them together. He pressed his lips against hers and stole her breath and every rational thought scattered in multiple directions like leaves in a sudden breeze.

His lips were gentle yet firm, and he smelled of the cool mint and leather scent she'd come to associate with him. The stubble on his jaw rubbed against her sensitive skin, and she shivered and pressed herself shamelessly against his hard body.

Tristan didn't seem to mind. He wrapped his arms around her, his broad shoulders holding her tight and deepening the kiss until Lillian forgot everything but the tug of his warm mouth on hers. For a while, they stood like that, tasting each other with their lips and tongues. Then his hands found her breasts, and she couldn't prevent the small whimper in the back of her throat. Desire shot through her, and she gasped and writhed underneath him.

"Tristan," she moaned in a voice that didn't sound like hers. "What are you doing?"

"Getting to know you better." She sensed the smile in his words.

"We can't do this."

He gazed down at her, his dimple on full display. "You want me to stop?"

"No…but we must."

He gazed into her eyes, the twinkle disappearing into seriousness. "Why must we stop, Zoey?"

His eyes held mysteries, and quite suddenly, she was tired. Tired of dodging questions and denying the attraction between them. Tired of telling lies and looking over her shoulder. Tired of being tired. Only one thing stopped her from tearing off the wig and pouring out her heart. If she let Tristan into her world, she was handing him a potential death sentence. And she didn't want that for him. She didn't want him to have to fight anxiety every day and pretend everything was all right.

"I can't do this." She pushed against his chest. To protect him, Lillian must disappear from his presence as fast as she'd entered it. "I'll get my things and then we need to see your mom."

"Zoey, wait."

She ignored his plea, nearly tripping in her haste to get away.

CHAPTER TWENTY

Tristan didn't talk much on the car ride over, except when he reminded Lillian again not to put herself in danger. In all fairness, he tried to engage in small talk, but she avoided his gaze and gave him one-syllable answers until he quit trying. By the time they pulled up to his mom's house, her throat burned with all she'd wanted to say but didn't.

"What is your name, honey?" Brenda King said now, squinting at Lillian from her recliner, her hands curled around a pair of wire-framed glasses in her lap.

Lillian had figured Tristan's mom might still be in bed, but Tristan had reassured her that wouldn't be the case, and he was right.

He crouched beside his mom's chair and captured her hands between his own, his voice taking on a gentle note. "Mom, this is Zoey Mills, remember? You met her yesterday when you were getting your tests."

Brenda frowned and put on the glasses with trembling hands. She blinked at Lillian, her eye movements not quite normal. "I did?

"Yes, you said it felt like someone hugged you."

"Oh, I remember now." A wide smile broke through. "You're Tristan's girlfriend."

"Just a friend," Lillian rushed to say. She didn't know whether she should be grateful she wasn't Tristan's girlfriend or disappointed. She was pretty sure she'd dreamt about him, and ever since she saw him this morning, she couldn't stop thinking about the intimacy they'd shared and how it felt to be in his arms.

His sharp gaze caught hers before she could look away, and he grinned. "I'm working on that, Mom."

Warmth flooded her cheeks, and she avoided his gaze by focusing on Brenda. Much as she wanted Tristan in her life, it was dangerous to allow herself to think it possible. The sooner she attempted the healing, the sooner she could get herself out of temptation's way. She stepped forward. "Is it okay if I hold your hands like I did before?"

"All right." Brenda's expression didn't change, making Lillian wonder if she had any idea what Lillian had asked or what was about to happen.

"Let me get you a chair, Zoey." Tristan lifted a blue padded armchair from the dining room table and placed it behind Lillian. "Can I get you something to drink—coffee, tea?

She shook her head. "I'm good."

He hovered over her, far too near.

"Why don't you sit over there?" She tilted her head toward the dining room table. She needed Tristan nearby but not so close she couldn't concentrate.

Tristan smiled because he understood exactly why she sent him away. "Of course." But still he didn't move, and despite herself, she found herself glancing up at him. His gaze locked on hers. "Remember what we talked about."

She nodded, and warmth flooded her body. Of course, she remembered. He did not want her overusing her talent. As anxious as he was to see if Lillian could cure his mom, he didn't want to put her own life at risk.

Once Tristan was seated, Lillian clasped Brenda's hands, closed her eyes, and focused on the dark shape in her mind. *Breathe in.* Power inflated Lillian's lungs, zipped through her veins, and poured into her central nervous system. She latched onto the light, and in seconds, a tiny spark of orange flame erupted between the two of them, shifting and multiplying.

Breathe out. The energy reversed direction, racing along her nerve endings, pulsing from Lillian's fingertips into Brenda's hands.

Breathe in. Lillian absorbed more of the energy in the room. Tristan's energy.

Breathe out. The energy rushed from her fingertips, pulsing and glowing orange, covering the dark figure in her mind.

Breathe in.

Breathe out.

Breathe in.

Breathe out.

Breathe in.

Breathe out.

Lillian wasn't sure how long she injected power into Brenda's body. Long enough for her foot to fall asleep and her arms to feel sluggish. Long enough for her to realize she was funneling too much energy from Tristan, and she needed to stop or risk harming him. Long enough to know she would not be able to cure Brenda King of Huntington's no matter how badly she wanted to. The disease had too strong a grip on Brenda's body, and as she'd suspected, their body chemistry was not a good match.

"Enough." Tristan gripped her shoulder, shaking her.

She released Brenda's hands and opened her eyes to see him glowering over her, his chiseled features creased in concern.

"Is she okay?" Brenda's voice sounded like she'd spoken into a long pipe positioned miles away. "Nancy, get her some water."

The room tilted and swayed, and Lillian closed her eyes and tried hard not to pass out. Thank goodness she was still sitting.

Tristan crouched to wrap an arm around Lillian's shoulder "Here, take a drink." He held a glass of cold water to her lips.

She did as he said, the drink and Tristan's cool energy clearing her head.

"Tristan, honey, have her lie down. She doesn't look well," Brenda said.

Before Lillian could object, Tristan picked her up in his strong arms and carried her to the couch, positioning her among the cushions.

She sighed. "I could get used to this."

He didn't answer but propped a pillow under her head. "Take it easy. Lay here and rest a while."

"I'm okay. I just need a minute."

His blue eyes seared into hers, his expression stern, and she realized he was angry with her and trying hard not to show it. "Your definition of okay and my definition of okay are obviously different."

"She's exhausted. Now's not the time to get upset with her," Brenda said. She had come behind Tristan and laid her hand on his shoulder.

Tristan's eyes widened, and his mouth dropped open. Lillian realized despite what she had told him about being able to heal, he had not quite expected to see such a major improvement in his mom's condition.

"Mom?"

"Relax, I feel great." She smiled at Lillian. "You have a magical touch."

"Thanks. I'm glad you're feeling better."

Tristan shot a look toward Lillian, wonder in his eyes.

She smiled but shook her head from side to side and sent a silent apology, trying to remind him without words that a total cure was not possible—would never be possible.

He must have understood because he frowned, turning to his mom. "How do you feel?"

"Wonderful. I've never been better. Listen, Nancy's making breakfast; why don't you both stay?"

Tristan flicked a glance at Lillian, his brows drawn. "Mom, I wish we could, but Zoey isn't feeling well. I want to get her home and into bed so she can rest."

"I understand." She winked at Tristan, and warmth flooded Lillian's cheeks. "You need to bring her back soon, though. Your Zoey is special."

"I'll do that." Tristan hugged his mom, leaning over to whisper something in her ear. Whatever it was made his mom laugh and kiss him on the cheek.

Lillian didn't bother telling Brenda she was not her son's girl, and they wouldn't have the opportunity to get to know one another better. She was leaving just as soon as she felt well enough to board an airplane.

Tristan must have guessed some of Lillian's thoughts because a stubborn look flashed across his expressive face. "Do you think you can make it to the car?"

She sat up, and thankfully, the room stopped spinning. "I think so."

He held out a hand, which she grasped, and he pulled her to her feet.

"I can manage on my own," she said.

"I'm not taking any chances." He must have collected her purse where she left it because he held it in one hand and curled his other around Lillian, guiding her toward the front door.

She should resist being this close to him. It would only make it harder when she had to leave. But her knees were weak, and her heart was racing, whether from the healing or being next to Tristan, Lillian wasn't certain.

His mom followed them, and Tristan turned to hug her when they reached the door. "You seem so much better, Mom. I'll have Nancy make an appointment with your doctor for an exam."

His mom must have been used to Tristan making the decisions for her care because she didn't argue. Instead, she patted Tristan's arm and smiled. "When will I see you next?"

"Tomorrow," he said. "I'll see if I can talk Zoey into coming with me."

Before Lillian could object, Tristan whisked her out the door. "Bye, Mom."

❧

Tristan kept his thoughts to himself on the way home, but he glanced over at Lillian from time to time to make sure she was resting. She'd closed her eyes as soon as she'd strapped herself into the vehicle, and he witnessed once again how healing took a toll on her physically.

He stepped on the accelerator and pulled onto the highway. The sooner he could get Lillian to his home and in bed, the better. What she had done for his mom was nothing short of a miracle. What would the doctors say when they saw how improved she was? He could hardly believe it himself.

It started to rain, so he turned on the windshield wipers and flicked a glance at Lillian. Right now, he was more worried about her than his mom, which was unusual enough to make him question his own motives. How had she become so important to his personal happiness in such a short space of time?

Her thin arms were tucked into her lap, and her eyes were shut. She looked exhausted, and no wonder. She'd thrown up the meal he'd prepared last night. This morning, she'd only eaten a small portion of her breakfast.

It rained harder now, which matched his mood, and he strained to see through the wiper blades. He'd be damned if he'd let Lillian leave without a decent meal in her. He'd be damned if he'd let her leave without getting her to first acknowledge what was happening between them. The more he thought about it, he'd be damned if he'd let her leave him at all until she'd completely recovered.

Despite the driving rain, in no time at all they had pulled through the gate and into the long driveway and around the back of his house. He parked the car and watched her a moment, the slight up and down movement of her chest confirming she still breathed. He hated to wake Lillian, but she'd sleep better in bed.

"Zoey." He shook her shoulder gently, careful to use her alias although he'd begun to think of her as Lillian the moment Brian had revealed her given name.

She opened her eyes and blinked. "Are we home already?"

Home. A thrill raced through him at the sound of the word on her tongue. He suspected she hadn't even realized she'd used it to describe his house. "Yes. Here, let me help you."

He came around to her side, but she'd unlocked her seatbelt and was stepping out of the car. She didn't reject his offer of help, though—another clue to how hard the healing process was on her body. He tucked her into his side and guided her through the side door.

She let out a small shriek of surprise when he scooped her up into his arms once they were inside.

"You can't keep picking me up every time you think I'm going to fall over." She sounded winded.

He laughed and continued moving. "Is that what I was doing?"

"Yes, put me down. I'm not sick—I'm just tired."

He ignored her. He wasn't about to let her walk up the long staircase in her present condition. Not when she was obviously drained and he could easily take the burden from her fragile frame.

She stopped the protests after the first few steps, winding her arms around his neck and laying her head on his shoulder as if she'd exhausted herself. Her hair smelled like a wild strawberry patch, and he had the crazy urge to never let her go. But all too soon they reached her bedroom.

He managed to twist the knob and kick the door open with her in his arms and place her on the bed. He lifted her foot and tugged on one of her shoes.

"What are you doing?"

"Getting you undressed so you can crawl under the covers. You need to rest." He removed the other shoe.

"Tristan…"

"Where are your pajamas?"

"I don't need them," she said, but he'd already found her suitcase and unzipped it.

"Found them." He pulled out what looked to be a pair of sleeping shorts and a T-shirt and offered them to her. "Your PJs, am I right?"

"Yes." She held the clothing he tossed her way to her chest like a shield.

He couldn't stop from teasing her. "Would you like me to help you in them?"

She tugged a hand through her hair, and her voice hitched. "I've got it."

Was her real hair short or would it tumble around her shoulders? Hell, he didn't even know if it were curly or straight.

"Spoil sport." He swallowed the dryness in his throat.

She shot him a look that managed to convey both exasperation and adorableness at the same time, and he grinned like a damn fool.

He meant to leave her alone to put on her pajamas then, but his fingers reached to caress her cheek, and she placed her hand on his. Their gazes connected, and suddenly, he no longer cared about the secrets she guarded or whether her eyes were brown or blue underneath the contacts or if she would leave him tonight. He cared only about the here and now—this moment—the incredible softness of her skin, her warm strawberry scent, the painful pounding of his heart, which threatened to beat its way out of his chest, and her red, red, lips.

"Zoey, I…" She needed her rest. He should go.

Her eyes were so large in her oval face, he was drowning in them—her irises such a clear green, he could see into her soul, and what he saw left him breathless. What he saw made him believe in happy ever after. His throat scratched, and he cleared it again, but he didn't move. He couldn't. He remained frozen in place, waiting.

She tugged him toward her. "Don't leave me."

That was all the signal he needed. He practically dived onto the bed, rolling with her in a tangle of arms and legs and pajamas. He held her close, stunned by her softness and the way her chest moved under his as she drew in air, and the taste of her skin and the fact that she was under him.

"Tristan," she gasped as his lips kissed every bit of flesh he could find. "Tristan, I…"

He was crushing her, of course. The knowledge crashed in on him with blinding clarity. What a selfish jerk he was. She'd only just recovered and all he could think about was burying himself in her softness.

It practically killed him, but he put a little space between then, propping himself on his elbows.

"I should leave. You're tired," he managed, but neither of them moved.

He brushed a piece of blonde hair from her eyes, and there his fingers lingered, seeming to have a will of their own, stroking down the line of her cheek.

She gazed up at him, a shyness in her expression, which tugged at his heart until it was almost painful. He lowered his head slowly, slowly, giving her plenty of opportunity to tell him where to go.

She didn't, and their lips connected. And then he was drowning in their perfect smoothness and their bowed shape. She moved under him restlessly, and his pulse rocketed when she wound her arms around his neck. He backed off, but she pulled him toward her.

"Please," she said. "Please."

Oh, he pleased alright. But his guilty conscious required him to give her one last chance to get away, so he pulled himself up to study her face. What he read in her eyes took his breath away. There was excitement and passion and a warm invitation.

"Zoey? Are you wanting…"

"You," she said and kissed him.

Chapter Twenty-One

Lillian was quite certain she'd never felt so secure as she did in Tristan's arms. She'd put up a good fight, but the ending was inevitable. She'd known it the first time he'd touched her, when she felt the rush of his energy and realized he was a burner. She'd known it last night when she'd had to hide in her bedroom. On some fundamental level she needed him, needed the safe haven he provided, and this was what made it impossible to fight the attraction between them any longer.

That was her last rational thought before she was drowning in a sea of sensation.

He tugged on her shirt, slipping it over her head, and then unhooked her bra. She drew in a breath at the intense look in his eyes and the tender way he touched her—like she was fragile and would break.

"Are you sure?" His breath caressed her skin like a warm breeze. "We don't have to do this if you don't want to. You can still tell me to go, and I will."

She shivered and silenced his words with a single finger over his lips. She did not want him to go. She did not want to be cautious any longer or have regrets. She'd grown weary of worrying about a future she could not control. She only wanted the here and now and the solid presence of Tristan to relieve the ache of loneliness and fear inside her. She needed to be selfish for once in her life—to take what he offered freely and to not think about the consequences. To touch him and be touched.

"I've never been surer of anything," she whispered.

He scooped her from the bed, rising up so that the room seemed to sway, and all she could do was cling tightly to his neck.

"Where are we going?" she asked as he carried her through the doorway and down the long hallway.

"To my room," he said, heading through the doorway and laying her down on the biggest bed she'd ever seen. "We'll have a little more leg room here."

"I'll say," she laughed, spreading her arms wide.

He laid down and pulled her into his arms. "I've dreamt of having you here in my bed."

"You…you have?" The admission had her blushing.

For an answer, he pulled her finger into his mouth and sucked on it, which had the immediate effect of creating a coiling tension inside her. It was a sensual, pleasurable sensation, and made her long for the feel of him moving inside her.

She would have to wait.

He would not be rushed, despite how much she writhed and twisted and rubbed against him. He finished suckling her finger, then moved to her palm and arm and neck before finding her breasts. His teeth nipped and grazed her nipples like he was feasting on a banquet.

She moaned, and he paused before bending to suckle her again, slow and agonizingly attuned to her every reaction. She gasped and gyrated under his touch, running her hands up the broad muscles of his back to wrap around his neck and press him close. Liquid heat spread between her legs, igniting a raging fire inside her.

"Please, Tristan. Please. I need you."

"Yes," he said and shrugged out of his shirt, tugged out of his pants with a little help from her. And then he rose above her like some Greek god of old, moving into her, hard and deep and oh so glorious, and she forgot everything except how right they felt together and how much she needed him.

ॐ

His Lillian lay sprawled across the comforter, gloriously naked and vulnerable. Funny how he thought of her as his after such a short time. There was still so much to learn about her.

He traced the mole on her stomach, the curve of her hip, enjoying the softness of her skin and the contrast between her pale tone and his darker one.

She shivered, and he pulled the blanket up and curled her into his side, throwing one leg over hers and rising up on his elbow to view her expression. "Cold?"

She blinked, granting him a flash of emerald—contacts, he reminded himself—before closing her eyes as if to hide from his gaze. "A little."

There would be no more hiding from this day forward. No more secrets. He would not allow it. He willed her to confide in him, to trust him with the truth of her situation so he could reassure her he would do everything in his power to protect her.

"What are you thinking?" She watched him, wariness in her expressive eyes.

He decided honesty was the best course of action. "That you're beautiful. That I've been wanting to make love to you since we first met. That although it's only been a few days since we met, I think I'm falling for a blonde-haired, green-eyed siren who refuses to reveal her whole self to me."

She lowered her eyes but stayed put, which he took as a promising start.

"I don't want to say goodbye," he said.

She raised her gaze to his, some secret emotion swirling in their emerald depths. "I don't, either."

He smoothed a hand across her forehead. "I won't force you to stay, but I'd like you to. Whatever this is that's happening between us, I don't ever want it to end." He placed her hand over his pounding heart. "You must feel it, too."

"Yes."

He tugged on a strand of her hair. "Will you remove this and show me what you look like? I don't want barriers between us. I want to see your whole self."

"I…I'm not quite ready."

"Zoey, whatever it is…whatever you're afraid of revealing, I promise, I won't run. But I won't tolerate lies or deception. I need to know I have your trust as you have mine."

"I know." A tear trembled at the corner of one of her eyes, and she drew in a breath, her lips parting. He waited in silent expectation for an answer that never came.

Instead, she twisted in his arms and kissed him, cloaking his body in her strawberry scent. He only meant to return the kiss, but she opened her mouth and stretched out her arms, pressing her breasts into him, and he was lost in a sensual haze of pleasure.

He'd learn the secrets of her flesh now. There would be time to learn her other secrets later.

❧

Lillian rested her cheek on Tristan's chest, enjoying the way it rose and fell as he slept and the long, lean length of him. She loved the way his hairs curled, matted against his skin and how they formed a dark V on his belly and lower. She loved everything about him.

She took a breath, amazed that the ache and haziness in her head she normally felt after a healing had vanished. Was that the effect of making love to a burner?

She moved her gaze down Tristan's body, toward his muscled thighs and calves and that part of him that gave her pleasure, marveling at his shape and how it had felt earlier to have free access to explore his body. He had watched her with dark-blue eyes glittering with want, and then he'd taken command, turning her over and thrusting deep inside until she couldn't be sure where he ended and she began.

Did she dare stay here with him? She wanted to…oh, how she wanted to. The longer she lingered, the harder it was to contemplate leaving. Maybe she could find a way.

She untangled her legs from his body, holding her breath when he murmured something unintelligible. When he didn't open his eyes, she released the air in her lungs. With the smallest movement possible, Lillian scooted to the edge of the bed and stood.

She paused again to look at him. In sleep, Tristan appeared boyish and vulnerable, one hand flung above his dark curls and the other resting over his heart.

She sucked in a breath and held it inside. It hurt to think of leaving…to destroy the fragile bond blossoming between them. Maybe if she confided in him they could find a way to put a stop to Kinetica? They wouldn't have to part.

She needed some space between them so she could think. With swift movements, she made her way to the door. When she opened it, he stirred again, and she held her breath until he settled into sleep. She studied his face, lingering on his chiseled jawline and the masculine beauty of his shape.

She twisted the doorknob, and without a sound, stepped into the long hallway. She made her way to her bedroom, found her bra and panties where he had tossed them, and slipped them on along with her clothing from earlier in the day. Then she stuffed her pajamas in the suitcase, zipped it, and grabbed her purse. She would go to his office to find a pad of paper and pen and consider her options.

It didn't take her long to reach his office door and make her way to the spot where she'd first asked Tristan to visit Hannah and he'd agreed. So much had taken place since then, it seemed a lifetime ago.

She spent a minute peeking out the large window, curious what the view from the office looked like in the daytime. A stone patio opened onto a crystal-blue zero entry pool, surrounded by white outdoor furniture and what looked like a bathhouse in matching white. Beyond the bathhouse a long stretch of land led to a wooded area. What a beautiful private oasis. Maybe she and Tristan could swim in the pool together? Maybe he could show her the garden as he'd promised?

She turned toward the desk to look for something to write on. She found a pen in a drawer, her gaze settling on a manila folder. Her heart stopped beating for a moment, and she couldn't catch her breath. Why was her full name written on the folder? Not Mills, but her real name, Lillian Abigail Milano?

Adrenaline shot through her veins, and for a moment, white spots formed in front of her eyes. Everything moved in slow motion—her heart heaved in her chest, the air froze in her lungs. She couldn't take her eyes off the bold, black print in Tristan's familiar handwriting. She recognized it from when he'd written his address on a napkin and given it to her with an invitation to his fundraising party. *Was it only a couple of days ago?*

How and when had he learned her real name, and why had he written it on a folder hidden in his desk?

Her heart resumed its furious beating as she flipped open the folder and skimmed through its contents. This was a report prepared by Townsend Security, whom Tristan apparently hired to investigate her. Her name jumped out at her from the paper. Her alarm grew with every word she read.

Her hands shook, and she had to lean against the desk to keep from pitching forward. His security firm knew who she was, knew her real name, which meant Tristan also knew, although he'd called her Zoey. Her gaze flew to the date on the report. *Yesterday.* All the while Tristan had made love to her, he'd known her real identity. *He knew, and yet he'd stayed silent.* He'd used her.

She forced air into her starved lungs. He knew who she was, he knew her family. He'd known she could heal before she'd confirmed it. He knew of Kinetica's involvement. It was all there in a typed memo, and yet, he hadn't told her. Instead, he'd slept with her. He slept with her so she would…the truth crashed around her shoulders like an icy thunderstorm, drenching her in panic.

Her legs buckled, and she sat in the chair, still clutching the folder, her hands and heart and lungs ice cold… so cold.

My God, he'd pretended like he hadn't known she could heal, when it was spelled out on page one of the report. He'd deliberately made her fall in love with him, then asked her to heal his mom, pretending ignorance. He'd taken advantage of what she freely offered. Could he be working with Kinetica? Was this an elaborate plan to use her to heal his mom and then hand her over to that horrendous organization?

Her stomach pitched, and she placed a hand over her mouth so she wouldn't vomit. She stood. She had to get out. *Now.*

She turned to go, but it was too late. Tristan stood in the doorway, watching, a frown on his handsome face.

Chapter Twenty-Two

"It's not what you think," Tristan said.

He held out his hand for the folder, but Lillian ignored him. She curled her lip and let some of the frigid cold in her veins leak into her voice. "It's not a detailed report on me given to you by a security firm you've apparently hired to investigate me?"

"I had no choice. I asked you numerous times to tell me what or who you were afraid of, and you refused to confide in me."

She had to hand it to him—he didn't back down. His voice rang with the confidence of a man used to going after what he wanted without regrets.

"Don't come near me. You're working with Kinetica."

He looked stunned by her accusation, but it could have been an act.

The stunned expression vanished, his lips thinned, and he clenched his jaw until it quivered. Energy shot toward her like a bullet to the heart. Quite suddenly, she was afraid, and it was not of Kinetica.

She took a step backward. She'd never seen Tristan so intensely furious.

"Think about it. If I was working with Kinetica, why would I have my security firm investigate you? I would have already known what you were capable of doing. I would have outed you to whomever was in charge."

Anger came to her rescue. "You didn't *out* me because you wanted me to heal your mom. Now I've done that, you plan to turn me in, don't you? Dumbass that I am, I practically threw myself at you, and you took what I offered. Why not, when it was a bonus, right?"

"This is what you really think of me?" He towered over her, his navy eyes shards of thick, dark ice. "I am *not* working with Kinetica. I didn't tell you because I figured you would freak out like you're doing now. I wanted you to trust me with the truth yourself, Lillian."

Panic fueled her fury. She was practically shrieking now. "Don't call me Lillian. You have no idea who you're dealing with. If Kinetica knows my identity—if they know I'm here—they'll kill you to get to me. Hell, they're probably already out there, watching your house. I have to get out of here."

She headed toward the door. She'd grab her things and nurse her shattered heart later.

"So, this is it? You're going to just walk out the door? I didn't take you for a coward, Lillian. Well, you won't have to worry about Kinetica for much longer at least. I've reported them to the FBI. They'll handle it from here."

Ice-cold fear stopped the blood coursing through her veins.

"What have you done?" She turned and looked around the room, although logically, she knew Kinetica couldn't come through the office walls. "Kinetica's spies are everywhere, including within the FBI. If they know I'm alive, they'll come after me, and trust me when I say they'll find me. You think the government will let someone like me go? Who do you think funded Kinetica? I can't stay here. I have to leave."

Tristan stepped in front of her, blocking the doorway. "I'll go with you."

She shook her head. "If you really aren't working with Kinetica, then don't try and follow me. It will only get you killed."

"Lillian, don't shut me out. I want to help you."

"How? It doesn't matter how rich you are. Kinetica won't stop until they find me. Do you really believe you can somehow protect me from an organization with no ethics, hell-bent on creating a super healer? That you'll persuade the government to let me go after they've spent years waiting and watching as other healers were used and discarded? They won't, you know. I'm far too valuable to their success. They'll lock me up and force me to cooperate."

"Kinetica can be bought. You forget, I know the company CEO. He won't want to lose the money I'll offer if they leave you alone. And they won't want the publicity my name will bring. As for the FBI, not everyone is corrupt, Lillian."

His voiced softened, and he reached a hand to wipe her cheek, which she realized was soaked with tears. "I have friends there."

She shook her head and backed away from his tenderness. "You have no idea the power this organization wields. They've been operating for years and getting away with it with the government's blessing. If you shut down their operations, they'll simply find a new location."

"Lillian, don't run. Trust me."

For a mad moment, she thought about leaning on Tristan's considerable strength and taking advantage of his money and resources. But her insanity was only temporary. Kinetica had captured, used, and ultimately, killed every healer in the program, including her mother. Lillian was one of the few people alive with the unique DNA they needed.

"I'm leaving." She moved toward the door.

He stepped in front of her, his jaw clenched. "Please don't. Give me your phone number so I'll know you're safe."

She studied the hard planes of his face, which contrasted with the wary vulnerability in his eyes. This was not a man who would stand in a corner and wait to see what would happen when she was threatened. No, this man would use the number to trace her and probably bring Kinetica to her doorstep.

Something tore inside her, breaking away from her heart and shattering into a million invisible pieces. Tristan wouldn't stay away, but she would never forgive herself if he or her dad or sister were hurt when Kinetica came for Lillian. She refused to lose another person she loved. It was best for everyone if she went back into hiding.

She tried to step around him, but he shifted to the right, blocking her path to the door. Her eyes dropped to his shirt, partially unbuttoned. He was not going to let her leave without a fight. She'd run out of options...but there was one.

She forced air into her lungs and raised her gaze until her eyes met his. She heard herself speaking like it was someone else—someone cold and uncaring—someone like Angelina. "You don't understand, Tristan. I should never have slept with you. It was a mistake."

"You can't mean that."

"I do. I don't love you. I was grateful to you for saving my sister…nothing more. I never had serious intentions toward you. I might someday want children… healthy ones. I could never be with a man who can't give them to me."

Her arrow struck home, a world of hurt flaring in his eyes before disappearing behind a hard mask. This time when she moved forward, he stepped aside.

Her stomach twisted, and bile rose in her throat.

Tristan believed her lies.

❧

Tristan clenched his fists, but he didn't try to follow Lillian as she gathered her suitcase from her bedroom and found the keys to the rental in the dish where he'd left them. He let her walk out the door, although everything inside of him urged him to stop her, to protect her. But she'd made her choice. She didn't want his help—she didn't want him. He'd never forced himself on a woman before, and he wasn't about to start now.

A deep chill settled in his gut. He set the folder on his desk and then deliberately walked to a different room with a window overlooking the driveway to watch her leave. Her words had pierced his heart and frozen his insides. She'd used him just like everyone else. She didn't love him. She'd believed the worst of him. She'd only slept with him to pay a debt. Nothing more.

She didn't look back at the house but got into her car and started the engine. His limbs were waking up, the blood returning to his heart, his brain beginning to function. Anger burned a scorching pathway through his veins.

The little white car sped down the drive and out of his line of vision. As quickly as she'd entered his life, Lillian was gone. He'd put himself on the line and lost. It was his fault for ignoring the warning signs and allowing himself to be vulnerable. Once again, he'd been played.

His phone buzzed and he checked the number. *Brian.* The old feelings of betrayal rose up like a ghost to haunt, urging him to let Lillian leave without a fight and to spend his time nursing his wounded heart. But he found he couldn't bury his protective feelings toward her entirely—not without first making sure she was safe.

⁓

Lillian turned on the second road to the right and headed south toward the airport, all the while looking in the rearview mirror to see if Tristan—or anyone else—was tailing her. She didn't know if the pain in her chest was caused by lack of food or disappointment that Tristan's fancy car wasn't behind her.

The sky broadcast a storm, seeming to echo her current mood, but at least it wasn't raining…yet. Her cell phone buzzed—her dad. She answered.

"Zoey, thank God you haven't left yet. Can you come to the hospital? Hannah isn't doing well." Her dad sounded distraught, but he'd remembered to use her alias."

"What is it? Is Hannah okay?"

"I don't know. The doctors aren't saying. But she's running a high fever again. It doesn't look good."

"Oh my God, Dad. Okay. Hang tight. I'm on my way."

She made an illegal U-turn and prayed a cop wasn't watching. Thankfully, no sirens or flashing lights went off. She would do what she had to do to save Hannah. She just hoped she could get in and out of the building safely.

By the time she reached the hospital parking lot, Lillian was determined not to leave her sister's side until she was cured. This time, she would not give up so easily. This time, she would heal Hannah once and for all.

She opened the car door and looked around, and when she didn't see anything out of the ordinary, made her way to the entrance.

The automatic doors opened, and she slipped inside, keeping her head down and avoiding the gazes of the other visitors and medical personnel she passed along the way. No one paid any attention to her, which helped to slow her breathing and calm her erratic heartbeat.

When she got to the elevators, as luck would have it, the doors were open, seeming to wait for her arrival. She ducked inside and hit the button for her sister's floor. In a moment, she was knocking on the door of her sister's room and heading inside.

"You're here, thank God," her dad said, getting up from where he'd been sitting by Hannah's bedside. He gestured toward her sister. "She's been like this for the past hour."

Hannah's face was as pale as the white sheets, and her eyes were closed, her breathing labored. A nurse whom Lillian didn't recognize hovered over her bed, checking the IV drip.

"What are you doing?" she asked the nurse.

"The doctor wants to give her a sedative."

"Please, before you do, can her dad and I have a moment with her?"

The nurse nodded. "Sure, honey, but be quick. I'll be back in a jiffy."

The moment the nurse left the room, Lillian turned to her dad. "I'm going to heal her." She reached for Hannah's hands.

"Be careful," her dad said.

"Lillian?" her sister whispered.

"Shhh, I'm here now. It's going to be okay. Try to relax."

Hannah didn't respond, so Lillian pulled in air and let her breath out slow and easy. Almost immediately, a dark shape encased in an orange glow formed behind her closed eyelids. The orange light swelled and shifted with each of Lillian's indrawn breaths, retracting when she emptied her lungs.

Deep breath in. Breathe out.

Each time she exhaled orange light, it absorbed a tiny spot of the vast darkness surrounding Hannah.

Breathe in. Breathe out.
Breathe in. Breathe out.
Breathe in. Breathe out.

Her legs grew sluggish, and her heartbeat fluttered.

A thud, like a hammer striking a pillow, sounded behind her. What was it? Why was she so cold?

❦

"Brian, I'm on my way out the door. What is it?"

Tristan shrugged on his jacket and grabbed his car keys. He'd made up his mind to follow Lillian and make sure she got on her flight, and then he'd come home and pour himself a tall glass of something strong. With any luck, he'd pass out by midnight and no longer feel her departure so intensely…or anything else for that matter.

"We've been watching the hospital like you asked, keeping a close eye on the buildings. A few minutes ago, one of my guys spotted two men lingering at a restricted entrance."

Beads of sweat formed on Tristan's brow, and his heartbeat broke into a gallop. He headed to his car, walking fast. "They're going after Hannah?"

"We don't know that. They didn't go inside and left after a few minutes. It could be nothing. But you asked us to report anything out of the ordinary."

He took a moment to calm himself. "That's right. Good work, Brian. Keep a close watch and alert the hospital's security. Call me if they return. Lillian headed to the airport a few minutes ago, and I'm following her to make sure she gets on her flight safely."

"Hold on…something's up."

There was a long pause, and he could hear Brian talking to someone in the background. Tristan used the

233

time to get into the vehicle and start the car, stepping on the accelerator and pulling out with a squeal of tires. If he floored it, he might be able to catch Lillian.

"Change of plans. Don't go to the airport. Lillian was just spotted pulling into the Clinic parking lot."

"The hospital?" Tristan frowned. "Something must be wrong with her sister. I'm on my way over now." Tristan headed north instead of south.

"She's going inside. Do you want us to stop her?"

Tristan thought a moment. If Hannah was ill again, Lillian might need to cure her. She'd never forgive him if he prevented her from trying. "No, but tail her and make sure no one else follows. Wait for me inside. I'm about ten minutes away."

"Roger that."

Tristan ended the call and sped up, passing the slower-moving vehicles in the other lane. His gut churned like a worn-out washing machine. Was Lillian all right? Had he put her in more danger, as she'd accused, by telling his friend at the FBI what he suspected? He turned left and headed down Chester Avenue toward the North Side Clinic, his heart pounding all the while. Could the men Brian spotted belong to Kinetica? Had they been tipped off by the FBI?

The light from Chester to East 93rd Street seemed to take forever. Tristan tapped the steering wheel and tried to keep his breathing in check. When the light changed, he navigated the turn and pressed on the accelerator, zipping down the street at warp speed.

The minute he turned into the hospital lot, he slammed the car into park and was out the door, running toward the entrance. All the while, his footsteps hammered out a frantic rhythm that seemed to keep time with the blood pounding through his body. What was happening in Hannah's room? Had Lillian cured her sister?

He moved through the sliding doors, run-walking as fast as he could, watching for Brian's crew. When he didn't find them inside, he hurried to the elevator and rode it to Hannah's floor. The doors opened, and he stepped out and looked around. A woman dressed in a white lab coat passed by, followed by a man in blue scrubs. Everything appeared normal. Where were the men Brian said would meet him?

He didn't spend time looking, preferring to make his way as fast as he could to Hannah's room. He'd verify for himself that Lillian, Hannah, and their dad were inside safe. Some instinct made him pause before entering the room.

A woman screamed.

He didn't hesitate, pushing the door open and rushing into the room, prepared for a fight. What he saw was a horrible dream come to life. Frank Milano was slumped on a chair, blood oozing from a nasty wound on his forehead. Next to him, a nurse lay crumpled on the floor in a pool of blood. Hannah Milano was sitting up in the bed, her eyes wide with terror, and Lillian was missing.

CHAPTER TWENTY-THREE

"Dad, are you okay? Dad? Tristan, help him!" Hannah Milano sat up in bed and pointed at her father in horror.

Tristan crouched by Frank to check his pulse. The regular beat reassured him the man was very much alive. "It's okay. He's just been knocked unconscious."

On cue, Frank groaned and lifted his head.

"Steady now. You'll be okay." Tristan motioned to the remote control on Hannah's bed. "Hannah, use your emergency button to call for help."

Hannah scrambled to comply. When Tristan was sure Frank wasn't going to tumble from the chair, he bent to check the nurse on the ground. Where was Brian's crew? Nurses and doctors streamed into the room, followed by several police officers.

He stepped back from the body, but he knew their efforts were pointless. No amount of medical personnel would bring the nurse on the floor back to life. She had been hit on the head so hard, her skull had been crushed.

Tristan squelched the fear pumping through his veins. What had they done to Lillian? She'd warned him what Kinetica's soldiers were capable of, but he hadn't really thought they would snatch her from a hospital, of all places. He'd been wrong, and now Lillian and her family would suffer for it.

As if echoing the thought, Frank groaned. The medical team placed him on a hospital bed and moved him to the room next to Hannah, where they hooked him up to an IV. Tristan followed to make sure Frank was okay and then returned to check on Hannah. A nurse was taking her vitals, but that didn't stop Hannah from beckoning him to her side.

"You have to find my sister."

"What did they look like?"

"I don't know. I was pretty sick and had my eyes closed, so I didn't see whoever it was. By the time I was well enough to understand what was happening, all I saw was my dad and the…the nurse on the ground. Is she going to be okay?"

Tristan shook his head. "No, Hannah, the nurse is dead." Where was Brian's security team?

Hannah's eyes widened in horror. "How's my dad?"

"He's conscious. I'll check on him again and let you know."

He went next door to visit Frank, who gazed at Tristan in fear and grabbed his arm.

"You have to find Zoey." Frank had a nasty bruise on his forehead. "They took her…men dressed like medical professionals…you have to find her. Please." For someone who had been knocked out, Frank's grip was surprisingly strong.

Tristan tightened his lips. "Who was it?"

"I don't know. I only got a glimpse, but there were more than one. They hit me from behind. I suspect it's a high-tech pharmaceutical company called Kinetica that's responsible. Zoey has…special gifts…which make her valuable to them. Promise me you'll find her."

Tristan pressed his palm against Frank's hand and squeezed. "You have my word." Tristan turned to leave, pausing a moment to talk to the nurse. "He'll recover?"

"We can't be sure until we do an MRI, but he most likely has a concussion. He was hit pretty hard on the head, but he's conscious and aware of his surroundings, which is a good sign."

"Please reassure his daughter who's in the room next door—she's extremely worried. I have something I need to do." He didn't wait around for the nurse's response but headed out the door, ripping his cell from his pocket and dialing Brian, who answered on the first ring.

"Where are the men you promised?"

"They were caught off guard, but don't worry, we have her."

"Thank God." Tristan stopped and bent over, letting out the breath he held. "Where?"

"In the parking garage, second floor. They didn't get far."

"Thank God," he said again. Tristan stood and raced toward the exit, holding the phone to his ear, his pulse pounding.

"Don't celebrate yet. She's unconscious. It's not looking good, Tristan."

His heart beat like a wild creature. "What do you mean it's not looking good? What did they do to her?" He quickened his pace, running to the elevator that would take him to the parking garage.

"The men who held her claim they did nothing. They could be lying. Paramedics are looking at her now."

The doors swung open. "Okay, I'm almost there." He pressed the glowing P for the parking garage and paced the small space. What if Lillian didn't make it? It would be his fault. He should have listened to her and not tried to delay her leaving.

The doors opened, and then he was out in the garage looking left and right.

"I'm here," he barked into the phone.

"Behind you," Brian answered.

He swerved the opposite direction and spotted men in the distance. He ran full out toward them, shouting, "Where is she?"

But even as he asked, he saw Lillian lying on the ground, surrounded by an emergency crew. The men lifted her stiff body onto a stretcher.

He took in the scene in a single glance and worked to stay calm. Lillian didn't need him freaking out right now.

Her eyes were closed, her face pale and drawn. The medical crew had strapped a mask on her face, he presumed to feed her oxygen, and had started an IV. Two men dressed in blue medical scrubs were on the floor next to her, their hands cuffed behind their backs, while the police stood over them. Several plainclothes men, probably Brian's gang, hovered nearby.

He caught up to the stretcher and crouched by Lillian's side, holding her cold hands in his, his heart a jackhammer in his chest. What was it she'd called him…a burner? If he could transfer his energy to her now, he'd gladly do it. If he only knew how.

"Lillian, it's me, Tristan. I'm here now."

"We need to get her inside," one of the paramedics said. "She has a pulse, but it's weak."

"Let's move, then," Tristan said.

He continued to walk beside Lillian, while the paramedics rolled the stretcher onto the elevator and up to the main floor.

❧

A fire raged, burning Lillian from inside out. Sweat matted the hair against her neck. *Water.* What she would do for a tall glass of cold water.

"Hang on, Lillian, hang on."

"Tristan?" She tried to speak but couldn't through dry, cracked lips. There was so much she wanted to tell him. Now it was too late.

Death comes to all of us eventually.

"Mom?" Her mother had warned her what would happen. Why hadn't she listened? She wasn't ready to die.

It's not your job to heal everyone, Lillian.

"Mom, is that you?"

A cool hand touched her forehead, offering some relief. The scent of roses filled the air.

"Please, stay with me, Mom. Don't leave. I'm afraid."

Her mother cast Lillian an understanding smile.

"Would you sing to me, Mom?" Lillian asked. "Like you used to?"

Her mother nodded and hummed a melody, familiar and comforting and haunting at the same time.

"You love him, don't you?" She had reached the end of the song.

Lillian blinked. "Love, who?" She had been half-listening, drifting in the dreamy lullaby. How could her mother possibly know about Tristan? She'd died long before they could be introduced. Lillian's mind stuttered over the thought.

"Oh, I think you know who."

Dead. Her mother was dead. This was a dream. Still, she wanted it to go on and on and on. "Yes. But there's no hope for us."

"Oh, darling, there's always hope."

Lillian's breath hitched. She'd spent the past two years on autopilot, not really living—researching Kinetica, afraid of every stranger, jumping at every sound, never daring to want anything for herself.

"Kinetica still wants me. I told Tristan lies and deliberately hurt him, so he wouldn't follow me. He won't forgive me. He asked me to trust him, but I didn't. I hurt him terribly—I could see it in his eyes."

Her mother smoothed the hair from Lillian's forehead. "My Lily, always so steadfast and loyal. Always so protective of those you love. Always ready to sacrifice your own happiness. The time has come to see if you're strong enough to grab happiness for yourself."

"What are you saying, Mom?"

Her mother's expression grew serious. "It will not be easy. You must be willing to humble yourself…to follow your heart."

"Her heart rate's too high. She's running a hundred and three-degree temp," a woman said over Lillian's head. Not her mother.

The clinical voice cut into the hallucination—it was a hallucination, wasn't it?—snapping Lillian back to her current circumstances. She watched from far above where she lay on a gurney, a team of medical professionals surrounding her. A doctor barked out orders.

Where was she? The hospital, of course. She was in the hospital and the doctor was putting paddles on her chest. A defibrillator?

"One, two, three…clear."

Pain radiated from her head to her toes.

"Sleep now, Lily," her mother said. "You'll feel better soon."

CHAPTER TWENTY-FOUR

"How is she?"

Tristan eyed Hannah through bloodshot eyes. He sat across from Lillian's bedside—he could have been there a day, or maybe it was longer. He couldn't remember. He couldn't remember when he'd last ate or slept, either.

He shook his head and pressed his lips together. "She went into cardiac arrest. The doctors shocked her heart and brought her back to life, but she's still unconscious."

"My God." Hannah brought her hand to her mouth, suppressing a sob. Her dark hair gleamed, shimmering with a rich chestnut color under the harsh hospital lights. If he hadn't seen her in a hospital bed earlier, Tristan would never have known the woman before him had been near death only a few days ago.

Hannah seemed to pull herself together, straightening her shoulders and casting him a fierce look. "We can't let her die. We must find a way to save her."

He shook his head, looking down at his hands in his lap to avoid her fiery gaze. He managed a single, painful breath and muttered. "I've tried. I've talked to every medical professional I know. She's in a coma. The doctors say there's only a slim chance she'll awaken."

"No, Tristan." Hannah laid a hand on his arm, a hesitant touch, but it opened something inside him.

He lifted his head until their eyes met. A mistake. He seemed to get pulled into their swirling amber depths, until he couldn't look away.

"You *can* save her. But you must act fast. Here's what you must do."

⌘

Something brushed Lillian's face, and she swatted at it like a fly. She blinked, but the fog was so thick in front of her, she couldn't see.

"Don't fight me," a woman whispered in a thick accent. "Soon you'll feel better. Davay ya tebe pomog."

Lillian strained to open her eyes, but they were sealed. Power whispered over her skin, and she trembled. "Who are you?" Had she spoken out loud? But no, she hadn't moved her lips.

"A friend. I'm here to help. Relax, my dear."

Easier said than done. Heat entered her veins—warm, thrilling, powerful heat. There was something familiar in the woman's touch, in the heat, but Lillian couldn't figure out what.

The woman mumbled something, and a low voice answered. It was then Lillian realized they were not alone. Someone else was there...a man.

"Tristan?" A mist formed and tightened its clammy fist around her throat. She gasped and shivered, and her mother wrapped her in a warm blanket.

"Thanks, Mom, I'm so cold."

"Sweetie, you can't stay here."

Tears slipped down her cheeks. "Please, Mom. I want to be with you."

"You can't, baby," her mother said, wiping away her tears. "Your time has not yet come. You must go back."

"No, please," she said, her voice shaking.

Her mother's serene expression didn't change. She smiled at Lillian and stroked her cheek. "Sweetheart, the choice is not yours to make."

She strained to gaze beyond her mother's face, but the mist had thickened, making it impossible to see. She reached out, snagging her mom's hand in hers. "I won't let you leave me."

Her mother's hand slipped like water in her grasp, but understanding shone from her warm brown eyes, and her voice was steady and clear in Lillian's ear, while the vision faded into the gray mist.

"Don't be afraid, my darling."

&

Tristan tapped his foot and waited for Tanya—the healer who'd been held at Oak Haven and Brian's men had tracked down—to tell him what to do next. What was taking her so long? Shouldn't they be getting started by now?

It had been a week since he'd located the healer, who had been in police custody, and pulled strings to have her come to Cleveland and attempt to cure Lillian. A week fraught with panic and frustration and anxiety, while he wondered if Lillian would live or die. She had slipped into a coma while Tristan held her hands, helpless to save her.

Now Tanya was finally settled into a chair next to Lillian's bed and her eyes were shut. That had been more than thirty minutes ago. Tristan swore she hadn't moved an inch since then.

He passed his gaze again over her slim figure dressed in jeans and a plain, white sweatshirt. She didn't look like she had extrasensory ability. She looked more like a small mouse than the heroine who could save the day. She wore her brown hair braided, her eyes were too close together and narrow, and her skin held a grayish cast, like she hadn't seen the sun in a good long while.

Tanya gasped, and his heartbeat sped up. He held his breath, but she didn't utter another sound or open her eyes. What if she were playacting, only pretending to have healing ability for the money? He'd paid her a tremendous sum to cure Lillian.

He let his breath out and tried to slow his beating heart. Really, if he'd been left to pick Tanya out as a healer among a room full of people, she'd be the last person he would have selected.

He hunched over his clasped hands and tried not to gaze at Lillian, who lay motionless. Every time his eyes rested on her slight figure, a rope of despair twisted his stomach into knots.

Tanya coughed, and he looked up, his gaze settling on Lillian's still figure in the hospital bed again. *A mistake.* A long, blue tube snaked oxygen into her lungs, and a spiderweb of cords crisscrossed her chest, feeding the drugs keeping her alive into her veins.

He bowed his head, his gaze fixing again on his hands, gripping them to counteract the vision of a lifeless Lillian he couldn't erase from his brain. She should have died. Only the fast action of the emergency room doctor shocking her heart into beating had kept her alive. Now she was on life support.

He breathed deep, the harsh smell of antiseptics and lemon mingling with the fresh scent of roses he had placed in the vase on the nightstand by her bed. Was he crazy to think a healing even possible? That Tanya—a twenty-two-year-old kid from Russia whom Kinetica had kidnapped, and until a week ago, had forced to conduct atrocious experiments—that Tanya could somehow awaken Lillian from a coma?

"It will work," Hannah said, as if she'd read his thoughts.

Lillian's sister had been a rock-steady shoulder to lean on, displaying an incredible resourcefulness and strength. Her presence was so soothing, he'd almost forgotten she was in the room sitting next to him.

He nodded, gripping his hands together and counting to ten—anything to counteract the despair overwhelming his hard-fought control. During the time he had been away from Lillian, he'd leaked the full story of what happened at Oak Haven to the news media, exposing Kinetica and forcing the government to shut down their operations.

Hannah touched his arm, somehow restoring a measure of his equilibrium. It had been Hannah who had urged him to find the healer. Hannah who had convinced Tanya to use his energy to try and save Lillian's life. He only prayed Hannah was right and their efforts today produced a miracle.

"You are sure you want to go through with this, da? That you understand the consequences?" Tanya asked him now in a thick accent.

That the healing may not work? That he could die in the process? Yes, he was well aware, and none of it mattered. "Just tell me what I need to do."

"Hold hands, keep calm." Tanya grabbed one of Lillian's pale hands and offered the other to Tristan.

"Got it." He pressed his lips together and slowed his breathing—a trick he'd learned to keep himself from panicking during his many ER visits with his mom—before taking Tanya's hand in his.

A warm, fuzzy feeling took hold. And then it seemed like all the oxygen in the room was swallowed up at once, and he was left thrashing around, like a fish out of water. Tanya had warned him the healing would be dangerous, but he had no idea he'd not be able to breathe.

White spots formed behind his eyelids. Someone gasped. *Hannah?* The room spun wild and free, forcing him to close his eyes so he wouldn't faint.

The last thing he recalled was the sound of a woman weeping.

Lillian blinked and opened her eyes. The fog had disappeared, giving way to glorious sunshine.

"She's awake," Hannah said, tossing her knitting aside and jabbing the button on the remote attached to the bed.

"Hannah?" Was she dreaming? Lillian closed her eyes and opened them again, but Hannah still sat next to her bed, knitting.

"Oh my God." Hannah leaned over Lillian wide-eyed, scanning her from head to toe. "How do you feel? They told me you would wake up soon, but I wasn't sure it would happen."

"I feel fine."

A nurse entered the room, coming immediately to her bedside and checking her vitals. "Can you tell me your name?"

"Yes, it's…Zoey."

The nurse wrinkled her brow and held up her hands. "How many fingers do you see?"

"Ten," Lillian said.

"Good. Do you know who this is?" She pointed at Hannah.

Lillian smiled. "That's my…that's Hannah."

"Good," the nurse said, a smile on her face. "I'll be back. We're paging your doctor."

As soon as she left, Lillian turned to Hannah. "Tell me you're not still working on that same pair of socks?"

Hannah stilled, the smile dying on her face.

"What's the matter?"

"Nothing, it's…I finished those socks weeks ago."

"Weeks ago? But you were just working on them earlier today…weren't you?"

Hannah shook her head, her forehead creasing. Now that Lillian took a closer look, her sister's eyes looked glassy, a deep weariness in their amber depths.

"What's wrong?"

"Lil, you've been in a coma for more than a month. Dad and I have been taking turns by your bedside night and day, praying you'd make it. For a while there, I wasn't sure you would. But then a few days ago, your hands and feet started twitching, and you opened your eyes a couple of times. The doctors said these were all good signs your brain was healing, and you'd be waking up soon."

A flashback of the doctor leaning over her chest with a pair of paddles came to Lillian's mind. "That's right, I saw them shock my heart."

"You saw that?"

"Yes."

"That's wild…then you know you nearly died. Tristan saved you."

"Tristan? What did he have to do with it?"

"I remembered what you told me about him being a burner." Hannah bit her lip. "I reminded him if we could find someone else with your ability, they might be able to use his energy to save your life."

"You found another healer?"

"Not me. Tristan tracked her down. Her name's Tanya Kovalenko. She's from Russia. Kinetica kidnapped her and was using her to heal women they infected with deadly viruses at Oak Haven—you remember, where Mom was working before she was killed?"

Lillian could only nod.

"Tristan discovered where their operations were based and paid a lot of money to the right people to have Tanya released. Since I had fully recovered after you healed me, I traveled with Tristan. I used my talent to open Tanya's heart and convince her to use her energy to cure you. It worked."

"What about Kinetica? They snuck up on me in your room. I was so weak, I couldn't scream. How did you find me and stop them?"

"I didn't. By the time I was aware of what was going on, they had already left with you. But Tristan hired a security team to protect us. The team had been watching the hospital, and they chased the kidnappers to the parking garage and were able to stop them until the police arrived. By then, though, you were too far gone. You'd expended too much energy curing me, and the additional trauma of being kidnapped put a strain on your heart. You were in a coma."

Lillian tried to sit up, adrenaline causing her heart to pound. "The kidnappers were arrested, but that doesn't mean Kinetica is no longer a threat."

"Take it easy, Lil. Kinetica is out of business. Tristan's security firm gathered strong evidence and then turned it over to a major TV network, who ran an exclusive story. It was all on national television and the government's involvement was exposed. There was nowhere for them to hide. The CEO was arrested and their operations in West

Virginia shut down. Tanya and many others were freed. Somehow Tristan kept your name out of the press."

The pressure in Lillian's chest eased a little, but now another thought had her pulse racing. "Tristan, he's…"

"Not here."

"Where is he? I should thank him."

Hannah hesitated, looking down at her hands, her expression hard to read. "I don't know. After he cured you, he was pretty sick. The nurses took him away. I figured to a hospital room for treatment. I didn't question it at the time because I was so worried about you, and I thought he'd return when he was better. Dad finally went to see him, and…well…"

"What is it?" Hannah looked up, and Lillian understood she was trying to mask her worry and sympathy.

"He has a fiancée. I'm so sorry, Lillian."

"Angelina."

"Yes, that's her name."

"Is he…how is he?"

"Dad wasn't able to see him, but Angelina said he's fully recovered. The nurses said he came to see you the day he was released. Dad and I had left your side for a few minutes to get a bite to eat, so we never saw him. But he's called the hospital every day since to get an update on your progress."

"Have you talked to him?"

Hannah swallowed. "Once on the telephone. He was concerned for you, but he was…distant. I couldn't get a good read. I'm sorry, Lillian. Angelina told Dad they're planning a large wedding. I know you loved him."

Lillian didn't deny the claim—she never argued with Hannah about matters of emotion. Her sister was always right—it was her gift.

A yawning crater opened in her heart and filled with despair. Tristan had felt responsible for what had happened, so he saved her. And he'd checked on her because he was a good person who cared. But she'd rejected him in the worst possible way, and he'd believed her, which was why he'd turned to Angelina for comfort.

His heart belongs to me...always has, always will.

Angelina's words were a taunting voice in her head. Lillian closed her eyes to block out her sister's concerned expression, but she couldn't shut down her thoughts.

"He'll come back to me eventually, and when he does, I'd hate to see your little heart get broken."

The phrase was like a death knell in Lillian's mind. She blinked, and the tears she had been holding back spilled over and rolled down her cheeks—far too many tears to hide from her perceptive sister.

Hannah held her in her arms like Lillian was a baby, rocking back and forth. "It'll be okay," she soothed.

Did she blame Tristan for going back to Angelina? What other reaction should Lillian have expected?

Her lies had condemned her forever.

Chapter Twenty-Five

The most surprising thing about being in a coma for more than a month and then in a rehabilitation center for another month while she recovered? Lillian had missed most of spring. Summer was in full glory by the time she was well enough to leave the hospital and return to her dad's house.

She set aside the magazine she had been trying to read and got up from her bed, crossing to the window to open the yellow drapes and look out into the backyard. Her dad fiddled with the riding lawnmower under the bright summer sun. Some sixth sense made him look up at Lillian, and when he saw she was out of bed, he waved and beckoned for her to come down.

How amazing she no longer needed to glance over her shoulder in fear she would be snatched. According to the FBI, Kinetica had been disbanded and was no longer operating. Lillian had a hard time believing it was true, but she supposed if it weren't she'd have been kidnapped from the hospital or her bedroom.

Lillian smiled and waved at her dad and closed the curtain. Incredible her dad had recovered completely from the trauma he'd suffered when Kinetica's men had attacked him. Now she could be with her family, enjoying a normal day, free to interact out in the open. Free to be a daughter and a sister again.

So why did she feel an aching loss inside that nothing could relieve?

She slipped on a pair of jean shorts and tennis shoes and the first T-shirt she could find and went downstairs to find her sister, sniffing the air.

"Is that French toast I smell?" Unlike Lillian, Hannah knew her way around a stove.

"You guessed right…and scrambled eggs and hash browns. I wasn't sure what you'd be up for."

"It all sounds great to me as long as I don't have to cook it."

"How are you feeling?"

"Fine. There's no need to fuss."

"Yes, there is. You nearly died."

"So did you."

Hannah smiled. "Touché. Okay, point taken. Get to work then. We're outta dishes. Here's a towel. You can dry the ones in the sink."

Lillian picked up the towel and rubbed her mother's pretty flowered dishes, placing them in a stack on the counter as she dried each plate and bowl.

Don't be afraid.

Hard not to be, knowing Tristan was in the past and the future was a great big unknown blur.

"What are your plans for the day?" Hannah asked when the silence stretched between them a little too long.

"Oh, you know, I may go to the park."

"You went to the park yesterday."

"I like the park."

Hannah flipped the French toast and put the jug of maple syrup on the table. "That's what you said yesterday and the day before. Lil, you've gone to the park every single day since you've been well enough to leave this house. It's been over two months since you've come home. Don't you think it's time to try something a little different?"

Lillian shrugged. "The park soothes my soul." In the park, she could feed the ducks and watch children play. She could eavesdrop on families and see flowers unfolding. She could close her eyes and feel the sun on her skin and tip her face to the sky to find faces in the clouds. For a brief time, she could avoid thinking about Tristan, wondering where he was and if he loved Angelina. Wondering if he ever thought about her as she thought about him— with a wretched loneliness and a terrible sense of loss.

Her sister raised her eyebrows and tossed her long hair to the side. "May I make a suggestion?"

"If I said no, would it stop you?"

Hannah smiled and turned off the burner, adding the last of the French toast to the stack on the table. "Of course not. So sit and eat and listen to your little sister for a change."

Although she wasn't in the least bit hungry, Lillian dutifully pulled out a chair and sat in front of the mound of food on her plate, and Hannah did the same.

"How many walks to the park will it take before you go after him?"

Lillian choked on a piece of French toast and took a sip of water. "He has a fiancée, remember? Besides, if he cared about me at all, he would have come to the hospital in person to make sure I survived."

"He saved your life, Lil. He obviously cares. And excuse my bluntness, but it's more than a coma putting that gloomy look on your face. You're mourning his loss, but he's not dead. Fiancée or not, why would you give up on him before you've told him the truth? I think he still has feelings for you."

Lillian rubbed a hand over her eyes. "You didn't see his face when I told him I used him."

"I'm sure by now he understands the pressure you were under. Don't you think you ought to try and explain?"

Lillian took a drink of orange juice, the sweet, citrusy flavor contrasting with the bitterness on her tongue. "Angelina broke up with him because he refused to be tested for Huntington's and to have children. Then she changed her mind, and he had a hard time accepting it. I told him I could never be with someone who couldn't give me healthy children. Now I'm going to come back and tell him it was all a lie? How can I ever expect him to believe me? I'm no better than Angelina."

"It's a chance I think you should take, Lil. Listen, tonight Tristan is hosting a large party at his home. I heard about it online this morning. It's some sort of local parade of homes. They're selling tickets to raise money for Huntington's research. They said there are still a few tickets remaining."

Lillian pushed her chair out and stood, nearly stumbling in her haste to end the conversation. Her heart tapped out a furious rhythm.

"Why don't we buy tickets? They're pricey, but it will be on me. It'll be fun."

"Are you crazy?"

"I'd like to see his home. I'm curious after listening to you describe it. I'll get us two tickets, and you can show me around. We'll make an adventure out of it."

"No, no adventure. I…I can't see him again yet." *Maybe ever.* "Thanks for breakfast. I'm heading out."

Hannah raised her eyebrows. "Just consider it. That's all I'm asking."

Lillian hesitated. Her sister had been so patient and considerate up to this point. Lillian could at least think about it before putting the kibosh on the idea. She nodded, then turned and headed to the back door and freedom.

"Be sure to take your phone and call me if you need anything."

"Yes, Mother."

"Don't be sarcastic. You need a mother right now. I know I'm no substitute for the real thing, but I'm all you've got."

Lillian's eyes stung and filled with tears, and she paused with her hand on the doorknob and turned.

"I know," she said. "I'm sorry. You are an amazing sister."

Hannah hugged her, and for a brief moment, Lillian drew comfort. A hug from Hannah was like drawing near the sun.

"Go on then, shoo. Enjoy your day in the park. I'll be here waiting with dinner when you get back."

"Thanks, Hannah." Lillian blew her sister a kiss and then opened the front door and followed the path to the park she had taken every day since she'd been home. The warm breeze kissed her skin, and she placed a straw hat on her head to keep the sun out of her eyes.

Gladys Morgan, the widow who lived next door, stopped digging at something in her flower bed long enough to wave a hand in Lillian's direction. "Going walking again? Lovely day for it."

"Thanks, Gladys," Lillian said. "Enjoy the sunshine."

This was all part of her daily routine. Every day, Gladys asked if she was going for a walk, and Lillian told Gladys to enjoy the sunshine—as long as there *was* sunshine. On cloudy days, Lillian advised Gladys to enjoy the day.

Lillian kept walking and turned left on the sidewalk. Three doors down, Rufus, the neighbor's dog woofed his daily greeting.

"Hi, Rufus. It's just me. No need to get riled up. Be a good boy now," Lillian said.

Rufus wagged his tail and barked again behind the neighbor's chain link fence, and Lillian had his blessing to continue her walk to the park.

Slap, slap, slap. Her sneakers scuffed the pavement until she hit the park entrance, where the pavement was replaced by soft grass.

She paused to take a swig from the water bottle she'd brought with her. A series of benches were scattered around the trail, leading past the pond. A couple wandered by, pushing a stroller. The big man, who Lillian mentally referred to as Fred, stood feeding the ducks as he usually did, nodding to her as she walked past and arriving at what she fondly thought of as *her* park bench.

Lillian brushed some twigs out of the way and sat. For a while she remained that way, watching the glimmering surface of the pond and the quacking of the ducks, her mind drifting to the earlier conversation with Hannah.

Maybe he still has feelings for you.

Lillian huffed. Highly unlikely Tristan still cared for her now so much time had passed. Angelina had probably moved her stuff into his lonely mansion by now. And they were planning their wedding. Wouldn't Angelina make a beautiful bride for a billionaire?

She gripped the side of the bench like she held on for dear life and watched as a few children ran in the park, their mothers hollering at them to slow down.

According to Hannah, Tristan had called every day to get an update on her condition when she'd been in a coma, but he'd stopped calling after he'd visited and saw she would recover. More than likely, he'd moved on with Angelina. Lillian should move on, too. But how could she, knowing he still believed her lies?

Since she'd been home, she'd kept herself away from social media and the local news, afraid she'd stumble upon news of Tristan. But maybe that had been the wrong tactic to take. Maybe Hannah was right. Maybe if she heard about and saw Tristan again, she could move past her feelings for him and get on with her life.

She pulled her phone from the pocket of her jeans and opened the browser. Before she changed her mind, she typed "Tristan King" in the window and the date and hit go. Almost immediately, a news article popped up with Tristan's picture.

Her hands trembled as she clicked on the headline, which read, "Software Mogul King Participates in Annual Gates Mills Parade of Homes Tonight." The article indicated Tristan's house would be the star attraction of the event. Those who paid the price could enjoy a tour of the mansion followed by a garden party under the stars.

The article didn't mention Angelina. Most likely, she'd be there, though.

Lillian swallowed hard. A counter on the website indicated there were still thirty-two tickets remaining. If Lillian saw Tristan again and how happy he was with Angelina, maybe she could gain some closure. She owed him a thank you for saving her life. Maybe this would be the best opportunity, and she wouldn't feel so awkward? Since she no longer faced a life-or-death situation, more than likely the bond between them wouldn't be as strong, and it would be freeing to see him again.

Her fingers hovered over the buy button. Her pulse sped up, and her chest tightened, but she couldn't bring herself to click. Who was she kidding? Wouldn't Tristan resent the intrusion again into his personal life? Wasn't that how he'd reacted when Angelina said she wanted him back after she hurt him? Lillian had already caused him enough trouble. He was soon to be a married man and happy with his choice. Her appearance would only cause stress and make him unhappy.

She closed the browser and shoved her phone back in her pocket before she could change her mind. Tristan deserved his happy-ever-after with Angelina, and Lillian had no business disrupting it. She would just walk around the duck pond and then make her way home to help Hannah with dinner.

She strolled toward a group of ducks, who were taking turns dunking themselves upside down in the water to search for food. Maybe tomorrow she would see about getting her nursing license back. Maybe tomorrow she could forget about Tristan for a little while. Maybe tomorrow she could think about her future without feeling this never-ending heartache.

She counted one, two, three, four, five, six, seven ducks. Their little bottoms looked white and fluffy, while their orange feet paddled furiously to keep them afloat.

She pulled out her phone and snapped a picture. It took several failed shots before she managed to capture one where all seven ducks had their bottoms up at the same time.

She smiled at their antics, and for the first time in a long while, she felt a glimmer of something other than overwhelming sorrow. It was a start.

Tomorrow, she would take another step toward getting her life back in order.

Chapter Twenty-Six

"You did what?" Lillian choked, her fork poised in the air.

Hannah remained unfazed by Lillian's reaction. She, Lillian, and their dad were sitting around the dinner table, eating pork chops and stuffing Hannah had made with no help from Lillian. She'd offered, but Hannah was wiser and had Lillian set the table instead.

"I ordered two tickets to the Parade of Homes tonight—Dad's not up for it, but I am." Hannah ignored Lillian's shocked gaze, her tone unapologetic.

"You had no right."

"If I left it up to you, nothing would happen."

"I told you I'm not ready to see him again."

"You're never going to be suddenly ready to face him, Lil. But you're carrying around a terrific burden—a heck of a lot of guilt and an irrational fear Tristan hates you. It's crippling you emotionally and preventing you from moving forward. I can't stand to watch your suffering any longer. It's time you release these feelings, don't you think?"

The trouble with having an empathic sister? Lillian couldn't argue with Hannah's assessment of her emotional state. And staring into her sister's auburn eyes, a fragile barrier inside Lillian crumbled, and she understood with clarity how important it was to see Tristan again, to be able to let go and move on, to reclaim her inner peace.

Lillian glanced at her dad, who raised his eyebrows to let her know he agreed with Hannah, but wisely said nothing. She stabbed at the pork chop with her fork and knife, cutting off a small piece and shoving it into her mouth. Hannah's talent made it impossible for Lillian not to see the truth of her own emotional state, but she didn't have to like it.

"Fine," she said around the bite of pork chop. "What time did you say it was?"

"I didn't, but it runs from seven to nine and there are around a dozen homes to see. Tristan's is the last one on the list, but we can skip the rest and just stop there if you want."

No, Lillian didn't want to stop there. Just the thought of seeing Tristan again made her stomach queasy and her legs shake and her palms sweat. She grabbed her glass of water to give herself time to formulate an answer, and in her haste, ended up tipping it over. Water and ice splashed across the table, spilling onto the floor and nearly landing in her dad's lap. He moved his chair out from the table in the nick of time.

"Oh, geez. I'm sorry, Dad."

"It's okay…a little water never hurt anyone," he said.

Lillian went to fetch a paper towel, but Hannah beat her to it, dabbing at the spill while her dad refilled her water glass.

"Thanks," Lillian said, feeling like a child.

"I take it you'd rather not be first to Tristan's house?" Hannah asked with an arch of her brows, referring to their earlier conversation.

Lillian sighed. "Last is better, I think."

Hannah smiled, her gaze sympathetic, and tossed the paper towel into the trash, brushing her hands together. "Well, then, let's leave at six thirty, so we'll have plenty of time to tour the other homes before we get to Tristan's, and you'll have plenty of time to think about what you'll say to him."

Lillian swallowed the piece of pork chop and tried not to think about what the next few hours would bring. While she did not expect Tristan to forgive her, she did hope seeing him with Angelina would provide the closure she needed. She could wish them well and put an end to dwelling on the situation.

Her dad offered to load the dishwasher, so all too soon, she and Hannah had changed their clothes and were on their way to the first stop on the Parade of Homes, a 1920s brick Tudor–style home with a round turret on one side.

Lillian glanced down at her brown skirt, flowered blouse, and wedges. She'd carefully chosen an outfit that was both casual and chic and cool enough for the warm June evening.

Hannah pulled behind a line of parked cars on the street—apparently, the tours were popular, as the line stretched around the block.

The first home on the list was both beautiful and practical. Its elegant bow window in the living room housed a window seat, and when they had made their way inside, Lillian eyed the books lining the built-in bookshelves.

The hosts were gracious, inviting their visitors to look around. The sisters passed through a gleaming kitchen and formal dining room and cozy bedrooms to make even the pickiest homeowner envious. The tour ended in the postage-stamp-size backyard, and they were moving on to the next house.

And so it continued, each house they visited both bigger and more expensive than the one before. With each stop, Lillian's stomach squeezed tighter, her mouth grew dryer, and every sentence she rehearsed in her mind for the coming meeting with Tristan seemed to be the wrong thing to say.

Should she simply say, "Thank you?" The words didn't seem grateful enough for the risk he'd taken to save her life. If she said, "Congratulations on your engagement," it would be insincere since she certainly didn't feel like celebrating the occasion. "I lied and am in love with you," was much too direct.

"This is it," Hannah said as they left the sixth house, a Frank Lloyd Wright–style ranch with a sunroom that seemed to bring the great outdoors inside. "Our last stop is Tristan's. Are you ready?"

Lillian cleared her throat, but it didn't seem to open her vocal cords. Maybe she was fretting for no reason? Maybe he wouldn't even be at home? Not all the owners were present to show guests around. Maybe Tristan had better things to do tonight than entertaining a bunch of ordinary citizens like herself?

"Lillian?"

"Er…yes, I'm ready…or I will be by the time we get there."

"It'll be fine. I promise. Just be honest and speak from the heart. The rest will take care of itself."

"What if…"

"He tells you to scram? He won't. I told you he cares for you. Be courageous."

Lillian hesitated. "Maybe I'm making a mistake? He's engaged to be married. He's obviously moved on."

"Seeing him again will help *you* move on. This is your chance to gain closure, remember? Telling him how you feel is the first stop on the road to recovery."

Lillian sighed and tried to calm her racing heart. Her sister was right. No matter what Tristan's reaction was to her arrival, what ultimately mattered was the chance for Lillian to talk to him one last time—to see for herself that he was happy with Angelina and moving forward with his life. Maybe then Lillian could move forward with hers.

"Are you ready?" Hannah asked a few minutes later when they pulled through the gate and into the familiar, long, winding driveway. They followed the signs, which pointed to a parking lot Tristan had on the grounds. A shuttle bus was parked there, and people were boarding it, probably to be driven to the house.

Lillian nodded, but she couldn't stem her anxious thoughts. What was she doing here, tonight, invading Tristan's home? Why did she think this visit would accomplish anything?

"Lil, you've got this." Her sister must have sensed her fear and doubt because as soon as they parked and exited the car, she linked her arm with Lillian's, and they walked together to the nearest shuttle bus.

The short walk felt a little like Lillian was being led to her doom.

"What's the worst he could say?" Hannah asked when the silence between them stretched a little too long.

"Get lost?" Lillian offered.

Hannah smiled, and if Lillian weren't so shaken up at the prospect of seeing Tristan again, she might have seen the humor in the situation and responded in kind. However, her brain had turned to mush, and her stomach was doing somersaults and backflips. Lillian was pretty certain the blood in her veins wasn't circulating because her legs were so damn weak.

"Buckle up, buttercup. You've got this. Be brave."

They were dropped off at the entrance to the house, where a lady with long dark hair and high cheekbones—a Cher lookalike—greeted everyone.

Not Angelina, thank God. Maybe Lillian had worried for no reason. Maybe Tristan wasn't even home. Maybe he was on a hot date with his fiancée.

"My name is Jasmine, and I'll be your tour guide this evening."

Three months ago, Lillian had stepped into the same foyer, as nervous and fearful as she was tonight. Now, she gazed up at the same chandelier and noticed the same security camera pointed her direction. She had the insane desire to wave.

"Follow me," Jasmine motioned.

The sisters trailed Jasmine into the same large room Tristan had held his fundraiser the night Lillian first met him. She looked around the room, but she didn't see Tristan. There was no live band or waiters with food and liquor, either. There was no party in progress. Her heart sank, but she wasn't sure if it was because the prospect of seeing him again had dimmed or because she had trouble dealing with the memories the room generated.

As Lillian and Hannah soon discovered, Jasmine was one of at least a dozen tour guides gathered with groups of twenty or thirty guests surrounding them. She beckoned to one corner of the room, and Lillian and Hannah followed along with the others in their circle.

Jasmine turned and flashed her entourage a welcoming smile. "Thanks for stopping by tonight and supporting our Parade of Homes, which raises money for scientific research. The tour should take approximately thirty minutes to complete, followed by a garden party for those who paid for that option. Before we get started, I'd like to remind you no pictures are permitted of the inside of the home to protect the privacy of the homeowner."

Lillian, who had pulled out her cell, thinking to snap a photo for memory's sake, shoved the device back in her purse.

Jasmine smiled and gestured around the room. "You are standing in the living room of the Hickory Farms estate, currently owned by software guru and local philanthropist Tristan King. The home has a long history, dating back to the 1920s. Located on over thirteen acres, as you will soon see, it includes twelve thousand, eight hundred square feet of living space, and is valued at two point nine million dollars."

The group oohed and aahed—everyone except Lillian, who searched for Tristan's tall form among the crowd with no success.

Jasmine went on to describe details of the architecture, including the marble in the grand foyer, the ornate crystal chandelier, and the white-washed brick walls, embellished with paintings by several well-known artists.

A few minutes later, they were heading up the winding staircase, which Lillian remembered led to the long hallway and Tristan's office, where she had pleaded with him to save her sister's life, and later, destroyed any affection he might have felt with her lies.

"Notice how every space flows effortlessly to the next and the tones are pleasing and warm. Each room contains plank hardwood floors, brick accents, and neutral walls, all lending to the home's understated elegance."

Jasmine continued, opening doors and leading the group through room after room, but Lillian was only half-listening. Memories haunted her…Tristan carrying her up the stairs and laying her on the bed in the ultra-feminine guest bedroom. She hadn't thought about it at the time, but now she wondered if he'd decorated the room for Angelina. Or worse, maybe Angelina had selected the furnishings.

"This is where the owner conducts his business," Jasmine continued, opening the door to Tristan's office. "The windows overlook the estate's backyard and the incredible garden, designed by renowned British landscape designer, Stu Wellington."

More oohs and ahhs followed.

"Notice the painting over the desk. It is called 'Cleveland by Night,' an original produced by local artist Henri Roberts."

Lillian paused at the window, recalling how haunted Tristan's eyes were the evening he'd revealed his hopelessness in the face of his mother's illness. The stray tree branch, which had insisted on tapping against the window that night so long ago, was silent, echoing the last couple months of Lillian's life.

"Lil?"

She turned to look at Hannah, who stood in the doorway, her brow creased. Where had all the guests disappeared to?

"Are you okay?"

"Yes, yes, of course." Lillian moved toward Hannah. "I didn't realize the tour had continued, that's all."

"It's okay if you want to cry, Lil. Tristan isn't here to see, and you know I won't tell anyone. It's not good to keep all that hurt inside. Let it out."

"No, no, that's not…I don't need to cry." She swiped at the tears at the corners of her eyes, and her sister wisely said nothing. "I'm just feeling sentimental, that's all. Let's catch up to the others."

She continued moving forward, and Hannah followed, but the next room was not one Lillian cared to see.

"This is the master bedroom," Jasmine was saying. "It was recently renovated to reflect the taste of its owner."

The tears were coming faster now, gushing from some unknown fount of sadness, spilling from Lillian's eyes in heavy rivulets. She couldn't do this…couldn't look at the spot where they'd first made love, where she had marveled at the glorious perfection of his body and fantasized about a future together. Couldn't hear again the whispered words, "You're mine." Couldn't remember the way his body had pressed against hers, filled her up, stamping out years of loneliness.

"I need some air," she whispered to Hannah.

"I'll come with you."

"Stay, enjoy the tour." Her voice sounded more forceful than she'd intended. Sometimes she needed a break from her sister's uncanny emotional antenna. "I've seen most of the rooms up here already, but you haven't. They're worth seeing."

"Are you sure?"

"Yes, I'll meet you downstairs." She didn't wait for her sister to respond, but turned and left the room, hoping Hannah wouldn't follow. She needed time to be alone, to release the feelings she'd been hanging onto, feelings which would never be reciprocated.

She moved down the grand staircase and into the open foyer. The double doors leading outside had been closed.

She gripped the railing to avoid falling down the stairs in case her trembling knees gave out. She must find a way to let Tristan—or at least the memory of him etched in her heart—go.

Chapter Twenty-Seven

A gentleman standing near the door turned to look at Lillian with a small frown.

"Can I help you?" he rasped, his cool gaze not without a tinge of suspicion.

He was handsome in a rugged sort of way, broad-shouldered and muscular. His golden-blond hair looked like it could use a comb, but his beard was neatly trimmed, and his silver eyes seemed to pin her in place.

She shook her head. "No, um…I'm waiting for my sister. She's still on the tour."

"You're not interested in finishing?"

"Oh, no, that's not it. I felt a little queasy upstairs, and I…I've seen a lot of the house before."

"Have you been here another time, then?"

"Yes, I…I know the homeowner."

"I see." The man's suspicious expression cleared, and he finally cracked a smile, which took the edge off his gruff exterior. "You're in luck. I believe he's in the solarium. Why don't you go on in and say hello? I suspect he'll be delighted to see you. Right this way."

The man moved forward but stopped when he realized Lillian wasn't following behind. "Aren't you coming?"

"He's…he's here…the homeowner? Right in the next room?"

"Yes, of course. There's an afterparty in progress for those who purchased the option. Do you have a ticket to the party?"

Lillian nodded, digging in her purse for her cell phone. "The garden party…that's right." Why was it so hard to formulate a coherent thought? All the other guests were probably in the solarium, as the man called it. That explained why this part of the house was empty.

She flicked through her texts and located the invitation she'd received, showing it to the guide, who nodded.

"Follow me, then, and I'll take you there." The man was much taller than she'd realized at first, towering over her. He turned and moved forward again, and Lillian found herself moving after him slowly as if in a dream.

She cleared her throat and tried to communicate her unease. "I'm not so sure the homeowner will want to see me."

Her guide glanced back at her and grinned. "A pretty girl like you? I'm sure he'll be more than happy to learn you went on the tour tonight. Have you seen the solarium during your other visits?"

"Not really. Not up close." Lillian put one foot in front of the other. This was her chance to see Tristan one last time—she shouldn't blow it. She could at least thank him for saving her life and congratulate him on his engagement. Although if her dad had somehow got things wrong…but no, she couldn't contemplate the possibility, couldn't let herself dream things were different. She only wanted to apologize for the lies she had told.

"Prepare yourself, then, because it's something to see," the man said.

"To see? Oh, yeah, the solarium." She nodded and attempted a smile, but it came out two parts adrenaline, one part anxiety.

The man didn't seem to notice, his gritty voice remaining even and calm. He seemed to be enjoying himself, rattling on like they were old friends. "I personally think it's the coolest part of the estate—kind of reminds me of one of those fairy gardens."

She nodded, half-listening, but refrained from responding, which didn't stop him from continuing his one-sided conversation.

"Right here's the living area. Pretty fancy, eh?"

They passed through a large room and entered another giant, open area with brick floors and skylights.

"Here we are. What do you think?"

Lillian paused at the entrance, taking in the numerous lanterns and twinkling lights scattered around the space. Waiters dressed in black and white outfits served sparkling glasses of champagne and an assortment of elegant hors d'oeuvres.

Her partner nabbed a glass of bubbly from a passing waiter and handed it to her. "Drink up. No doldrums here. This is a party, remember?"

She dutifully took the glass and had a sip, peering over the rim at groups of people gathered around the swimming pool and walking in the backyard beyond, where more lights twinkled.

Realization dawned, and she gasped. The backyard was the garden Tristan had promised to show her one day. Now she'd see it for herself. She swallowed hard and scanned the crowd for Tristan, first left, then right—he wasn't there. She let out the air she realized she was holding.

"Over here." Her tour guide motioned behind her.

She looked where he was pointing, and her heart stopped beating for an instant. Tristan stood in the center of a small crowd, looking cool and confident and oh, so handsome. In a single glance, she took in the pair of white slacks and the charcoal-gray shirt he wore and the look on his face, which was animated as if he told a joke. As she watched, his gaze slid past his companions and met Lillian's, and her heart beat once again, although much faster.

Something tightened in Tristan's expression, or dimmed, she wasn't sure. He didn't speak or otherwise gesture, nothing to give a clue to his emotions or if he wanted to talk to her. Lillian's gaze naturally flicked to his partner, and her heart nosedived into her shoes.

As she had feared whenever she imagined seeing Tristan again, he wasn't alone. Angelina stood next to him, dazzling in a white shimmering dress with a slit up one side and cute, strappy sandals. Unlike Tristan's un-readable expression, the glare Angelina directed Lillian's way was enough to knock her to the ground. Angelina stiffened her shoulders and drew herself up like an out-raged peacock, tucking her arm in Tristan's to send a not-so-subtle territorial message.

Keep away. He's mine.

Although Lillian only stared at the couple for a few seconds, it felt like an eternity. Her gaze took in the scene with devastating clarity. Tristan and Angelina were together, and Lillian was a third wheel—she shouldn't be here. What had she been thinking? She should have never let Hannah talk her into this madness.

She might have turned and fled the party, but she couldn't escape her tour guide's clutches. He had latched on to her forearm and pulled her toward Tristan, grinning at him like they were old friends.

"Wait…" she said, but it was too late, she was already within a foot of the couple.

"I brought you a present," the man said to Tristan.

She dug her sandals into the ground to stop the forward momentum, but all she managed was to lose her footing and stumble. The drink she held went flying in the air with perfect comedic timing. Her horrified gaze watched the action like some sort of silent Charlie Chaplin film.

Tristan sprang into action, dragging Angelina with him, and deftly caught the glass before it hit the brick pathway. It would have been a marvelous feat of athleticism if it were not for the glasses' contents, the majority which flew toward Angelina like a homing pigeon, drenching her in a champagne glow.

"You bitch," Angelina hissed, her face registering shock and anger.

"I'm sorry," Lillian said, and she meant it. The heat rushing to her cheeks could have toasted a pile of marshmallows. "It was an accident. I'll go now."

"Not so fast," the man holding her arm grunted, turning to Tristan. "This is the woman who caused all the ruckus, isn't it?"

"Yes," Tristan said, handing her what remained of her champagne without changing inflection. Their fingers brushed, which sent a tingle through Lillian, but his expression seemed distant.

Was he excited to see her, annoyed? She couldn't tell, so she scanned the place to see if her sister had returned from the tour. Why could Hannah never be present with her emotion detector when Lillian needed her?

"I…I didn't mean to disrupt your conversation. I should go now," Lillian said again and tried to keep her knees from knocking together.

"Yes." Angelina bared her teeth, dabbing at the liquid on her dress with a napkin a waiter brought her. "Good idea."

"Wait," Tristan said, taking a step toward Lillian. "Why are you here?"

"I…I took the tour," she said dumbly.

Angelina made a disgusted sound. "Let her go. She obviously didn't come here to see you."

Tristan said nothing but continued staring at Lillian, a question in his gaze.

Lillian pulled in air and dug deep for courage. She'd promised herself if she had the opportunity to see Tristan again, she would tell him the truth. The moment had arrived, and she wouldn't get another opportunity. What was she waiting for?

She took a deep breath. "I came to thank you for saving my life. Hannah told me what you did…how ill you were as a result."

He shrugged as if it were nothing. "Is that all? I'd do it again if I had to."

"I…thank you, Tristan. I should have trusted you when you asked me to. I was wrong to lie the way I did."

"Oh, please," Angelina said, turning to Tristan with a scowl. "Are you really buying her bullshit? This woman lied to you, repeatedly, the entire time you were acquainted. Why would you believe she's telling the truth now?"

Tristan said nothing, just continued to stare at Lillian with that hard-to-decipher expression, as if his computer-brain was analyzing all the inputs and outputs.

She swallowed. "Angelina's right…you have no reason to trust me. But I am being honest with you. I have no cause to lie."

"Oh, please." Angelina snorted and tugged on Tristan's arm. "I'd say she has billions of reasons to lie…as in dollars. C'mon, let me get you out of here."

Tristan didn't move, so Lillian rushed on before she lost her courage. "I didn't mean what I said—that last day. I was terrified of being discovered and of…of your being hurt, and so I told a lie I thought you would believe. I need you to know that. I'm truly sorry."

"What was it she lied about?" Angelina rolled her eyes, still dabbing at her dress with the napkin. "Oh, let me guess. She told you she hated you when she supposedly loves you. That's the biggest scam in the book."

"That's enough, Angelina."

Angelina stiffened at Tristan's authoritarian tone. "Don't tell me you believe her story? Can't you see what's she trying to do? She's trying to wheedle her way into your life again."

Lillian's tour guide, who had been listening to the entire conversation, a rapt expression on his face, latched onto Angelina with a snicker. "I think it's time you and I, little lady, got better acquainted. C'mon, let me get you a drink."

"What? Never." Angelina objected, but the man was already dragging her away from Tristan. As Lillian knew all too well, the gentleman had a powerful grip.

"Let me go, you filthy jerk. I don't want a drink."

"You can clean your dress, then. Your choice. Let's just leave these two to get reacquainted."

"Thanks, Brian," Tristan nodded at the tour guide as they passed by in a flail of arms and muscles.

"Just because you're his bodyguard doesn't mean you can tell me what to do…" Angelina's voice screeched and trailed off into the distance as the man hauled her away.

"Wait…he's your bodyguard?" Lillian turned to Tristan and narrowed her gaze. "Now who's being deceptive?"

Tristan smiled, and it sent a small jolt through Lillian's heart, igniting her talent.

"He's the head of my security team, actually, but he pretends to be my bodyguard when he's in the mood."

"He's the one who investigated me and prepared the report, isn't he?"

"Yes." Tristan's voice was smooth and calm, but he narrowed his gaze, and his rising energy had Lillian shifting from one foot to the other. "As I told you before, it was the only way I could discover the truth. But let's get back to the topic at hand, shall we. You were saying?"

"Saying?" Lillian asked.

"Earlier, about lying." Tristan's gaze registered impatience and something else, something that looked a lot like anticipation.

Lillian gulped when she thought about what she needed to do. The moment of truth had arrived, and she needed to pull up her big girl panties and say what she'd come here to tell him. Her throat seemed to close but she managed to squeeze the words out on a single rushed breath. "IliedwhenItoldyouIonlysleptwithyouasathankyou…IsleptwithyoubecauseIwantedto."

"Wanted to? You mean…"

She had looked down at her feet, but now she raised her head until their eyes met, and she was looking into those familiar deep-blue irises, which seemed focused on her with laser-sharp intensity.

"I didn't tell the truth when I said the reason I didn't want to be with you was because I wanted healthy children. You're a burner, Tristan. Burners can't inherit diseases like Huntington's."

"They can't?" Tristan looked stunned.

"No, they can't. And even if if they could, my DNA is…different. If we had children, there would be an approximate fifty percent chance they'd inherit a talent like mine or some other paranormal gift."

"A talent like yours."

Lillian didn't know what she expected to see in his eyes…disbelief, irritation, anger, disgust? But his expression never altered, and whatever emotion flickered in their ocean depths remained hidden. If only Tristan said something, anything, a single sentence indicating he accepted Lillian's apology. If only he said he forgave her for lying and still cared for her. If only his silence didn't tell her all she needed to know.

She looked past him to see a large man, standing about a foot away, his gaze on her. Wasn't that Fred from the park? What an odd coincidence. She waved, but he didn't acknowledge the gesture.

Tristan turned to look where she was waving. "Someone you know?"

"Yes…I mean no. But I've seen him before…at a park near my house."

"Oh."

Tristan's face lost a bit of color, which seemed odd, but maybe her being here embarrassed him. After all, she'd drenched his fiancée in champagne then admitted she'd lied to him more than once.

She dropped her gaze. It was time to gather her tattered pride and beat a fast exit.

"I'll go now. I wish you every happiness with…." She couldn't bring herself to say Angelina, but managed to fling a hand in the lady's direction, forgetting about the champagne glass she was holding. The last of its contents sloshed onto Tristan's shirt.

She watched in horrified silence as he glanced down at the stain.

"Oh, God, Tristan. I'm sorry. I didn't mean…I'll pay for the dry cleaning," she stuttered, while he examined the damage with a bemused expression.

At least he didn't seem angry. But what a disaster the evening had turned out to be.

"Goodbye." Before she could make a bigger fool of herself, Lillian turned and fled the solarium.

This time, no one stopped her.

Chapter Twenty-Eight

Lillian gasped for air as she tore open the front door and hightailed it out of Tristan's mansion, blood pumping fast and furious through her veins. Had she honestly expected he'd believe her after she'd told so many lies earlier in their acquaintance? And then to dump champagne on him after doing the same thing to his fiancée? What a klutz.

Her cheeks burned, but she wasn't sure if the cause was the mad dash to the shuttle or the shame filling her chest. Thank God the bus was waiting. She climbed onto it and made her way to the back, searching for Hannah in every seat she passed, but her sister was nowhere in sight. Most of the seats were empty of passengers since the guests were still at the party. Maybe she should get off the bus and look for Hannah at the house?

Too late.

Before she could make up her mind, the driver pulled away from the curb and headed toward the vast parking lot. A few minutes later, the shuttle stopped next to Hannah's car, and the doors opened.

Lillian got out and studied the vehicle, then turned and watched as the bus pulled away, heading back to pick up more passengers. She slumped against the car, then dug for her phone and sent a quick text to Hannah.

I'm at the car. Her sister had the keys.

A minute later, her cell phone buzzed with an answering text. *Just finishing up the tour. Won't be long.*

Lillian tapped her foot and scanned the parking lot, but it was empty of people, so she made a conscious effort to slow her heart rate and try not to think about her rapid exit and the bemused look on Tristan's face when she'd flung the last of her champagne at him.

She shuddered. How horrible this would be her last memory of him.

She closed her eyes and imagined herself on a beach, enjoying the warm rays of the sun. The mental imagery seemed to work, her breaths evening out. The squeal of the hydraulic brakes on the bus reentering the parking lot to unload its next set of passengers jolted her back to the present. A young couple got off, followed by a group of women, and a single man—Tristan.

Her heartbeat tripped into overtime. His hair looked a bit windblown from when she'd last seen him, and he glanced in every direction with a determined air until his gaze found hers.

Lillian's pulse leaped, and she looked for somewhere to leap as well, but there was no way out, unless she wanted to run across the open parking lot in wedges, which she did not.

Tristan didn't increase his gait, but his long legs made short work of the concrete. And then he was in front of her, smelling like his minty pine cologne and sweat and champagne and more than a few fantasies she'd had of long summer nights with him underneath the covers.

Lillian couldn't stop a shiver. What the hell was wrong with her? She had no business dreaming of nights under the covers with Tristan. He was engaged to be married.

Even so, she took a deep gulp of his unique scent and held it in her lungs while he peered into her eyes like he would read her soul.

He touched a strand of her hair. "I wondered what color it would be…underneath the wig. They had you hooked up to so many machines the last time I saw you in the hospital that I wasn't exactly sure."

She swallowed the lump in her throat. "I'm sorry I didn't show you myself when you asked. I was trying to protect you."

"Did you mean everything you said back there?"

She nodded, then took a step backward, which solved nothing since he took a step forward, cornering her against the vehicle.

"I don't have Huntington's?"

"No," she shook her head. "It's not possible."

"Your leaving had nothing to do with my inability to give you healthy children?"

He was going to make her spell it out. She could see it in his eyes. He would settle for nothing less. And why did he have to look and smell so damn good? Where was Hannah when Lillian needed her most?

"No, it did not." She cleared her throat. "It's the opposite, actually."

"What?" His intense look was replaced with puzzlement. "You mean…"

"I can't give you healthy children, Tristan. As I told you, burners are immune to most illnesses. They don't get inherited diseases like Huntington's, so they wouldn't pass it to their children. But any children I have will have a genetic disorder. They will likely inherit my gift and be hunted. I didn't think you'd want that."

He leaned a little closer, which had the effect of making Lillian want to fan her chest, if only she had a fan.

"You have no idea what I want."

The grit in his voice sent goosebumps up and down her arms. She couldn't hold his gaze any longer and dropped hers to look at the blacktop.

But he wasn't having it. He put two fingers under her chin and raised it until their eyes met. "You didn't sleep with me out of gratitude, then?"

She licked her lips, which had become dry. "Definitely not."

"So why did you?"

There it was…the million-dollar question. Her heart beat a rapid staccato against the walls of her chest, and her breaths came short and fast. She wanted to flee across the parking lot and not look back. She wanted to return to the safety of her dad's house and her pink bedroom and the daily walks to the park. She wanted not to feel so damn vulnerable.

But more than that, she wanted Tristan to know the truth.

All these thoughts flashed across her brain in an instant but were zapped to smithereens under the razor intensity of his gaze. "Um…er…um."

She couldn't seem to get her tongue moving, or any other body parts for that matter, while he waited for an answer, seemingly calm and unruffled, rather than a basket case like Lillian. But even as she had the thought, the expectation in his gaze changed to disappointment and he dropped his fingers from her chin, stepped backward and turned to go.

"Wait," she held out a hand. "Wait, please."

He paused and turned around.

"Ididitbecauseiwas…becauseiaminlovewithyou." There, she'd said it. Why wasn't he reacting? He still stood in the same spot, rooted to the ground, staring at her with a combination of confusion and disbelief.

"You…what did you say?"

She rushed on, desperate to get her pent-up feelings out now the dam had broken. "I know you're engaged to be married. I'm not expecting you to change your plans because I've developed feelings for you. I only want your happiness, Tristan, that is all. I want you to be able to think of me fondly in the years ahead whenever you do think of me. I want you to know I told the truth for once. That I fell in love with you. That I want—"

Before Lillian could finish her next sentence, Tristan exploded forward and wrapped his arms around her, cutting off the last of her words and pulling her up in his arms, swinging her high off the ground. "Why the hell didn't you just start with that, woman?"

And then she was sliding down his chest, and he was kissing her like he was dying, and she was the oxygen that kept him alive.

"We shouldn't be kissing," Lillian said when she could take a breath and a glimmer of rational thought took over and guilt set in.

"Hmm," he said, ignoring her. He tasted like champagne and heaven and a thousand wishes, and she never wanted the kiss to end, but she knew it must.

"Wait…stop…" She pushed on his chest. "You…we can't be doing this."

"Of course, we can."

He tried to pull her to him, but she resisted. "I know we *can*…but we shouldn't be. It's wrong. You have a fiancée, remember?"

"What the hell are you talking about?"

"Angelina…your fiancée? You know, the one who had her arm around you twenty minutes ago? Why are you looking at me like I'm crazy?"

"Because you are. Angelina's not my fiancée. We're not engaged."

"You're not? But Hannah said my dad came to your house and talked to Angelina when I was still in the hospital. She told him she was engaged to be married to you."

Tristan's wrinkled brow cleared, and his shock gave way to a superior smirk. "She lied, obviously. She does that."

"Then," she gulped. "Then why was she at your house?"

"She was there to help plan tonight's party. She leads the hospital fundraising committee, and I agreed to participate only if the committee would make all the arrangements."

"So, you're not engaged?"

"Nope, although she likes to think she has a claim. I haven't thought about Angelina in that way since the night of the party we attended together. Now, will you kiss me again?"

A flop of his dark curly hair had fallen into his eyes, and Lillian brushed it away, her hands trembling. "Why didn't you call me afterwards…when I woke up from the coma? I never heard from you. I thought you hated me after the terrible things I said…the lies I told. I thought you never wanted to see me again. I thought…"

He placed a warm hand over hers to stop the shaking and brought it to his chest. "*Never.* I've never hated you. I may have been angry or frustrated or even disappointed at times. But I didn't hate you. I think I fell in love with you the moment we first kissed."

He pressed kisses against her cheek, nose, eyes, lips, before continuing. "I was in agony. I wanted to call many times. But you said you didn't love or want me around because I couldn't give you healthy children, and I believed you. I was hurt, and I promised myself if you recovered, I wouldn't force myself on you. If you wanted me, you had to come to me and tell me. I wouldn't believe it any other way. I waited and prayed when you came out of the coma, but you never contacted me…until tonight."

"I didn't think you'd want to see me. I'm sorry I ever said those horrible words, Tristan. You don't know how often I wished I could take them back. I thought I lost you. I thought you had moved on with Angelina and…" A hiccup interrupted her next sentence, and she tasted the saltiness of her own tears. "I was miserable without you."

"Shhh..."

Tristan wiped her eyes with the pads of his fingers, and there was such warmth shining from his gaze, her heart was about to explode into a million fragments.

"I hope those are tears of joy and you're no longer miserable because I don't think I can live without you in my life."

What was he saying? Did he mean...?

He laughed and set her from him. "Don't look so shocked. You really don't think I'm going to let you slip away from me now, do you? Lillian Abigail Milano, I don't think I can go another day without you. I can call you Lillian, can't I?"

She nodded and hiccupped, and he used his fingertips to wipe the lingering wetness from her cheeks, then replaced his fingertips with his lips, pressing light kisses everywhere.

She didn't know how long they stayed like that. It was probably only minutes, but it felt like hours before the kisses ended and her heartbeat slowed to a more manageable rate and the thick lump in her throat dissolved.

Could this be real? Would she wake up and find it had all been a dream?

He smiled and smoothed the hair from her forehead with such tenderness in his gaze, her heart stuttered.

"I do have a confession to make, though. I don't want any more lies between us."

Her heart knocked against her chest. "What is it?"

"The big guy you saw in the park—you nicknamed him Fred—his real name is Glenn. He works for Brian."

"Your security guy? You mean you paid Glenn to spy on me? Why?"

"To protect you. I didn't want to take a chance after you warned me the FBI was working with Kinetica… although I was ninety percent sure the government had shut them down and put the leaders behind bars."

"I see."

"You're angry."

"No…surprised is all. I wish I had known."

"I couldn't tell you at the time since I thought you didn't want to see me. But I wanted to make sure you were safe. I had almost lost you once. I wasn't going to take another chance with your life."

"Even though I had told you I didn't love you?"

"Yes, even then. I wanted you to have a life free from worry and fear."

She smiled. "You are an amazing man."

He returned the smile, and his eyes seemed to glow. "I am a man desperately in love with you. Come and live with me in my lonely house, Lillian, and let's be amazing together. We'll have children one day…or not. Whatever you decide you want. I need you by my side."

"What about…"

"Or if you want, we can sell the place and move to Boston—your dad told me you live there and not Denver. Whatever it takes to get you to say yes."

Did Tristan sound a little panicked? She wrinkled her brow. "You're asking me to live with you?"

"Yes, although I'd like to put a ring on your finger and make it official."

"But you love Cleveland, and your mom lives here. How could you live in Boston?"

"My mom is feeling much better these days, thanks to you. I will go wherever you want. I only want you to be happy—and to say yes."

The shock was wearing off, and a sob broke through, opening the floodgates and drenching her in happy tears.

"Yes," she said. "Yes. Of course, I'll say yes. A million times yes. And we don't have to move to Boston. Cleveland is my home now. I'd be thrilled to move into your big ole' lonely mansion with you."

Tristan's grin was wider than Lillian had ever seen it, and he got up and tugged her into his arms, holding her against his chest and the comforting sound of his steady heartbeat.

There was an explosion of sound from the shuttle bus, where a group of passengers had gathered, which was the moment Lillian realized they had an audience—Tristan, too, by the look of surprise on his face.

Lillian turned to see the crowd clapping and carrying on, led by Hannah, who stood in their midst. She gave Lillian a big thumbs-up and a wink, the little troublemaker, but Lillian was too ecstatic to care if her sister had used her talent to excite the crowd and instigate the impromptu celebration.

After all, Lillian had bigger items to think about. She had a wedding to plan.

Chapter Twenty-Nine

"Where did you put my bouquet?" Lillian asked her sister, searching the dressing room frantically for the gorgeous arrangement of pale pink and white roses the florist had crafted.

"It's right here, Lil, where you set it a minute ago," Hannah said, handing Lillian the flowers from where they lay on the table behind her. Her sister's dark hair was twisted into an elegant knot on the top of her head, and she wore the midnight-blue maid-of-honor dress they'd selected together. She would be Lillian's only attendant, paired with Brian, who was Tristan's best man.

"Thanks…I'm a wee bit nervous," Lillian said.

"Don't be. You look absolutely beautiful. Tristan is going to fall in love with you even more than he already has if that's even possible. Are you ready?"

"You go ahead. I'll be just a minute."

Hannah stared at her a moment, her golden-brown eyes shimmering, before patting Lillian's shoulder. "Mom would be so happy for you, Lil."

Lillian sniffed. "I know."

"He's a good man, and he loves you so much. You're perfect together. Now, if only he had a brother," she winked.

Hannah was so earnest, Lillian laughed. "You'll meet your Prince Charming one day. You won't go through the doubts I went through, either. You'll take one look at him and know from the start. The lucky guy will never be able to hide from your emotion detector."

Hannah grinned. "That's the heart of the problem, though. There are far too many insincere men out there. That's why I don't date. Your guy, though, he's the real deal. I knew you were meant for each other the first time I met him."

"Thanks, sis, for everything." Lillian swiped at her eyes—she couldn't seem to stop the tears from flowing. "I am happy...so happy. I don't know why I'm crying."

Hannah hugged her, and warmth flooded Lillian's heart. "I do. You're missing Mom, and you're scared of getting married." She released Lillian but held her hands. "I dreamt about her, you know."

"When?"

"When you were in the hospital, and I wasn't sure you'd make it. She told me not to worry, that she was taking care of you, and it would be up to me to take care of you when you woke up. That's why I pushed so hard for you to see Tristan and bought the tickets to the Parade of Homes, even though I knew you'd be mad."

Lillian squeezed her hands. "I might have been a little annoyed at the time, but I'm so grateful you did."

"You've found your happily ever after, and Mom knows it, Lil. Don't be afraid. Dry your eyes and make those tears of joy. I'll head into the church now and send Dad to come get you in a few minutes. I love you, sis."

"I love you, too."

Lillian waited until Hannah left the dressing room before turning and considering her reflection in the mirror. Her dark chestnut hair glimmered under the fluorescent lights and seemed to bring out the glittery silver in her gown. Gone were the days of the long blonde wig and green contacts. The golden-brown eyes of the girl in the glass looked weepy and happy and like she could use a glass of wine to ease her anxiety.

"There's my girl," Lillian's dad said, coming into the room with a big smile on his face. "Are you ready to walk down the aisle? You have one nervous and impatient groom waiting at the altar."

Lillian managed a smile through watery eyes. In a few minutes, she would take her father's arm and be led into the arms of the man she loved. She should be ecstatically happy, and she was, but she'd be lying to herself if she didn't also acknowledge the day was laced with an edge of sorrow.

"What is it?"

"I wish Mom were here," she choked out, grabbing a tissue from the box on the nearby table.

"Ahh, my Lou-Lou," her dad said, taking her into his arms and patting her back. "I've been thinking about her, too, today. She was so proud of you girls, but she worried as mothers do."

"Most of the time, I can deal with Mom being gone but sometimes," she sniffed., "there's a hole in my heart that can't be filled by anyone else. Today's one of those days, Dad."

Her dad pulled away to look at her. "She had an incredible intuition, your mother. She could often predict things before they would happen. And she was especially sensitive to you girls. I suppose that's how she thought to give you this." Her dad reached into his pocket and pulled out a shiny silver jewelry box and folded it into Lillian's palm.

"What...what is this?"

"I don't know. Your mother didn't tell me. Hannah and I found it when we cleaned out her dresser after her death. You were in Boston by then. The box was sealed, but there was a note attached with your name that said it was meant for your birthday. You left before we got to celebrate it, remember? I had planned to give it to you when you came home, but with Hannah being so ill at the time, it escaped my mind. I thought today might be an appropriate occasion."

Lillian stared at the shiny silver box, her hands trembling. A whisper of power hit her hard—her mother's energy. She'd know it anywhere.

"Aren't you going to open it?"

Lillian sucked in a breath, her fingers tingling. She broke the seal and opened the lid, letting out a gasp. A tiny silver angel with a shiny halo encrusted with sparkling diamonds on a delicate chain glittered at her. She reached in with shaking fingers to touch it, absorbing the last remnants of her mom's spirit in the process. Underneath the necklace lay a folded letter.

Still clutching the necklace, she somehow managed to pull out the letter and open it without tearing the paper. She sat on the couch and smoothed the wrinkles so she could read what was written. Her mom's familiar hand jumped out at her, and Lillian's pulse leaped madly as she read.

My Dearest Lily,

In a few days, I will be leaving. I won't be here to celebrate your twenty-fifth birthday next month. It saddens me to miss it. I will ask your dad to give you this gift and will plan to celebrate with you when I return.

Although I feel bad about missing your birthday, it helps to know you want me to make the trip. How like you to be more concerned for others than yourself! I will be able to use my gift to help so many, and in that light, the time away from you is a small sacrifice we must make.

I thought about giving this gift to you before I leave, but you are working overtime right now, putting in long exhausting hours in the ER. Your patients and their families love you for it, but they don't understand the toll using your ability has on your spirit as I do.

I am so proud of you, Lily, but I'm afraid for you, too. You feel responsible for those who suffer. You continually put their needs before your own, and it worries me. The life of a healer can be lonely. You are always the strong one, always the dependable one, always the one everyone leans on. But there will come a day when you will not be able to cure someone you love, when you will try your hardest to use your talent and fail, when you can no longer be the strong one and stand alone.

I have enclosed the angel necklace to remind you I am always here for you. You are never alone. Please come to me any time you are feeling afraid or lonely or need a listening ear.

I hope one day you find your Prince Charming. The greatest happiness I have known has been with your dad, and the family we've created.

Happiest of birthdays, my sweet Lily. Be brave and kind and trust your instincts always.

I love you,
Mom

The tears were dropping on the paper, smearing the ink, and Lillian set the letter aside.

"Are those tears of happiness, I hope?" her father asked, handing her a tissue. "Would you like to wear the necklace?"

She nodded and dabbed at her eyes, standing and turning so her dad could fasten the clasp around her neck. She fingered the glittering angel, her mother's presence filling the room.

"Your mother understood you, Lou-Lou. She only ever wanted to see you happy. I think her wish has come true."

"Yes," Lillian said. "Yes, it has."

"Are you ready, then?" Her dad offered an arm, and Lillian looped hers through.

"I am."

They walked from the dressing room, through the hall, and into the back of the old historic church in her hometown where she was to be married. Hannah signaled the musicians and began her march down the aisle, following little Annie Logan, who had agreed to be Lillian's flower girl. Then, Lillian and her dad began the long walk.

Tristan's mom and a small group of cousins and aunts and uncles and friends turned to look. Lillian managed to stay calm by fixing her gaze on Tristan, who stood tall and handsome in his black tuxedo, the familiar wave in his dark hair.

And then they reached his side, and her dad was placing her arm in Tristan's. Her skin tingled, her heart pounded, and she was bolstered by Tristan's strength and the love shining from his dark-blue eyes.

The preacher turned to Lillian. "Will you have Tristan to be your husband? Will you love him, comfort, and keep him, forsaking all others remain true to him, as long as you both shall live?"

"I will," she said, gazing into Tristan's eyes, her voice clear and loud enough to be heard by the entire congregation.

Tristan smiled, as the preacher turned to him and asked him the same question. He squeezed Lillian's hands, and an electric current seemed to jump from his heart to hers. "I will."

"Lillian and Tristan, by the power vested in me by God and man, I pronounce you wife and husband. You may now kiss the bride."

And then Tristan tilted his head down and Lillian tilted her head up, and their lips met somewhere in the middle. And the sparks that had been igniting along her skin turned into a fiery blaze.

Chapter Thirty

Epilogue
Three Years Later

"What's the story with the hot bodyguard?" Hannah asked from where she lounged by the pool.

She set her knitting down to fan her cheeks and hoped Lillian put it down to the sun and not the heat in her belly. Brian Townsend was the most striking man she'd ever met. He was also one of the most mysterious. And since he'd been on some secret assignment for one of his clients the past year, Hannah hadn't seen him since her sister's wedding.

Her sister put her hand to her forehead to shield her eyes and looked across the patio at the men, who were tending the grill. "There's not much to tell as far as I know. Why are you asking?"

"He's not happy."

"He seems happy enough to me," Lillian said.

Hannah's gaze returned to Brian. Tristan was gesturing, and Brian was laughing at whatever he said. He was shirtless, his skin and hair a golden brown, his hands propped against lean hips. If there was a definition for casual male beauty, Brian possessed it in spades.

"When he's not grumbling, he's joking; that's just the way he acts."

"He jokes to cover the pain, Lil."

Brian shifted his stance and turned his head, and his unusual eyes caught Hannah's, as if he knew he was the subject of their discussion. Her heart thudded in her chest, but she refused to look away until his gaze returned to Tristan's.

"What's his issue then?" Lillian asked.

"I can't quite put my finger on it."

Her sister's mouth dropped open.

"Why are you acting so surprised? I'm empathic, not a mind reader."

"Because in the twenty-five years since you were born, I've never heard you say you couldn't figure someone out. Are you sick?"

Hannah made a face. "No, I'm not sick. He's challenging, that's all. He's not what he seems."

"Crusty on the outside, soft on the inside?"

She stared at Brian. "I'm not sure. He's scarred in some way I can't fathom. What has Tristan told you about him?"

"Not much, really. He's a chick magnet and moody. He likes his privacy."

"He must have told you something more than that."

"I know they went to high school together. Tristan said Brian was a star athlete and smart. I guess he took home about every award there was to take home and received several football scholarships. He turned them all down to join the military. Tristan lost touch with him for a few years, but when Brian got discharged and started his own security firm, Tristan was one of his first customers."

"No woman in his past who broke his heart?" Hannah found her gaze returning to Brian.

"Not that Tristan mentioned. Why do you keep staring at him with that puzzled look on your face? Are you interested? I can do some investigating of my own. He's cute in a lumberjack sort of way. I can see why women like him."

Hannah's gaze returned to Lillian, and she deliberately relaxed her face. "You know I don't date. How many times do I have to tell you, men are all the same—not to be trusted. Well, everyone but yours." She patted Lillian's hand. "Speaking of which, what are you holding inside? You're bursting at the seams."

Lillian's shining gaze met Hannah's. "I'm pregnant."

Hannah squealed and jumped up to hug her sister, trying not to let the worry inside taint Lillian's happiness. "I'm so, so happy for you, Lil. How long have you known?"

"Since this morning."

Hannah smiled. "Did you tell Tristan?"

"Tell me what?" Tristan had come up on them unexpectedly, attracted to their squeals, no doubt. Brian trailed close behind.

Lillian's expression went from excited to nervous in an instant, and she went to her husband, grasping his hands.

Hannah got herself out of the way. *He doesn't know?* she mouthed from behind Tristan's back.

The deer-in-the-headlights look in Lillian's eyes told Hannah all she needed to know.

"I swear I planned to tell you tonight before anyone else. Hannah guessed it before I could, though."

"Guessed what?" Tristan's puzzled expression grew more intense, his emotions heightening to a fever pitch. "Are you sick? What's wrong?"

Hannah put her hand over her heart in a feeble attempt to slow the furious pounding. Being around strong emotions tended to cause this effect. Brian's gaze moved to her, and somehow, she knew he'd noticed her reaction. The man didn't miss much, that was for sure.

"I'm…we're pregnant. You're going to be a father."

Tristan's stunned expression told Hannah the news was totally unexpected.

"You're not happy? Say something, so I know what you're feeling." Lillian burst into tears, the intensity of the situation too much for her to bear.

"Sweetheart, don't cry. I'm overjoyed. I'm surprised, that's all. I thought you didn't want children because you were afraid they'd inherit your talent."

"I'm still afraid, and I don't know how it happened. Well, I know how it happened, but I didn't think I would get pregnant. But I have, and oh, Tristan, I want this baby so much."

"Me, too." Tristan pulled his wife into his chest and held her against his heart. "Me, too."

Hannah could hear Lillian's muffled sobs from where she stood. She closed her eyes and sucked in air.

"What's wrong?"

The low voice next to her ear startled her, and she popped her eyes open. Brian stood over her, puzzlement in his gaze. His curiosity, concern, and attraction fluttered across her spine like a butterfly, before settling in her heart.

"I'm fine." She gasped, heart galloping. "I'm just so happy for them. They're going to be wonderful parents. They're so in love, don't ya think?"

Brian turned his attention to the couple, and Hannah's heartbeat settled into a more normal rhythm.

"If such a thing exists," Brian said. Was there a hint of wistfulness wrapped within the cynicism?

Tristan turned with Lillian in his arms and smiled at Hannah and Brian. "I'm going to be a dad. Can you believe it?"

Brian released his grip on her arm and moved forward, his affection for his friend evident.

"I'm thrilled for you, buddy," he said, slapping him on the back. "Congratulations. I see lots of diaper changes in your future." He turned to Lillian and shook her hand. "And you, too. This is one lucky baby."

"Thanks, Bri," Lillian said.

Hannah hugged the couple, and caught up in their happiness, turned to Brian and hugged him, too. It was an instinctual reaction, but she forgot he didn't have on a shirt. The moment their skin touched, electricity rippled through her system like she handled a live wire. She let go of him and stepped away as fast as she could. Warmth flooded her cheeks, and she didn't dare look at him. Something sizzled in the air between them.

"You guys make a cute couple," her sister said, oblivious to the tension surrounding them.

"You're delirious," Hannah said, avoiding Brian's gaze.

"Yeah, delirious with happiness. I wish everyone could be this happy," her sister said. She laughed, and the sound was so joyous, the feeling flooded into Hannah, like a soothing balm, settling her stomach. What did it matter if she never found happiness herself? She had played a part in healing two hearts. Wasn't that her mission in life?

And she would make one hell of an aunt, if she did say so herself.

Lillian and Tristan still held hands, lost in each other's eyes, while Brian went to find his shirt.

Hannah turned to fetch her knitting, hollering over her shoulder. "Time to start on a baby blanket."

THE END

Other Books by Amanda Uhl

Mind Waves, Mind Hackers Series, Book 1
Cross Waves, Mind Hackers Series, Book 2
Dark Waves, Mind Hackers Series, Novella
Charmed By Charlie

Praise for Award-Winning Author Amanda Uhl

Healing Kiss

"The heroine is especially compelling in this story, and there's a nice degree of emotion and heart that draws the reader in. I loved everything about this book. I was so disappointed to get to the end."

— On The Far Side Contest,
First Place, Light Paranormal

"This is polished writing with a clear voice and a well laid out plot. I love the initial scene, which pulls the reader in, and I love Lillian's first meeting with Tristan. One can see her powers without being overwhelmed or saying 'what the heck.' The scene is vivid, the desperation palpable, and altogether drew me in. I thoroughly enjoyed it."

— Rudy Writing Contest,
First Place, Paranormal

"The concept behind the story is a brilliant one, and the threat of Kinetica gives this a fresh genre balance between romantic suspense and paranormal that is so interesting! I breezed right through this story and wanted more."

– *Diamonds in the Desert Contest*,
Second Place, Paranormal

Dark Waves

"Uhl somehow manages to not only instill a fascinating plot into this short story but has also developed two characters that the reader can deeply connect with and understand...a short punchy and fascinating read I can highly recommend..."

– *Readers' Favorite*,
Gold Medal, Novella Category

"This novella held my attention from the first page to the last...complex and surprising. I didn't want it to be over..."

– *Paranormal Romance Guild*,
Reviewer's Choice Award Winner

"A fun and absorbing read!"

– *InD'tale Magazine*

Cross Waves

"...a fascinating and irresistible paranormal romance. From the beginning, the conflict between Geneva and

Rolf held me spellbound, and I couldn't put the book down until I found how their dilemma was resolved."

— Readers' Favorite,
5-Star Review

"I read this book in one sitting, and the excitement didn't let up for a minute."

— Paranormal Romance Guild,
Reviewer's Choice Award Nominee

"Amanda Uhl has invented a fresh brand of psychic paranormal romance with an imaginative and captivating theme."

— InD'tale Magazine

Mind Waves

"It was a mixture of genres and it was woven together in such a way that you did not see the distinction between genres. It just works!"

— The Genre Minx Book Reviews

"I look forward to reading more books by this author! The concept is intriguing, and I loved how she incorporated it into the modern world. Great book!"

— Lady With a Quill Book Reviews

"What a spectacular story for a debut book and definitely a book I would love to see converted into a movie or a miniseries on TV! Yes, it was that good and didn't fall into the cookie cutter PNR mold."

— Star Angel Reviews

"This book grabbed me from the very beginning and held me until the very last page. The characters were amazing and it was filled with suspense, secrets, surprises and romance. It was everything I love in a book and more. I loved it so much, I finished it in just one day."

– Paranormal Romance Guild,
Reviewer's Choice Award Nominee

Charmed By Charlie

"Uhl's latest is a sweet and cozy romance with genuine feelings and experiences to be worked through and overcome. A lighthearted and engaging read."

– School Library Journal

"…a romantic read with just the right amount of conflict to keep the story moving…it is about life, relationships, and learning to seize the day."

– Genre Minx Book Reviews

"…I enjoyed the dialog…the drama, the misunderstandings, the suspense/mystery, the chemistry, the banter and even the moments of heartbreak. The plot with the characters was brilliantly orchestrated into a "charming" romance story…I couldn't put the book down."

– Long and Short Reviews

A Word About the Author...

Amanda Uhl has always had a fascination with the mystical. Having drawn her first breath in a century home rumored to be haunted, you might say she was "born" into it. After a brief stint in college as a paid psychic, Amanda graduated with a Bachelor of Fine Arts in theatre and a Master's degree in marketing. Over the past twenty years, she has worked as an admissions representative and graphic designer, owned her own freelance writing company, and managed communications for several Fortune 500 companies, most recently specializing in cyber security and data. Amanda is an avid reader and writes fast-paced, paranormal romantic suspense and humorous contemporary romance from her home in Cleveland, Ohio. When she's not reading or writing, you can find Amanda with her husband and three children, gathering beach glass on the Lake Erie shoreline or biking in Cuyahoga Valley National Park.